FIVE GREAT
GREEK TRAGEDIES

DOVER THRIFT EDITIONS

Sophocles, Euripides
and Aeschylus

DOVER PUBLICATIONS, INC.
MINEOLA, NEW YORK

DOVER THRIFT EDITIONS
GENERAL EDITOR: PAUL NEGRI

Performance

This Dover Thrift Edition may be used in its entirety, in adaptation or in any other way for theatrical productions, professional and amateur, in the United States, without fee, permission, or acknowledgement. (This may not apply outside of the United States, as copyright conditions may vary.)

Copyright

Copyright © 2004 by Dover Publications, Inc.
All rights reserved.

Bibliographical Note

This Dover edition, first published in 2004, is a new collection of plays by Aeschylus, Sophocles, and Euripides. A new introductory Note has been prepared for this edition.

Library of Congress Cataloging-in-Publication Data

Five great Greek tragedies / Sophocles, Euripides, and Aeschylus.
    p. cm.—(Dover thrift editions)
  Contents: Prometheus bound / Aeschylus—Oedipus rex / Sophocles—Electra/ Sophocles—Medea / Euripides—Bacchae / Euripides.
  ISBN-13: 978-0-486-43620-3
  ISBN-10: 0-486-43620-9
  1. Greek drama (Tragedy)—Translations into English. 2. Mythology, Greek—Drama. I. Sophocles. II. Euripides. III. Aeschylus. IV. Series.

PA3626.A2 2004
882'0108—dc22

2004041436

Manufactured in the United States by LSC Communications
43620909   2019
www.doverpublications.com

Note

Aeschylus, Sophocles, and Euripides, the most important playwrights in fifth-century Greece, can be said to have "invented" Greek tragedy as we know it today.

Greek drama at the time of Aeschylus (525-456 B.C.) was derived from choral song and dance. Beside the chorus, only one actor appeared in a given scene. Aeschylus' great contribution was to add a second actor, thereby vastly increasing the dramatic possibilities. *Prometheus Bound*, believed to be one of his last plays, was written as the first play in a trilogy; unfortunately, the other two plays were lost.

Sophocles (born ca. 496 B.C., died after 413) wrote 123 plays, only seven of which survive. The violence of his plays rises out of intense emotional agony, and signifies nothing less than the psychological rebirth of the hero

The youngest of the three, Euripides (ca. 485 B.C. to ca. 406 B.C.) is represented by the largest number of extant plays (nineteen, as compared with seven each for Aeschylus and Sophocles). He is, in the opinion of many scholars, the cruelest of the three in his view of the indifference or vindictiveness of the gods.

Sources of the Text

Prometheus Bound is an unabridged republication of the English translation by George Thomson, M. A., as it appeared in *Aeschylus, The Prometheus Bound*, edited by George Thomson, first published by the Cambridge University Press, Cambridge, England, 1932.

Electra is an unabridged republication of the play *Electra* and *Oedipus Rex* is an unabridged republication of the play *Oedipus Tryrannus*, both from the volume *The Dramas of Sophocles Rendered in English Verse Dramatic & Lyric by Sir George Young*, as published by J. M. Dent & Sons, Ltd., London, in 1906. (The Dent edition was the second, the first having been published by George Bell & Sons, London, in 1888). In this edition, Sir Geoge's own notes (exclusively concerned with problems of the Greek text and its interpretation) have been omitted, and several new, very brief footnotes have been added.

Medea is an unabridged republication of the translation by Rex Warner originally published by John Lane, The Bodley Head Limited, London, in 1944. Explanatory footnotes have been added.

Bacchae is an unabridged, unaltered republication of the work translated by Henry Hart Milman as *The Bacchanals*, in *The Plays of Euripedes*, volume two, originally published in 1908 by J. M. Dent, London, as part of Everyman's Library. (Milman's translation was first published in 1865.)

Contents

Prometheus Bound

AESCHYLUS

Characters

Prometheus, *a Titan*.

Io

Hermes, *messenger of Zeus*.

Hephaestus, *god of fire*.

Oceanus, *god of the ocean*.

Might

Violence

Chorus of Oceanids (*daughters of Oceanus*).

Prometheus Bound

(*Enter* PROMETHEUS, *escorted by* MIGHT *and* VIOLENCE, *and accompanied by* HEPHAESTUS, *who carries the implements of his craft*)

MIGHT

> To Earth's far-distant confines we are come,
> The tract of Scythia, waste untrod by man.
>   And now, Hephaestus, thou must mind the task
> Ordained thee by the Father — to enchain
> This malefactor on yon mountain crags
> In indissoluble bands of adamant.
> Thy flower, fount of the arts, the light of fire,
> He stole and gave to mortals. Such the sin
> For which he must make recompense to heaven,
> And so be taught to accept the tyranny
> Of Zeus, and check his charity to man.

HEPHAESTUS

> O Might, and Violence, for you the word
> Of Zeus hath been fulfilled — your part is done.
> But I have not the heart by force to bind
> A god, my kinsman, in this wintry glen.
> And yet I must brazen myself to do it; ·
> For grave it is to scant the Father's word.

True-counselling Themis' lofty-ambitioned Son,
Not by my will, nor thine, shall rigorous bonds
Imprison thee in this unpeopled waste,
Where neither mortal form shall greet thine eye
Nor voice thine ear, but, parched in the sun's pure flame,
Thy beauty's bloom shall perish. Welcome to thee
Shall starry-kirtled Night enshroud the day,
Welcome the sun dispel the frosts of dawn;
And the anguish of thy state shall gnaw thy heart
For ever — unborn is thy deliverer.
        Such thy reward for charity to man:
A god, thou didst defy the wrath of gods,
On men their powers bestowing unrighteously.
So on this cheerless rock must thou stand guard,
Upright, unsleeping, unbending the knee,
And with many a groan of unavailing grief
Cry out. Implacable is the heart of Zeus,
And harsh is every king whose power is new.

MIGHT

Enough: why this delay? why waste your pity?
Do you not hate the god all gods abhor,
Betrayer of your privilege to man?

HEPHAESTUS

The tie of kin and comradeship is strange.

MIGHT

True, but is't possible to disregard
The Father's word? do you not revere that more?

HEPHAESTUS

Ah, you were ever pitiless and proud!

MIGHT

>To grieve for *him* cures nothing; so do you
>Labour no more where labour is in vain.

HEPHAESTUS

>O most abhorrent handicraft of mine!

MIGHT

>Why do you hate it? In plain truth, your art
>Is guiltless of the work that's now to do.

HEPHAESTUS

>Yet would that it had fallen to another!

MIGHT

>All things are troublesome, save to rule the gods:
>Liberty is the privilege of Zeus.

HEPHAESTUS (*pointing to chains*)

>These teach me that, and I can make no answer.

MIGHT

>No more delay then — in these chains bind *him*,
>For fear the Father see your faltering.

HEPHAESTUS

>Here are the curb-chains, ready to my hand.

MIGHT

>Then manacle his hands with all your might,
>Uplift the hammer, strike, and nail him down!

HEPHAESTUS

>See, 'tis not vain, the work proceeds apace.

MIGHT

> Strike harder, pin him, leave no fetter loose.
> His wit can circumvent the closest strait.

HEPHAESTUS

> *That* arm is fixed, fastened inextricably.

MIGHT

> And now encase the other, that he may learn,
> For all his craft, he is no match for Zeus.

HEPHAESTUS

> Of none, save him, have I deserved reproach.

MIGHT

> Now drive this stubborn adamantine edge
> Deep through his breast and nail it firmly down.

HEPHAESTUS

> Aiai, Prometheus! — for *thy* pains I groan.

MIGHT

> Once more you falter, weeping for the foes
> Of Zeus. Beware lest you should need your pity.

HEPHAESTUS

> The spectacle thou seest doth wound the eye.

MIGHT

> A knave I see repaid with his deserts.
> Come, cast this iron girth about his ribs.

HEPHAESTUS

> It must be done, you need not shout me on.

MIGHT

> And yet I *will* shout — ay, I will hound you on.
> Step down. Enclose his ankles in these rings.

HEPHAESTUS

> See, without length of labour, it is done.

MIGHT

> Now thrust these penetrating spancels home,
> For hard it is to please our taskmaster.

HEPHAESTUS

> How like your looks the utterance of your tongue!

MIGHT

> Be soft yourself, so please you, but do not chide
> My stubborn spirit and temperament severe.

HEPHAESTUS

> His feet are netted. Let us go our ways.   (*Exit*)

MIGHT

> Here now wax proud and plunder powers divine —
> Thy gifts to creatures of a day! How can
> Mortals relieve thee in thy present state?
> Falsely we named thee the Foresighted One,
> Prometheus — thine the need of foresight now,
> How from *this* art to extricate *thyself!*
>
> > (*Exeunt* MIGHT *and* VIOLENCE)

PROMETHEUS

> O divine Sky, and swiftly-winging Breezes,
> O River-springs, and multitudinous gleam
> Of smiling Ocean — to thee, All-Mother Earth,

And to the Sun's all-seeing orb I cry:
See what I suffer from the gods, a god!

    Witness how with anguish broken
    Through ages of time without number
    I shall labour in agony. Such are the bonds
    That the new-throned Lord of the Blest hath designed
    For my shame and dishonour.
    Pheu, pheu! for the pain that is now and to come
    I groan, and I cry, where is the destined
    Term of my trial and my travail?

And yet what say I? All things I foreknow
That are to be: no unforeseen distress
Shall visit me, and I must bear the will
Of Fate as lightly as I may, and learn
The invincible strength of Necessity.
Yet of my present state I cannot speak,
Cannot be silent. The gifts I gave to man
Have harnessed me beneath this harsh duress.
I hunted down the stealthy fount of fire
In fennel stored, which schooled the race of men
In every art and taught them great resource.
Such the transgression which I expiate,
A helpless captive, shackled, shelterless!

Ah ah, ea ea!
    What echo, what fragrance unseen wingeth nigh me?
Is it divine or mortal, or of mingled blood?
    Visiting this desolate edge of earth,
Spectator of my agony—with what purpose else?

Behold in chains confined an ill-starred god,
>The detested of Zeus and rejected of all
>The celestial band that assembleth aloft
>In the heavenly courts of the Highest,
>For my too great love of the children of men!
>Pheu, pheu! what again is the murmur I hear
>As of birds hard by?
>And the air is astir with the whispering beat
>Of their hurrying wings.
>Oh, fearful is all that approacheth.

CHORUS OF OCEANIDS (*Strophe 1*)
>O be not fearful — as a friend in flight contending to this
>>rock my airy voyage have I winged.
>>Eager for this adventure, my father's leave hardly I won.
>>Swiftly I rode on the flying breezes.
>I heard afar off the reverberating echoes in my hollow cave,
>>and unflushed with the shame of maidens
>I sped on my chariot-steed unsandalled.

PROMETHEUS
>Aiai, aiai!
>Daughters of Tethys, the bride many-childed of
>Oceanus, who with unslumbering tides
>Doth encompass the earth,
>Bear witness, behold how cruelly bound
>And enchained in a wild and precipitous glen
>I shall keep my disconsolate vigil!

CHORUS (*Antistrophe 1*)
>I see, Prometheus, and a mist of grief descendeth on my
>>vision, tears are springing to my eyes

Thus to behold thy beauty by day and night blasted in
these
Adamant shackles of shame and torment.
For new the rulers who are throned above in heaven, and
the laws of Zeus are new, framed for a harsh dominion.
The mighty of old he hath brought to nothing.

PROMETHEUS

O would in the boundless abyss of the earth,
Bottomless Tartarus,
Where Hades doth welcome the souls of the dead,
In invincible bondage my body were crushed,
That nor god nor another might mock my estate!
But here I am hung as a plaything of storms
And a mark for my enemies' laughter!

CHORUS (*Strophe 2*)

What god is he so hard of heart that such a spectacle could
delight?
Who doth not share thy sufferings, save Zeus? For in his
spirit is no pity. Inflexibly
Fixed on vengeance, still his wrath smiteth the Sons of the
Sky; ay, and shall not soften
Till his heart have its fill of revenge, or a mightier
Hand from him plunder his stolen kingdom.

PROMETHEUS

Yet of me, yet of me, though battered and bent,
Limb-pierced by his shackles of insolent wrong,
Shall the prince who presideth in heaven have need,
To reveal him the new-found plan whereby

Of his sceptre and sway he shall be stripped bare.
And then I, unappeased by his charms honey-tongued
And unmoved by his merciless threats, will withhold
From him all that I know, till he grant me release
From the bonds that encompass my limbs and atone
For the shameful disgrace that I suffer.

CHORUS (*Antistrophe 2*)

Nay, *thou* art bold and dost not bow before thy keen adversities,

And too unbridled is thy tongue. I tremble, and my spirit is
a-quiver with a piercing fear,

With terror for thy future state, when is it fated for thee rest
from these thy labours

To behold? Unapproachable, hard to appease is the

Heart in the breast of the Son of Cronos.

PROMETHEUS

Full well do I know he is harsh and a law
To himself, but in time, notwithstanding, I ween,
Crushed by this danger, his heart shall be humbled,
And, becalming his irreconcilable rage,
He shall hasten to union and friendship with me
Eagerly, eagerly waited.

CHORUS

All things unveil, make manifest to us
Upon what pretext seizing thee doth Zeus
Outrage thee with such agony and shame?
Teach us, unless to speak should bring thee harm.

PROMETHEUS
>   Painful it is for me to speak of this,
>   Painful is silence — 'tis misery every way.
>
>   As soon as war among the gods began
>   And strife internal broke the peace of heaven,
>   Some eager to cast Cronos from his throne
>   That Zeus might reign, and others contrary
>   Intent that Zeus should never rule the gods,
>   Then I, though wise the counsel that I pressed
>   Upon the Titans, Sons of Heaven and Earth,
>   Could win no hearing. All my cunning wiles
>   Counting as nought, in arrogance of heart
>   They hoped by force for easy mastery.
>   But often I had heard my mother, Earth
>   And Themis, one form under many names,
>   Predict the future as it would come to pass,
>   How not by strength nor by the stouter hand,
>   By guile alone the reigning powers would fall.
>   Such was the tale they heard revealed by me
>   But deemed unworthy even of a glance.
>
>   And then, it seemed, my best remaining choice
>   Was, with my mother's aid, to take my stand
>   Where help was welcome, at the side of Zeus;
>   And through my counsels in the nether gloom
>   Of Tartarus ancestral Cronos lies
>   With all his comrades. Such are the services
>   I rendered to the tyrant of the gods,
>   And these cruel penalties are my reward.
>   For tyranny, it seems, is never free
>   From this distemper — faithlessness to friends.
>
>   But to your question, on what pretext he

Outrages me thus, I will now reply.
No sooner was he on his father's throne
Seated secure than he assigned the gods
Their several privileges, to each appointing
Powers, but held the hapless race of man
Of no account, resolving to destroy
All human kind and sow new seed on earth.
And none defied his will in this save me,
I dared to do it, I delivered man
From death and steep destruction. Such the crime
For which I pay with these fell agonies,
Painful to suffer, pitiful to see.
For pitying man in preference to myself
I am debarred from pity; and thus I stand
Tortured, to Zeus a spectacle of shame.

CHORUS

Oh, iron-hearted he and wrought of stone,
Whoe'er, Prometheus, grieveth not for thy
Calamities — a sight I never hoped
To see, and now behold with broken heart.

PROMETHEUS

Ay, to my friends, I *am* a sight for pity.

CHORUS

Canst thou perchance have carried thy daring further?

PROMETHEUS

I stayed man from foreknowledge of his fate.

CHORUS

And what cure for that malady didst thou find?

PROMETHEUS

First, I implanted in his heart blind hopes.

CHORUS

A blessing, truly, hast thou given to man.

PROMETHEUS

And furthermore, I bestowed fire upon him.

CHORUS

Have creatures of a day the flame of fire?

PROMETHEUS

They have, and many arts shall learn therefrom.

CHORUS

Such then the accusation whereon Zeus —

PROMETHEUS

Outrages me and ceases not from wrong.

CHORUS

What, is no end appointed for thy labours?

PROMETHEUS

No end, save when *he* thinks it meet to end them.

CHORUS

When will he? Oh, what hope? Dost thou not see
That thou hast sinned? And yet that word gives me
No pleasure, and pains thee. Let us dismiss
Such thoughts, and from thy labours seek release.

PROMETHEUS

Easy for him who keeps his foot outside
The miry clay to give advice to one

In trouble. All this was known to me:
I willed to sin, I willed it, I confess.
My help to man brought suffering to myself.
Not that I thought that with such pains as these
I would be wasted on precipitous heights,
The tenant of this solitary rock.
But for my present sorrows mourn no more,
Step down to earth and to my future fortunes
Give ear and learn all things from end to end.
O hearken to me, hearken, take compassion
On him who suffers now, for, ever-restless,
Trouble alights on one now, then another.

CHORUS

To thy eager appeal will thy hearers respond
Gladly, Prometheus.
Lo, fleet-footed I step down from my wind-
Swift seat on the ways of the fowls of the air
And alight on the chill earth, eager to hark
To the tale full-told of thy labours.

(*Enter* OCEANUS, *mounted on a sea-horse*)

OCEANUS

To the end of my long journey, Prometheus,
Am I come, from afar have I travelled to thee,
Mounted on this wing-swift bird who is quick
To obey my command without bridle or bit;
And in this thy affliction, believe me, I share.
For indeed I am drawn to thy side by the strong
Constraint of our kinship, and, kinship apart,
There is none that I hold in a higher regard.

I will prove thee the truth of my words — it is not
In my nature to flatter with blandishing tongue, —
For behold, make known to me what is thy need,
And ne'er shalt thou say that Oceanus failed
As a friend to thee faithful and stedfast.

PROMETHEUS

Ah, what is this? Hast thou too come to gaze
Upon my labours? How didst thou dare forsake
The stream that bears thy name and vaulted caverns
Of self-grown rock, to journey to this land,
The mother of iron? Is it thy wish to see
My state and share the burden of my sorrows?
Then look on him who was the friend of Zeus
And fellow-founder of his tyranny,
In what fell agonies he bends my limbs!

OCEANUS

I see, Prometheus, and I would commend
To thee, so quick of wit, the wisest course.
Prepare to know thyself and change thy ways
Anew, for new the tyrant of the gods.
If with such barbed and bitter words thou criest
Defiance, Zeus, though far from hence enthroned
On high, might hear thee, and thy present host
Of ills would seem no more than child's play then.
Nay, most unhappy, lay aside thy rage
And from misfortune seek deliverance.
Antique, perchance, may seem my counsel to thee:
Yet such, Prometheus, is the penalty
Paid by the arrogance of a lofty tongue.
Unhumbled yet, thou dost not bow to trouble

But to these ills thou hast would others add.
No longer, if thou wouldst be schooled by me,
Wilt thou thus kick against the pricks, aware
That our harsh monarch owes account to none.
And I will now depart and do my best
To find release from thy adversities.
But hold thy peace and curb thy turbulent speech;
Or, over-subtle, hast thou not wit to see
A price is set upon an idle tongue?

PROMETHEUS

I count thee happy to be free from blame,
Though in my perils all participant.
And now have done, take no concern for me.
Thou canst not move him — he is immovable, —
And watch that no misfortune waylay *thee*.

OCEANUS

Ay, thou wast born to teach thy neighbours wisdom
But not thyself — thy works are proof of that.
Yet, since I have the will, oppose me not.
For I declare that Zeus will grant to me
This favour and release thee from thy pains.

PROMETHEUS

So far I praise thee, and praise thee ever shall —
Thy willingness lacks nothing. Even so
Spare thyself trouble, for labour spent on me
Will yield no profit, despite thy will to spend it.
So, hold thy peace, beyond the reach of harm.
    For I, though ill my fortune, would not seek
Relief in the distress of others too.

Indeed not so; for even now I mourn
My brother Atlas, who in the far west
Bears on his shoulders in no tender clasp
The massive pillar of the Earth and Heaven.
And the earth-born inmate of Cilicia's caves
I saw likewise and pitied, monster dread,
The hundred-headed Typho, as he fell
Subdued, a god who stood against the gods,
Hissing forth terror from his horrid jaws
And from his eyes darting disastrous fire
In challenge to the tyranny of Zeus,
Till on him fell the Lord's unslumbering bolt,
The swift-descending lightning-blast of heaven,
Which struck him low for all his overbold
And high-mouthed arrogance; pierced to the heart,
His cindered strength was thundered out of him.
And now his limp and outstretched body lies
Beside the passage of the ocean straits
Crushed by the roots of Etna's deep foundations;
Upon whose summit stands Hephaestus' smithy,
Under the rumbling ground, whence yet shall spring
Rivers of fire with ravenous jaws devouring
The level fields of fruitful Sicily:
Such are the shafts that Typho's buried wrath,
Though turned to ashes by the bolt of Zeus,
Shall hurl in seething cataracts of fire.

　　Nay, thou hast seen; there is no need for me
To school thee. Save thyself as thou knowest how,
And I will bear my sufferings until
The heart of Zeus with spleen is surfeited.

OCEANUS

> Hast thou, Prometheus, never learnt that words
> Are the physicians of distempered rage?

PROMETHEUS

> If in due season they assuage the spirit
> And not by force constrict the swollen heart.

OCEANUS

> What is the penalty thou seest prescribed
> For willingness and courage? Teach me that.

PROMETHEUS

> Pains to no purpose and light-headed folly.

OCEANUS

> Then do not seek to cure my malady:
> Prudence, miscounted folly, profits most.

PROMETHEUS

> Indeed the charge of folly would fall on me.

OCEANUS

> Plainly your words would send me home again.

PROMETHEUS

> Let not your tears for me make enmity—

OCEANUS

> With him new-throned in heaven's omnipotence?

PROMETHEUS

> Beware of him, lest thou provoke his wrath.

OCEANUS
        Thy fate, Prometheus, is my teacher there.

PROMETHEUS
        Make haste, begone, preserve thy present mind.

OCEANUS
        To willing ears that word of thine is spoken:
        For see, my winged horse impatiently
        Fans the smooth paths of heaven, and travel-tired
        In his own stall would gladly bend the knee.

CHORUS (*Strophe 1*)
        I weep for thee, weep for thy hapless fate, Prometheus.
        From a full eye are the warm fountains of sorrow on a
                tender cheek descending
        And its bloom with tears bedewing;
        For enthroned in dire oppression by his self-appointed
                edict
        To the gods of old the lord Zeus doth reveal o'erweening
                power.

Antistrophe 1
        And all the earth lifteth her voice in lamentation,
        And the mortals who on earth dwell for thy lost splendour
                lament and mourn thy brethren's
        Immemorial age of grandeur;
        And the peoples who inhabit the expanse of holy Asia
        In thy loud-lamented labours do partake through grief's
                communion.

Strophe 2

Those who rule the coast of Colchis,
Maids in battle unaffrighted,
Ay, the Scythian swarm that roameth
Earth's far verges around the wide
Waters of Lake Maeotis;

Antistrophe 2

Araby's flower of martial manhood
Who upon Caucasian highlands
Guard their mountain-cradled stronghold,
Host invincible, armed with keen
Spears in the press of battle.

Epode

But one god else in labours have I seen,
In fetters of adamant held,
The Titan Atlas, who with unequalled strength
The massy pillar of the sky
Alone upholds and weeps his hard fate.
The waves of Ocean cry aloud
Falling, full of sighs the deep,
And Hades stirs with subterranean moan;
Yea and the pure river-fountains are poured
In streams of sad compassion.

PROMETHEUS

     Think not my silence is enforced by pride
     Or obstinacy — by bitterness of heart
     To see myself so savagely outraged.

And yet for these new deities who else
Prescribed their powers and privileges but I?
Of that no more, for the tale that I could tell
Is known to you; but hearken to the plight
Of man, in whom, born witless as a babe,
I planted mind and the gift of understanding.
I speak of men with no intent to blame
But to expound my gracious services:
Who first, with eyes to see, did see in vain,
With ears to hear, did hear not, but as shapes
Figured in dreams throughout their mortal span
Confounded all things, knew not how to raise
Brick-woven walls sun-warmed, nor build in wood,
But had their dwelling, like the restless ant,
In sunless nooks of subterranean caves.
No token sure they had of winter's cold,
No herald of the flowery spring or season
Of ripening fruit, but laboured without wit
In all their works, till I revealed the obscure
Risings and settings of the stars of heaven.
Yea, and the art of number, arch-device,
I founded, and the craft of written words,
The world's recorder, mother of the Muse.
I first subdued the wild beasts of the field
To slave in pack and harness and relieve
The mortal labourer of his heaviest toil,
And yoked in chariots, quick to serve the rein,
The horse, prosperity's proud ornament;
And none but I devised the mariner's car
On hempen wing roaming the trackless ocean.
  Such the resources I have found for man,

Yet for myself, alas, have none to bring
From this my present plight deliverance.

CHORUS

Thy plight is cruel indeed: bereft of wit
And like a bad physician falling sick,
Thou dost despair and for thine own disease
Canst find no physic nor medicament.

PROMETHEUS

Nay, hear the rest and thou wilt marvel more,
What cunning arts and artifices I planned.
    Of all the greatest, if a man fell sick,
There was no remedy, nor shredded herb
Nor draught to drink nor ointment, and in default
Of physic their flesh withered, until I
Revealed the blends of gentle medicines
Wherewith they arm themselves against disease.
And many ways of prophecy I ordered,
And first interpreted what must come of dreams
In waking hours, and the obscure import
Of wayside signs and voices I defined,
And taught them to discern the various flight
Of taloned birds, which of them favourable
And which of ill foreboding, and the ways
Of life by each pursued, their mating-seasons,
Their hatreds and their loves one for another;
The entrails too, of what texture and hue
They must appear to please the sight of heaven;
The dappled figure of the gall and liver,
The thigh-bone wrapt in fat and the long chine

I burnt and led man to the riddling art
Of divination; and augury by fire,
For long in darkness hid, I brought to light.
Such help I gave, and more — beneath the earth,
The buried benefits of humanity,
Iron and bronze, silver and gold, who else
Can claim that he revealed to man but I?
None, I know well, unless an idle braggart.
  In these few words learn briefly my whole tale:
Prometheus founded all the arts of man.

CHORUS

Render not aid to man unrighteously,
Neglectful of thine own misfortunes — thus
I have good hope that, from these bonds released,
Thou shalt return to power, the peer of Zeus.

PROMETHEUS

Not so nor yet hath all-determining Fate
Ordained the end, but, when ten thousand pains
Have crushed my body, from bonds shall I escape.
For Art is weaker than Necessity.

CHORUS

Who then is helmsman of Necessity?

PROMETHEUS

The Fates three-formed and the remembering Furies.

CHORUS

Is Zeus himself less powerful than these?

PROMETHEUS

He could not alter that which is ordained.

CHORUS

What *is* ordained for Zeus save power eternal?

PROMETHEUS

Question no more — I will not answer that.

CHORUS

Some solemn secret doth thy heart embrace.

PROMETHEUS

Nay, turn to other things — I must not yet
Make *that* tale manifest, but keep it veiled
Most jealously — by guarding that shall I
From these fell bonds and agonies escape.

CHORUS (*Strophe 1*)

Ne'er may the Ruler of all, Zeus, athwart my purpose array
his supreme power,

Ne'er may I be slow to present to the gods burnt-offerings
tended with prayer

Nigh my father's waters, the slumberless stream which
faileth not;

Ne'er may I sin with my lips — may this prayer abide with
me and ne'er within me perish!

Antistrophe 1

Happy is he who doth pass length of life in sureness of hope
and doth feed his

Heart on gladness sprung from a conscience clear: for truly
I shudder as I

View the thousand sufferings fated for thee. Almighty Zeus

Dauntlessly hast thou defied, ay with froward purpose
　　prized mankind too high, Prometheus.

Strophe 2

What reward for thy favours, and where is there succour at
　　hand to save thee
In the things of a day? Or have thine eyes not seen how
In a vain, unavailing, dreamlike impotence the purblind
　　peoples
Of the earth are imprisoned eternally? Ne'er shall the
Harmony ordered of Zeus be turned awry by mortal coun-
　　sels.

Antistrophe 2

Thus indeed am I taught by the sight of thy hapless fate,
　　Prometheus.
For alas! unalike the song that now I sing thee
To the tune that of old around thy bridal bath and bed was
　　chanted,
As thou camest with gifts to my father to win from him
Beautiful Hesione for thy marriage-bed, a bride to sleep
　　beside thee.

(*Enter* IO, *horned like a cow*)

IO

　　What people and place is this? whom do I see
　　Bridled in boulders and harnessed in stone,
　　Laid bare to the storm?
　　What offence hath condemned thee to such bitter pain?

O declare to me, where
In the world have my wanderings borne me?

Ah, ah!
Again the gadfly's sting — unhappy maiden!
The ghost of earth-born Argus wakes again.
I see the Herdsman hundred-eyed approach me.
Ever he follows, fixed on me his crafty eye;
Whom even after death the earth conceals not.
Ever he tracks me down out of the land of death,
He hunts me hungry, far astray, hapless wanderer on
    sand-strewn shores.

Strophe
Ever the sleepy music is around my ears,
Melody shrill whispered on waxen reed.
Alas, where, alas,
Where do these wand'rings lead, wanderings aimless, wild?
How have I, O Cronian King,
How have I given offence that I am maltreated so, bound
    and yoked fast to these miseries, woe is me!
What cause hast thou to madden a helpless maid
With terror of goading torment?
Give me to flames to burn, bury me underground,
Ay, to sea-monsters cast my flesh.
Grudge me not, I pray thee, grant my prayer, O king!
Enough my restless wanderings,
I can no more endure, and know not where to find
Respite from this anguish.
The cow-horned maid cries to thee: hear her cry!

PROMETHEUS

> I hear indeed the gadfly-hunted maid,
> Daughter of Inachus, who fired the heart
> Of Zeus with love, and now by Hera's hate
> Is doomed to run her lengthy race of pain.

Io (*Antistrophe*)

> How dost thou know to call me by my father's name?
> Tell me, speak to an unhappy maid,
> Who art thou, hapless one,
> Quick to greet me by my true name with knowledge sure
> Of the distemper heaven-sent to waste my limbs, pangs that
> spur feet afar wandering, woe is me!
> Distraught with pain and leaping in frenzy high
> I come, to spiteful Hera's
> Venomous wiles a victim, and I ask, of all
> Evil-starred mortal kind, alas,
> Who hath known such anguish? Nay but tell me true,
> Declare to me what sufferings
> Remain, what physic can assuage my plague—
> Show me, if thou knowest!
> O speak, hear the far-wandering maiden's cry!

PROMETHEUS

> I will tell clearly all thou seek'st to know,
> No riddles weaving, but a plain-told tale,
> Even as 'tis meet to open the lips to friends.
> Thou seest Prometheus, giver of fire to man.

Io

> O common benefactor of mankind,
> Prometheus, why art thou condemned to this?

PROMETHEUS

Even now I ceased to mourn my own misfortunes.

IO

Wilt thou not grant the gift I ask of thee?

PROMETHEUS

Say what thou askest: all shalt thou be told.

IO

Declare who prisoned thee in this rocky glen.

PROMETHEUS

The will of Zeus worked by Hephaestus' hand.

IO

Of what offence is this the penalty?

PROMETHEUS

If I reveal so much, that will suffice.

IO

Nay, show me also when shall I behold
The term of my unhappy wanderings.

PROMETHEUS

Better remain in ignorance of that.

IO

O hide not from me that which I must suffer!

PROMETHEUS

'Tis not that I am jealous of the gift.

IO

Then why so loth to make all manifest?

PROMETHEUS

>I grudge it not, but fear to break thy heart.

IO

>Nay, spare me not against my own desire.

PROMETHEUS

>Since thou dost wish it, I must speak. Attend.

CHORUS

>Not yet: to me likewise vouchsafe a favour.
>First let us learn her malady and hear
>The tale of her wild wanderings, before
>She learns from thee what agonies yet remain.

PROMETHEUS

>Io, thy task it is to grant them this.
>Remember, too, they are thy father's sisters,
>And to bemoan the bitterness of fortune
>To listeners who are like to be moved
>To weep with thee, is labour worth the pains.

IO

>I know not how I can deny your wish:
>All that you seek to know shall in plain words
>Be told. And yet I blush even to recall
>How I, unhappy girl, was seized by that
>Tempest from heaven and beauty's swift decay.
>   Night after night dream-visions haunting me
>Came to my chamber and beguiled me thus
>With winning words: O greatly blessed maid,
>Wherefore so long a virgin, when 'tis thine
>To wed the Highest? Zeus with sharp desire

Of thee is smitten and longs for the embrace
Of Cypris. O my child, do not disdain
The bed of Zeus, but get thee to the deep
Meadows of Lerna, thy father's pasturage,
That there the eye of Zeus may ease desire.

Such were the dreams that each night restlessly
Beset and troubled me, until I dared
To tell my father of those night-fantasies.
Then he sent forth his wise interpreters
To Pytho and Dodona's oaks, to enquire
What might be said or done to please the gods.
With dimly-worded messages they returned,
Obscure reports of dark significance,
Till Inachus received at last a clear
Reply enjoining on him this command,
That he must drive me out from hearth and home
To wander to the confines of the earth,
And, if he disobeyed, the bolt of Zeus
Would visit him, destroying all his house.

Such were the oracles of Loxias,
And he, as they commanded, cast me forth
Against his will and mine, constrained to do
That which he would not by the curb of Zeus.
Then suddenly, my wit and woman's form
Distorted, with horned temples, as you see,
I sped distraught to the Cerchnean streams
And springs of Lerna, savagely pursued
By Argus, the fierce earth-born Herdsman, who
Kept watch upon me with his hundred eyes,
Till wing-swift death, descending unawares,
Did cut him off; but, gadfly-hunted, I

Before God's scourge still flee across the world.
　　Such is my story, and, if thou canst tell
What yet awaits me, speak, and let not pity
Temper the true with false, for I abhor
Above all plagues the tale compact of lies.

CHORUS

O horrible!
Words so strange, words so full of fear
I never dreamed would come to beat against my ears,
Terror and torture, a sight that doth wound the eye,
Smite my soul with scourging anguish.
Alas, O Fate, Fate, I shudder
With fear to behold the state of Io.

PROMETHEUS

Too soon thou criest, thy heart surcharged with fear.
Keep back thy tears till thou hast learnt the rest.

CHORUS

Speak, teach us all: to those who are in sickness
Foreknowledge of their suffering brings relief.

PROMETHEUS

Your first request you have obtained of me
With ease; for first from her you sought to hear
The unhappy tale of her past sufferings.
Now hear what is to come, what agonies
This young girl must endure from Hera yet.
And thou, O seed of Inachus, lay to heart
What I shall tell, and learn thy journey's end.
　　First turn thy face towards the rising sun

Across the unploughed meadow-lands, until
Thou com'st unto the Scythians, wanderers
Who dwell on wheels in wicker chariots,
Armed with far-flying shafts of archery.
Approach not these, but, skirting the long strand
Beside the moaning ocean-surf, pass on
Till on thy left hand thou shalt find the tribe
Of Chalybs, iron-craftsmen, whom beware,
A savage people and inhospitable.
And thou shalt come to the Violent Stream, well-named,
Whose swollen flood must not be forded till
The highest top of Caucasus confront
Thy gaze, from whence that river pours his strength
Sheer from the summit; then, the star-neighbouring peaks
Behind thee, turn thy steps towards the south,
Till thou shalt come unto the Amazons,
Man-hating people, who in Themiscyra
Shall dwell beside Thermodon, by the rock
Of rugged Salmydessus, whose welcome waits
The fearful seaman, stepmother to ships.
And they will gladly lead thee on thy way,
Till at the gateways of the lake thou comest
To the Cimmerian Isthmus, whence pass on
And with stout heart tread the Maeotic Sea.
And of that passage shall mankind relate
The wondrous tale for ever, and shall name
Those waters Bosporus in thy memory.
Thence, leaving Europe, thou shalt come unto
The land of Asia.
    (*To Chorus*) Is it plain to you
The tyrant of the gods is violent

In all his ways? A god, lusting to lie
With mortal woman, he persecutes her thus.
A brutal lover seeks thy hand, my child;
For that which I have now revealed hath scarce
Opened the prelude of thy agony.

CHORUS

Oh me, alas!

PROMETHEUS

Again that cry of pain! What wilt thou do
When thou hast heard the sorrows that remain?

CHORUS

Are further sufferings in store for her?

PROMETHEUS

Ay, a tempestuous sea of misery.

IO

What profit then to live? Let me in haste
Cast myself down from yonder dizzy height,
And buy with one swift leap deliverance
From all my labours! Once to die is better
Than length of days in sorrow without end.

PROMETHEUS

How ill wouldst thou endure *my* sufferings,
Who am by Fate appointed not to die.
That were indeed deliverance from pain,
But for my labours now there is no date
Decreed till Zeus from tyranny hath fallen.

IO

What, can it be the power of Zeus shall fail?

PROMETHEUS
> Glad wouldst thou be, I think, to see that day.

IO
> And who would not, whom Zeus made suffer so?

PROMETHEUS
> Then be assured that it shall come to pass.

IO
> But who shall strip his tyrant sceptre from him?

PROMETHEUS
> Himself by his own empty-headed counsels.

IO
> But how? Declare, if 'tis no harm to tell.

PROMETHEUS
> A marriage shall he make which he will rue.

IO
> Divine or mortal? If 'tis lawful, speak!

PROMETHEUS
> What matter? 'Tis not lawful to say more.

IO
> A bride of his shall cast him from his throne?

PROMETHEUS
> A son shall she bear stronger than his sire.

IO
> And from this destiny has he no escape?

PROMETHEUS
> None, save myself, freed from captivity.

IO

> Who shall deliver thee in despite of Zeus?

PROMETHEUS

> One of thine own descendants shall it be.

IO

> What, shall a son of mine deliver thee?

PROMETHEUS

> The tenth generation and three besides.

IO

> Hard to interpret is that prophecy.

PROMETHEUS

> And of thine own pains seek to learn no more.

IO

> Do not first promise, then withhold, thy gift.

PROMETHEUS

> Two gifts I offer: one or other choose.

IO

> What are they? Speak, that I may make my choice.

PROMETHEUS

> Resolve which thou wouldst hear expounded thee —
> Thy future trials, or my deliverer.

CHORUS

> Nay, grant to her one favour, and accord
> To us the other. Do not grudge the tale:

To her, her future path make manifest,
Declare to us thine own deliverer.

PROMETHEUS

Since you desire it, I will not refuse
To manifest all that you seek to know.
First, Io, learn thy tearful wanderings
And write them on the tables of thy heart.
    Having passed the stream that parts two continents,
Take the bright paths trod by the rising sun
Beside the roar of ocean, until thou come
To the plains Gorgonian of Cisthene, where
Dwell the ancient hags, daughters of Phorcys three,
Swanlike in shape, sharing one common eye,
One-toothed, on whom the sun hath never shed
His radiant beam nor the night-wandering moon;
And near them their three sisters, clothed in wings,
The serpent-cinctured Gorgons, foes of man,
On whom no mortal e'er shall look and live.
Such is the prelude to thy pilgrimage.
And now to another fearful sight give ear:
Beware the savage, sharp-mouthed hounds of Zeus,
The griffins, and the one-eyed thievish host
Of Arimaspian horsemen, who beside
The banks of Pluto's golden river dwell.
Approach not these, but at the ends of earth
Seek out the swarthy tribesmen who abide
At the Sun's fount by the brook of Ethiop,
Along whose verges journey till thou come
To the cataract where from the Bybline Hills
Are spilt the holy waters of the Nile,

Leading thee on to that three-cornered land,
Nilotis, where thou, Io, and thy sons
Shall found at last a far-off colony.

   If there is aught in this of dark import,
Repeat your questions, till the tale is clear.
I have much leisure, more than I desire.

CHORUS

If aught remain, passed over or to come,
Of her unhappy wanderings, speak on.
If all hath been made manifest, vouchsafe
My share in that which thou hast promised us.

PROMETHEUS

The end of all her travels she hath heard;
But, lest she should misdoubt my prophecy,
What she endured before her coming hither
I will relate, to prove my story true.

   The bulk of that long tale I will pass over
And to thy latter wanderings proceed.
When thou didst walk the wide Molossian plains,
Even to the lofty ridges of Dodona, where
Thesprotian Zeus holds his prophetic seat
And stands the marvel of the Speaking Oaks,
By whom in plain and unambiguous words
Thou wast proclaimed the glorious Bride Elect
Of Zeus — Ah, is thy memory touched by that? —
Then, gadfly-hunted down the long sea-shore,
Thou didst press on to the Gulf of Rhea, whence
Upon thy tracks the tempest beat thee back;
Wherefore, in time to come, that hollow sea,

Believe me, shall be called Ionian
By all mankind in memory of thy passage.
    Accept this testimony of my understanding,
That it perceives more than the eye beholds.
And now the rest will I reveal to all,
My steps retracing to my former tale.
    A city stands, Canobus, at the extreme
Of Egypt, on the silted mouth of Nile;
And there shall Zeus, thy wits restoring with
A touch, lay on thee his unfearful hand;
And, of that touch begot, thereafter named,
Thou shalt bear swarthy Epaphus, who shall till
The wide lands watered by the spacious Nile.
His fifty children, fifth in descent from him,
Against their will to Argos shall return,
A band of maidens, fleeing from the bed
Of fifty cousins, who with hearts astir,
Hawks after doves, in hot pursuit shall follow,
Unrighteous huntsmen, coveting a match
Unlawful, to be cut off by jealous heaven.
For Pelasgia shall welcome them with deeds
Of blood by woman dared in the dark of night:
Each bride shall rob each bridegroom of his breath,
Steeping in slaughter the dagger's double blade.
Thus may the Cyprian greet *my* enemies!
One daughter only, softened by desire,
Her hand shall hold and blunt the edge of her
Resolve, electing rather to endure
The taunt of coward than of murderess;
And she shall bear a race of kings in Argos.
Too long it were to trace the tale in full,

But from her seed at last shall spring a brave
And glorious Archer, who from bondage shall
Deliver me!
               Such is the oracle
My age-old Mother, Titan Themis, spake.
So shall it be, but how, 't would take me long
To tell, and thee to hear would profit not.

IO

Eleleu! eleleu!
Yet again is my mind set aflame by the scourge
Of the maddening goad, and the arrow unforged
Driveth me onward;
And my heart is a-plunging with fear in my breast,
And my eyes to and fro wildly are glancing,
And distracted I veer far out of my course
On the wind of my frenzy, unbridled my tongue,
And a torrent of speech falls broken upon
Irresistible waves of disaster.   (*Exit*)

CHORUS (*Strophe 1*)
Wise in exceeding wisdom
He who first did weigh in his heart and declare this saying
    in speech to his neighbours:
Blest are they who seek not a marriage above their own
    degree;
May not the meek and lowly aspire to the hand
Full of gold and exalted in riches, or seek
Wedlock with the nobles of the world.

Antistrophe 1

Ne'er may it fall to my lot, O
Fate all things fulfilling, to be called to the bed of Zeus as
    the bride of the Highest;
Ne'er may I by lords of the heavenly host be woo'd or won;
I tremble ev'n to look on the maiden who hates
Her Olympian wooer, destined to wander in pain
Far and wide, pursued by Hera's jealous rage.

Epode

For me, when even-matched the union,
Naught is there to fear, but only
Ne'er may god above let fall love's glance upon me!
O helpless agony, fruitful in fruitless tears!
What the end might be I know not.
Yea, the plan that Zeus designs
None shall avail to alter.

PROMETHEUS

And yet shall Zeus, so obstinate of spirit,
Be humbled, such a marriage will he make
Which shall o'erthrow him from his tyranny's
Celestial seat for ever; and then the curse
His father Cronos uttered as he fell
From his ancestral throne shall be fulfilled.
Such is his fate, which to avert can none
Of all the gods instruct him, only I —
I know the manner of it. So let him sit
Proudly exultant in his airy thunders
And brandishing his bolt of lightning fire;
For nothing can avail to save him from

Downfall disastrous and dishonourable.
Such is the wrestler he now trains against
Himself, a prodigy unconquerable,
Whose strength shall battle down the lightning blast
And master the mighty roar of heaven's thunder;
And then that brandished spear which plagues the Earth,
The trident of Poseidon, shall be shattered,
And, stumbling upon disaster, Zeus shall learn
How far from sovranty is servitude.

CHORUS

Thy wish has fathered this proud threat to Zeus.

PROMETHEUS

I speak what shall be, likewise what I desire.

CHORUS

Is it possible that Zeus shall serve another?

PROMETHEUS

Yea, and be yoked to harsher pains than *these*.

CHORUS

Hast thou no fear to hurl such menaces?

PROMETHEUS

What should I fear, predestined not to die?

CHORUS

He will devise yet greater anguish for thee.

PROMETHEUS

Then let him do it! All things have I foreseen.

CHORUS

The wise are those who bow to Adrasteia.

PROMETHEUS

 Bow down, adore, cringe on thy present master;
 To me is Zeus a thing of no account.
 Nay, let him reign supreme and work his will
 For his brief day — he shall not rule for long.

  But see where comes the courier of Zeus,
 The lackey of the new tyrant of the gods.
 Some news, assuredly, he has to tell.

HERMES

 Thou, cunning wit, outbittering bitterness,
 Who gave to creatures of a day the gods'
 High privileges, thee, thief of fire, I call.
 The Father bids thee instantly reveal
 This vaunted marriage, whate'er it be, whereby
 His power shall fail, and that not riddlingly
 But clear in each particular, and so spare me
 A second journey; for thou seest, Prometheus,
 The heart of Zeus is softened not by this.

PROMETHEUS

 How solemn-mouthed and puffed with arrogance
 The announcement, as befits a gods' attendant!
 New, new are you to power, and yet you think
 Your citadel is impregnable. Have I not seen
 Two tyrants cast already from their thrones? —
 Ay, and shall see the third, your present sovran,
 In shame hurled headlong: and dost thou think that I
 In fear of these new gods will cower and quake?
 Far, far am I from that. And, as for thee,

> Begone, retrace the path that brought thee hither;
> For thou shalt learn nothing thou seek'st to know.

HERMES

> Such was the obstinate spirit which called down
> Thy present calamities upon thy head.

PROMETHEUS

> I have no wish to change my adverse fortune,
> Be well assured, for thy subservience.

HERMES

> Better indeed to wait upon this rock
> Than serve as trusted minister of Zeus.

PROMETHEUS

> Such arrogance befits the arrogant.

HERMES

> In thy present state, it seems, thou dost exult.

PROMETHEUS

> Exult! May I behold my enemies
> Exulting so, and thee I count among them.

HERMES

> What, dost thou blame me also for thy plight?

PROMETHEUS

> In simple truth, all of the gods I hate,
> Who, served by me so well, maltreat me thus.

HERMES

> 'Tis plain, most sorely is thy mind diseased.

PROMETHEUS

> Is hate of enemies sickness? Then heal me not.

HERMES

    Thou wouldst be insufferable in prosperity.

PROMETHEUS

    Ah me!

HERMES

    Ah me! That is a cry unknown to Zeus.

PROMETHEUS

    Yet all is being taught by aging Time.

HERMES

    Ay, *thou* hast yet to learn a wiser mind.

PROMETHEUS

    True, or I'd not have spoken to a slave.

HERMES

    Thou wilt not grant, then, what the Father asks.

PROMETHEUS

    I would repay him if I owed him aught.

HERMES

    Thou hast reviled me as though I were a child.

PROMETHEUS

    And art thou not more simple than a child
    If thou dost hope to learn one jot from me?
    No rack nor pillory can Zeus devise
    To move me to make manifest these things
    Till he release me from these insolent bonds.
    So, let him hurl his sulphurous flames from heaven,
    With white-winged snow and subterranean thunder

Make chaos and confusion of the world!
Not thus will he constrain my tongue to tell
By whose hand he from tyranny shall fall.

HERMES

Take thought, consider, art thou helped by this?

PROMETHEUS

These things were seen and thought on long ago.

HERMES

Nay, bring thyself, infatuate, to learn
From this thy present state a sounder mind.

PROMETHEUS

'Tis vain, thy words might sooner stem the waves.
Or dost thou deem that I, fearing the purpose
Of Zeus, will, woman-hearted, supplicate
My hated adversary with bow abased
And abject inclination of my palms,
To free me from my bondage? It cannot be.

HERMES

Much to no purpose have I said, it seems.
Unmelted art thou yet nor softened by
My prayers, but, like a newly-bridled colt,
Dost champ and chafe against the irksome rein.
Yet the conceit that gives thee strength is frail:
For obstinacy, sustained not by a mind
Of healthy judgment, has no strength at all.
    Consider, if thou wilt not hearken to me,
What dreadful tempest and wild waves of woe
Will overwhelm thee. First, this icy cliff

The Father's thunder-clap and lightning-flame
Shall blast asunder, and thy body, clasped
In the rock's embrace, bury beneath the earth:
Till, having outlived an endless expanse of Time,
Thou shalt return to light, and then the hound
Of Zeus, the blood-red eagle, ravenously
Shall tear thy tattered body limb from limb,
An uninvited, day-long banqueter
Feasting upon thy liver's blackened flesh.
Such woe awaits thee, whereto expect no end
Until some god appear, relieving thee
Of toil, content to face the lightless glooms
Of Hades and the pit of Tartarus.
    Even so take counsel with thyself, for this
Is no fictitious menace, but too true:
To speak false is unknown to the mouth of Zeus,
Each word shall be accomplished. So then, do you
Take heed, deliberate, and do not hold
Good counsel cheaper than an obstinate spirit.

CHORUS

To us it seems that Hermes speaks in season,
Bidding thee lay aside thy obstinacy
And with good counsel walk the path of wisdom.
Yield! It is baseness for the wise to err.

PROMETHEUS

Known to me, known was the message that he
Hath proclaimed, and for none is it shameful to bear
At the hands of his enemies evil and wrong.
So now let him cast, if it please him, the two-

Edged curl of his lightning, and shatter the sky
With his thundering frenzy of furious winds;
Let the earth be uptorn from her roots by the storm
Of his anger, and Ocean with turbulent tides
Pile up, till engulfed are the paths of the stars;
Down to the bottomless blackness of Tartarus
Let my body be cast, caught in the whirling
Waters of Destiny:
For with death I shall not be stricken!

HERMES

Nay, such are the feverish cries of a mind
Distorted, the crazed counsels of madmen.
What but the depth of distraction that desperate
Boast? what sign yet that his fury abates?
Be it so; and do you, who have come to his side
In compassion, begone, make good your escape,
That you may not be struck down senseless and stunned
By the roar of the thunder of heaven.

CHORUS

To a different tune must thou speak to persuade;
That turbulent threat is beyond sufferance.
Wouldst thou have me a coward, betraying a friend?
What he must I am willing to bear at his side.
For disloyalty I have been taught to detest—
The disease above all
That repels me with hatred and loathing.

HERMES

Be it so, but remember I warned you away,
Nor, embroiled in the meshes of ruin, complain

Of your fortune, nor feign that unwarned, unawares
Zeus suddenly smote you, but blame yourselves:
Yea, wittingly, willingly, folly-beguiled,
Will your feet be entrapped
In the far-flung nets of disaster!

PROMETHEUS

O mark, no longer in word but in deed,
Earth has been shaken;
The reverberant thunder is heard from the deep,
And the forked flame flares of the lightning, the coiled
Dust flieth upward, the four winds are at play
Frolicking wildly in ruin and riot,
And the sky and the sea in confusion are one:
Such is the storm Zeus gathers against me,
Ever nearer approaching with terrible tread.
O majestical Mother, O heavenly Sky,
In whose region revolveth the Light of the World,
Thou seest the wrongs that I suffer!

Oedipus Rex

SOPHOCLES

Characters

OEDIPUS, *King of Thebes*.

PRIEST *of Zeus*.

CREON, *brother to Jocasta the Queen*.

TIRESIAS, *a Prophet, with the title of King*.

A *Messenger from Corinth*.

An *old Shepherd*.

A *Second Messenger, servant of Oedipus' household*.

JOCASTA *the Queen, wife to Oedipus, formerly married to Laius, the last King*.

ANTIGONE,
ISMENE, } *daughters to Oedipus and Jocasta*.

The CHORUS *is composed of Senators of Thebes*.

Inhabitants of Thebes, Attendants.

A *Boy leading Tiresias*.

Oedipus Rex

Scene, before the Royal Palace at Thebes. Enter OEDIPUS; *to him the Priest of Zeus, and Inhabitants of Thebes.*

OEDIPUS   Children, you modern brood of Cadmus* old,
        What mean you, sitting in your sessions here,
        High-coronalled with votive olive-boughs,
        While the whole city teems with incense-smoke,
        And paean hymns, and sounds of woe the while?
        Deeming unmeet, my children, this to learn
        From others, by the mouth of messengers,
        I have myself come hither, Oedipus,
        Known far and wide by name. Do thou, old man,
        Since 'tis thy privilege to speak for these,
        Say in what case ye stand; if of alarm,
        Or satisfaction with my readiness
        To afford all aid; hard-hearted must I be,
        Did I not pity such petitioners.
PRIEST   Great Oedipus, my country's governor,
        Thou seest our generations, who besiege
        Thy altars here; some not yet strong enough
        To flutter far; some priests, with weight of years
        Heavy, myself of Zeus; and these, the flower
        Of our young manhood; all the other folk
        Sit, with like branches, in the market-place;

* Founder of Thebes.

By the Ismenian hearth oracular*
And the twin shrines of Pallas.** Lo, the city
Labours—thyself art witness—over-deep
Already, powerless to uprear her head
Out of the abysses of a surge of blood;
Stricken in the budding harvest of her soil,
Stricken in her pastured herds, and barren travail
Of women; and He, the God with spear of fire,
Leaps on the city, a cruel pestilence,
And harries it; whereby the Cadmean home
Is all dispeopled, and with groan and wail
The blackness of the Grave made opulent.
Not that we count thee as the peer of Heaven,
I, nor these children, seat us at thy hearth;
But as of men found foremost in affairs,
Chances of life and shifts of Providence;
Whose coming to our Cadmean town released
The toll we paid, of a hard Sorceress,***
And that, without instruction or advice
Of our imparting; but of Heaven it came
Thou art named, and known, our life's establisher.
Thee therefore, Oedipus, the mightiest head
Among us all, all we thy suppliants
Implore to find some way to succour us,
Whether thou knowest it through some voice from heaven,
Or, haply of some man; for I perceive
In men experienced that their counsels best
Find correspondence in things actual.
Haste thee, most absolute sir, be the state's builder!
Haste thee, look to it; doth not our country now
Call thee deliverer, for thy zeal of yore?
Never let us remember of thy rule

* Referring to Ismene, a legendary Theban woman.
** Athena.
*** The Sphinx, whose riddle Oedipus guessed.

That we stood once erectly, and then fell;
But build this city in stability!
With a fair augury didst thou shape for us
Our fortune then; like be thy prowess now!
If thou wilt rule this land (which thou art lord of),
It were a fairer lordship filled with folk
Than empty; towers and ships are nothingness,
Void of our fellow men to inhabit them.

OEDIPUS   Ah my poor children, what you come to seek
Is known already—not unknown to me.
You are all sick, I know it; and in your sickness
There is not one of you so sick as I.
For in your case his own particular pain
Comes to each singly; but my heart at once
Groans for the city, and for myself, and you.
Not therefore as one taking rest in sleep
Do you uprouse me; rather deem of me
As one that wept often, and often came
By many ways through labyrinths of care;
And the one remedy that I could find
By careful seeking—I supplied it. Creon,
Menoeceus' son, the brother of my queen,
I sent to Pytho, to Apollo's house,
To ask him by what act or word of mine
I might redeem this city; and the hours
Already measured even with today
Make me solicitous how he has sped;
For he is longer absent than the time
Sufficient, which is strange. When he shall come,
I were a wretch did I not then do all
As the God shews.

PRIEST   In happy time thou speak'st;
As these, who tell me Creon is at hand.

OEDIPUS   Ah King Apollo, might he but bring grace,
Radiant in fortune, as he is in face!

PRIEST   I think he comes with cheer; he would not, else,

Thus be approaching us with crown on brow,
All berries of the bay.

OEDIPUS   We shall know soon;
He is within hearing.

Enter CREON, *attended.*

                              My good lord and cousin,
Son of Menoeceus,
What answer of the God have you brought home?

CREON   Favourable; I mean, even what sounds ominously,
If it have issue in the way forthright,
May all end well.

OEDIPUS   How runs the oracle?
I am not confident, nor prone to fear
At what you say, so far.

CREON   If you desire
To hear while these stand near us, I am ready
To speak at once—or to go in with you.

OEDIPUS   Speak before all! My heavy load of care
More for their sake than for my own I bear.

CREON   What the God told me, that will I declare.
Phoebus our Lord gives us express command
To drive pollution, bred within this land,
Out of the country, and not cherish it
Beyond the power of healing.

OEDIPUS   By what purge?
What is the tenor of your tragedy?

CREON   Exile, or recompense of death for death;
Since 'tis this blood makes winter to the city.

OEDIPUS   Whose fate is this he signifies?
CREON   My liege,
We had a leader, once, over this land,
Called Laius—ere you held the helm of state.

OEDIPUS   So I did hear; I never saw the man.
CREON   The man is dead; and now, we are clearly bidden
To bring to account certain his murderers.

OEDIPUS   And where on earth are they? Where shall be found
      This dim-seen track-mark of an ancient crime?
CREON   "Within this land," it ran. That which is sought,
      That may be caught. What is unheeded scapes us.
OEDIPUS   Was it at home, afield, or anywhere
      Abroad, that Laius met this violent end?
CREON   He went professedly on pilgrimage;
      But since he started, came back home no more.
OEDIPUS   Nor any messenger nor way-fellow
      Looked on, from whom one might have learnt his story
      And used it?
CREON   No, they perished, all but one;
      He fled, affrighted; and of what he saw
      Had but one thing to say for certain.
OEDIPUS   Well,
      And what was that? one thing might be the means
      Of our discovering many, could we gain
      Some narrow ground for hope.
CREON   Robbers, he said,
      Met them, and slew him; by no single strength,
      But multitude of hands.
OEDIPUS   How could your robber
      Have dared so far—except there were some practice
      With gold from hence?
CREON   Why, it seemed probable.
      But, Laius dead, no man stood up to help
      Amid our ills.
OEDIPUS   What ill was in the way,
      Which, when a sovereignty had lapsed like this,
      Kept you from searching of it out?
CREON   The Sphinx
      With her enigma forced us to dismiss
      Things out of sight, and look to our own steps.
OEDIPUS   Well, I will have it all to light again.
      Right well did Phoebus, yea and well may you
      Insist on this observance toward the dead;

So shall you see me, as of right, with you,
Venging this country and the God together.
Why, 'tis not for my neighbours' sake, but mine,
I shall dispel this plague-spot; for the man,
Whoever it may be, who murdered him,
Lightly might hanker to serve me the same.
I benefit myself in aiding him.
Up then, my children, straightway, from the floor;
Take up your votive branches; let some other
Gather the tribes of Cadmus hitherward;
Say, I will make clean work. Please Heaven, our state
Shall soon appear happy, or desperate.

PRIEST   Come children, let us rise; it was for this,
Which he himself proclaims, that we came hither.
Now may the sender of these oracles,
In saving and in plague-staying, Phoebus, come!

                              [*Exeunt* CREON, PRIEST *and* THEBANS.
                                        OEDIPUS *retires.*

Enter THEBAN SENATORS, *as Chorus.*

Chorus.

I. 1.

O Prophecy of Jove, whose words are sweet,
With what doom art thou sent
To glorious Thebes, from Pytho's gilded seat?
I am distraught with fearful wonderment,
I thrill with terror, and wait reverently—
Yea, Io Paean, Delian lord,* on thee!
What matter thou wilt compass—either strange,
Or once again recurrent as the seasons change,
Offspring of golden Hope, immortal Oracle,
Tell me, O tell!

* Apollo.

I. 2.

Athena first I greet with invocation,
Daughter of Jove, divine!
Next Artemis thy sister, of this nation
Keeper, high seated in the encircling shrine,
Filled with her praises, of our market-place,
And Phoebus, shooting arrows far through space;
Appear ye Three, the averters of my fate!
If e'er before, when mischief rose upon the state,
Ye quenched the flames of evil, putting them away,
Come—come to-day!

II. 1.

Woe, for unnumbered are the ills we bear!
Sickness pervades our hosts;
Nor is there any spear of guardian care,
Wherewith a man might save us, found in all our
          coasts.
For all the fair soil's produce now no longer springs;
Nor women from the labour and loud cries
Of their child-births arise;
And you may see, flying like a bird with wings,
One after one, outspeeding the resistless brand,
Pass—to the Evening Land.

II. 2.

In countless hosts our city perisheth.
Her children on the plain
Lie all unpitied—pitiless—breeding death.
Our wives meanwhile, and white-haired mothers in
          their train,
This way and that, suppliant, along the altar-side
Sit, and bemoan their doleful maladies;
Like flame their paeans rise,
With wailing and lament accompanied;

For whose dear sake O Goddess, O Jove's golden child,
Send Help with favour mild!

III. 1.

And Ares the Destroyer, him who thus—
Not now in harness of brass shields, as wont—
Ringed round with clamour, meets us front to front
And fevers us,
O banish from our country! Drive him back,
With winds upon his track,
On to the chamber vast of Amphitrite,*
Or that lone anchorage, the Thracian main;
For now, if night leave bounds to our annoy,
Day levels all again;
Wherefore, O father, Zeus, thou that dost wield the
      might
Of fire-fraught light,
Him with thy bolt destroy!

III. 2.

Next, from the bendings of thy golden string
I would see showered thy artillery
Invincible, marshalled to succour me,
Lycean King!**
Next, those flame-bearing beams, arrows most bright,
Which Artemis by night
Through Lycian highlands speeds her scattering;
Thou too, the Evian, with thy Maenad band,
Thou golden-braided patron of this land
Whose visage glows with wine,
O save us from the god whom no gods honour! Hear,
Bacchus! Draw near,
And light thy torch of pine!

Enter OEDIPUS, *attended.*

* The sea.
** Apollo.

OEDIPUS   You are at prayers; but for your prayers' intent
           You may gain help, and of your ills relief,
           If you will minister to the pestilence,
           And hearken and receive my words, which I—
           A stranger to this tale, and to the deed
           A stranger—shall pronounce; for of myself
           I could not follow up the traces far,
           Not having any key. But, made since then
           A fellow-townsman to the townsmen here,
           To all you Cadmeans I thus proclaim;
           Whichever of you knows the man, by whom
           Laius the son of Labdacus was slain,
           Even if he is afraid, seeing he himself
           Suppressed the facts that made against himself,
           I bid that man shew the whole truth to me;
           For he shall suffer no disparagement,
           Except to quit the land, unscathed. Again,
           If any knows another—say some stranger
           To have been guilty, let him not keep silence;
           For I will pay him the reward, and favour
           Shall be his due beside it. But again,
           If you will hold your peace, and any man
           From self or friend in terror shall repel
           This word of mine, then—you must hear me say
           What I shall do. Whoe'er he be, I order
           That of this land, whose power and throne are mine,
           None entertain him, none accost him, none
           Cause him to share in prayers or sacrifice
           Offered to Heaven, or pour him lustral wave,
           But all men from their houses banish him;
           Since it is he contaminates us all,
           Even as the Pythian oracle divine
           Revealed but now to me. Such is my succour
           Of him that's dead, and of the Deity.
           And on the guilty head I imprecate
           That whether by himself he has lain covert,
           Or joined with others, without happiness,

Evil, in evil, he may pine and die.
And for myself I pray, if with my knowledge
He should become an inmate of my dwelling,
That I may suffer all that I invoked
On these just now. Moreover all these things
I charge you to accomplish, in behalf
Of me, and of the God, and of this land,
So ruined, barren and forsaken of Heaven.
For even though the matter were not now
By Heaven enjoined you, 'twas unnatural
For you to suffer it to pass uncleansed,
A man most noble having been slain, a king too!
Rather, you should have searched it out; but now,
Since I am vested with the government
Which he held once, and have his marriage-bed,
And the same wife; and since our progeny—
If his had not miscarried—had sprung from us
With common ties of common motherhood—
Only that Fate came heavy upon his head—
On these accounts I, as for my own father,
Will fight this fight, and follow out every clue,
Seeking to seize the author of his murder—
The scion of Labdacus and Polydore
And earlier Cadmus and Agenor old;
And such as disobey—the Gods I ask
Neither to raise them harvest from the ground
Nor children from the womb, but that they perish
By this fate present, and yet worse than this;
While you, the other Cadmeans, who approve,
May succouring Justice and all Gods in heaven
Accompany for good for evermore!

1 SENATOR   Even as thou didst adjure me, so, my king,
I will reply. I neither murdered him,
Nor can point out the murderer. For the quest—
To tell us who on earth has done this deed
Belonged to Phoebus, by whose word it came.

OEDIPUS   Your words are just; but to constrain the Gods
    To what they will not, passes all men's power.

1 SENATOR   I would say something which appears to me
    The second chance to this.

OEDIPUS   And your third, also—
    If such you have—by all means tell it.

1 SENATOR   Sir,
    Tiresias above all men, I am sure,
    Ranks as a seer next Phoebus, king with king;
    Of him we might enquire and learn the truth
    With all assurance.

OEDIPUS   That is what I did;
    And with no slackness; for by Creon's advice
    I sent, twice over; and for some time, now,
    'Tis strange he is not here.

1 SENATOR   Then all the rest
    Are but stale words and dumb.

OEDIPUS   What sort of words?
    I am weighing every utterance.

1 SENATOR   He was said
    To have been killed by footpads.

OEDIPUS   So I heard;
    But he who saw it is himself unseen.

1 SENATOR   Well, if his bosom holds a grain of fear,
    Curses like yours he never will abide!

OEDIPUS   Whom the doing awes not, speaking cannot scare.

1 SENATOR   Then there is one to expose him: here they come,
    Bringing the godlike seer, the only man
    Who has in him the tongue that cannot lie.

Enter TIRESIAS, *led by a boy.*

OEDIPUS   Tiresias, thou who searchest everything,
    Communicable or nameless, both in heaven
    And on the earth—thou canst not see the city,
    But knowest no less what pestilence visits it,
    Wherefrom our only saviour and defence

We find, sir king, in thee. For Phoebus—if
Thou dost not know it from the messengers—
To us, who sent to ask him, sent word back,
That from this sickness no release should come,
Till we had found and slain the men who slew
Laius, or driven them, banished, from the land.
Wherefore do thou—not sparing augury,
Either through birds, or any other way
Thou hast of divination—save thyself,
And save the city, and me; save the whole mass
By this dead corpse infected; for in thee
Stands our existence; and for men, to help
With might and main is of all tasks the highest.

TIRESIAS   Alas! How terrible it is to know,
Where no good comes of knowing! Of these matters
I was full well aware, but let them slip me;
Else I had not come hither.

OEDIPUS   But what is it?
How out of heart thou hast come!

TIRESIAS   Let me go home;
So shalt thou bear thy load most easily—
If thou wilt take my counsel—and I mine.

OEDIPUS   Thou hast not spoken loyally, nor friendly
Toward the State that bred thee, cheating her
Of this response!

TIRESIAS   Because I do not see
Thy words, not even thine, going to the mark;
So, not to be in the same plight—

1 SENATOR   For Heaven's sake,
If thou hast knowledge, do not turn away,
When all of us implore thee suppliant!

TIRESIAS   Ye
Are all unknowing; my say, in any sort,
I will not say, lest I display thy sorrow.

OEDIPUS   What, you do know, and will not speak? Your mind
Is to betray us, and destroy the city?

TIRESIAS   I will not bring remorse upon myself
           And upon you. Why do you search these matters?
           Vain, vain! I will not tell you.

OEDIPUS   Worst of traitors!
           For you would rouse a very stone to wrath—
           Will you not speak out ever, but stand thus
           Relentless and persistent?

TIRESIAS   My offence
           You censure; but your own, at home, you see not,
           And yet blame me!

OEDIPUS   Who would not take offence,
           Hearing the words in which you flout the city?

TIRESIAS   Well, it will come, keep silence as I may.

OEDIPUS   And what will come should I not hear from you?

TIRESIAS   I will declare no further. Storm at this,
           If't please you, to the wildest height of anger!

OEDIPUS   At least I will not, being so far in anger,
           Spare anything of what is clear to me:
           Know, I suspect you joined to hatch the deed;
           Yea, did it—all but slaying with your own hands;
           And if you were not blind, I should aver
           The act was your work only!

TIRESIAS   Was it so?
           I charge you to abide by your decree
           As you proclaimed it; nor from this day forth
           Speak word to these, or me; being of this land
           Yourself the abominable contaminator!

OEDIPUS   So shamelessly set you this story on foot,
           And think, perhaps, you shall go free?

TIRESIAS   I am
           Free! for I have in me the strength of truth.

OEDIPUS   Who prompted you? for from your art it was not!

TIRESIAS   Yourself! You made me speak, against my will.

OEDIPUS   Speak! What? Repeat, that I may learn it better!

TIRESIAS   Did you not understand me at first hearing,
           Or are you tempting me, when you say "Speak!"

OEDIPUS   Not so to say for certain; speak again.

TIRESIAS   I say that you are Laius' murderer—
       He whom you seek.

OEDIPUS   Not without chastisement
       Shall you, twice over, utter wounds!

TIRESIAS   Then shall I
       Say something more, that may incense you further?

OEDIPUS   Say what you please; it will be said in vain.

TIRESIAS   I say you know not in what worst of shame
       You live together with those nearest you,
       And see not in what evil plight you stand.

OEDIPUS   Do you expect to go on revelling
       In utterances like this?

TIRESIAS   Yes, if the truth
       Has any force at all.

OEDIPUS   Why so it has,
       Except for you; it is not so with you;
       Blind as you are in eyes, and ears, and mind!

TIRESIAS   Fool, you reproach me as not one of these
       Shall not reproach you, soon!

OEDIPUS   You cannot hurt me,
       Nor any other who beholds the light,
       Your life being all one night.

TIRESIAS   Nor is it fated
       You by my hand should fall; Apollo is
       Sufficient; he will bring it all to pass.

OEDIPUS   Are these inventions Creon's work, or yours?

TIRESIAS   Your bane is no-ways Creon, but your own self.

OEDIPUS   O riches, and dominion, and the craft
       That excels craft, and makes life enviable,
       How vast the grudge that is nursed up for you,
       When for this sovereignty, which the state
       Committed to my hands, unsought-for, free,
       Creon, the trusty, the familiar friend,
       With secret mines covets to oust me from it,
       And has suborned a sorcerer like this,

An engine-botching crafty cogging knave,
Who has no eyes to see with, but for gain,
And was born blind in the art! Why, tell me now,
How stand your claims to prescience? How came it,
When the oracular monster was alive,
You said no word to set this people free?
And yet it was not for the first that came
To solve her riddle; sooth was needed then,
Which you could not afford; neither from birds,
Nor any inspiration; till I came,
The unlettered Oedipus, and ended her,
By sleight of wit, untaught of augury—
I whom you now seek to cast out, in hope
To stand upon the steps of Creon's throne!
You and the framer of this plot methinks
Shall rue your purge for guilt! Dotard you seem,
Else by experience you had come to know
What thoughts these are you think!

1 SENATOR   As we conceive,
His words appear (and, Oedipus, your own,)
To have been said in anger; now not such
Our need, but rather to consider this—
How best to interpret the God's oracle.

TIRESIAS   King as you are, we must be peers at least
In argument; I am your equal, there;
For I am Loxias'* servant, and not yours;
So never need be writ of Creon's train.
And since you have reproached me with my blindness,
I say—you have your sight, and do not see
What evils are about you, nor with whom,
Nor in what home you are dwelling. Do you know
From whom you are? Yea, you are ignorant
That to your own you are an enemy,
Whether on earth, alive, or under it.

* Apollo's.

Soon from this land shall drive you, stalking grim,
Your mother's and your father's two-edged curse,
With eyes then dark, though they look proudly now.
What place on earth shall not be harbour, then,
For your lamenting? What Cithaeron-peak*
Shall not be resonant soon, when you discern
What hymen-song was that, which wafted you
On a fair voyage, to foul anchorage
Under yon roof? and multitudes besides
Of ills you know not of shall level you
Down to your self—down to your children! Go,
Trample on Creon, and on this mouth of mine;
But know, there is not one of all mankind
That shall be bruised more utterly than you.

OEDIPUS   Must I endure to hear all this from him?
Hence, to perdition! quickly hence! begone
Back from these walls, and turn you home again.

TIRESIAS   But that you called me, I had not come hither.

OEDIPUS   I did not know that you would utter folly;
Else I had scarce sent for you, to my house.

TIRESIAS   Yea, such is what we seem, foolish to you,
And to your fathers, who begat you, wise.

OEDIPUS   What fathers? Stop! Who was it gave me being?

TIRESIAS   This day shall give you birth and death in one.

OEDIPUS   How all too full of riddles and obscure
Is your discourse!

TIRESIAS   Were you not excellent
At solving riddles?

OEDIPUS   Ay, cast in my teeth
Matters in which you must allow my greatness!

TIRESIAS   And yet this very fortune was your ruin!

OEDIPUS   Well, if I saved this city, I care not.

TIRESIAS   Well,
I am going; and you, boy, take me home.

* Mountain associated with many myths; see also page 37.

OEDIPUS   Ay, let him.
    Your turbulence impedes us, while you stay;
    When you are gone, you can annoy no more.

                                                          [*Retires.*

TIRESIAS   I go, having said that I came to say;
        Not that I fear your frown; for you possess
        No power to kill me; but I say to you—
        The man you have been seeking, threatening him,
        And loud proclaiming him for Laius' murder,
        That man is here; believed a foreigner
        Here sojourning; but shall be recognized
        For Theban born hereafter; yet not pleased
        In the event; for blind instead of seeing,
        And poor for wealthy, to a foreign land,
        A staff to point his footsteps, he shall go.
        Also to his own sons he shall be found
        Related as a brother, though their sire,
        And of the woman from whose womb he came
        Both son and spouse; one that has raised up seed
        To his own father, and has murdered him.
        Now get you in, and ponder what I say;
        And if you can detect me in a lie,
        Then come and say that I am no true seer.

                                        [*Exeunt* TIRESIAS *and Boy.*

Chorus.

I. 1.

            Who is he, who was said
            By the Delphian soothsaying rock
            To have wrought with hands blood-red
            Nameless unspeakable deeds?
            Time it were that he fled
            Faster than storm-swift steeds!
            For upon him springs with a shock,
            Armed in thunder and fire,

The Child of Jove, at the head
  Of the Destinies dread,
That follow, and will not tire.

I. 2.

For a word but now blazed clear
From Parnassus' snow-covered mound,*
To hunt down the Unknown!
He, through the forest drear,
By rocks, by cavernous ways,
Stalks, like a bull that strays,
Heartsore, footsore, alone;
Flying from Earth's central seat,
Flying the oracular sound
  That with swift wings' beat
For ever circles him round.

II. 1.

Of a truth dark thoughts, yea dark and fell,
  The augur wise doth arouse in me,
    Who neither assent, nor yet gainsay;
And what to affirm, I cannot tell;
  But I flutter in hope, unapt to see
    Things of to-morrow, or to-day.

Why in Polybus' son** they should find a foe,
  Or he in the heirs of Labdacus,
    I know no cause, or of old, or late,
In test whereof I am now to go
  Against the repute of Oedipus,
    To avenge a Labdakid's unknown fate.

* Mount Parnassus is also associated with Apollo.
** Oedipus.

II. 2.

True, Zeus indeed, and Apollo, are wise,
    And knowers of what concerns mankind;
        But that word of a seer, a man like me,
Weighs more than mine, for a man to prize,
    Is all unsure. Yea, one man's mind
        May surpass another's in subtlety;

But never will I, till I see the rest,
    Assent to those who accuse him now.
        I saw how the air-borne Maiden came
Against him, and proved him wise, by the test,
    And good to the state; and for this, I trow,
        He shall not, ever, be put to shame.

Enter CREON.

CREON   I am come hither, fellow citizens,
    Having been told that Oedipus the king
    Lays grievous accusations to my charge,
    Which I will not endure. For if he fancies
    He in our present troubles has endured
    Aught at my hands, either in word or deed,
    Tending to harm him, I have no desire
    My life should be prolonged, bearing this blame.
    The injury that such a word may do
    Is no mere trifle, but more vast than any,
    If I am to be called a criminal
    Here in the town, and by my friends, and you.

1 SENATOR   Nay, the reproach, it may be, rather came
    Through stress of anger, than advisedly.

CREON   But it was plainly said, by my advice
    The prophet gave false answers.

1 SENATOR   It was said;
    But how advised I know not.

CREON   Was this charge

Of a set mind, and with set countenance
Imputed against me?

1 SENATOR   I do not know.
I have no eyes for what my masters do.
But here he comes, himself, forth of the palace.

Enter OEDIPUS.

OEDIPUS   Fellow, how cam'st thou hither? Dost thou boast
So great a front of daring, as to come
Under my roof, the assassin clear of me,
And manifest pirate of my royalty?
Tell me, by heaven, did you detect in me
The bearing of a craven, or a fool,
That you laid plans to do it; or suppose
I should not recognize your work in this,
Creeping on slily, and defend myself?
Is it not folly, this attempt of yours,
Without a following, without friends, to hunt
After a throne, a thing which is achieved
By aid of followers and much revenue?

CREON   Do me this favour; hear me say as much
As you have said; and then, yourself decide.

OEDIPUS   You are quick to talk, but I am slow to learn
Of you; for I have found you contrary
And dangerous to me.

CREON   Now, this same thing
First hear, how I shall state it.

OEDIPUS   This same thing
Do not tell me—that you are not a villain!

CREON   If you suppose your arrogance weighs aught
Apart from reason, you are much astray.

OEDIPUS   If you suppose you can escape the pain
Due for a kinsman's wrong, you are astray!

CREON   You speak with justice; I agree! But tell me,
How is it that you say I injured you?

OEDIPUS   Did you persuade me that I ought to send
To fetch that canting soothsayer, or no?

CREON   Why yes, and now, I am of the same mind, still.

OEDIPUS   How long is it since Laius—

CREON   What? I know not.

OEDIPUS   Died—disappeared, murdered by violence?

CREON   Long seasons might be numbered, long gone by.

OEDIPUS   Well, did this seer then practise in the craft?

CREON   Yes, just as wise, and just as much revered.

OEDIPUS   And did he at that time say one word of me?

CREON   Well, nowhere in my presence, anyhow.

OEDIPUS   But did not you hold inquest for the dead?

CREON   We did, of course; and got no evidence.

OEDIPUS   Well then, how came it that this wiseacre
            Did not say these things then?

CREON   I do not know.
            In matters where I have no cognizance
            I hold my tongue.

OEDIPUS   This much, at least, you know,
            And if you are wise, will say!

CREON   And what is that?
            For if I know it, I shall not refuse.

OEDIPUS   Why, that unless he had conspired with you
            He never would have said that Laius' murder
            Was of my doing!

CREON   If he says so, you know.
            Only I claim to know that first from you,
            Which you put now to me.

OEDIPUS   Learn anything!
            For I shall not be found a murderer.

CREON   Well then; you have my sister to your wife?

OEDIPUS   There's no denying that question.

CREON   And with her
            Rule equal, and in common hold the land?

OEDIPUS   All she may wish for she obtains of me.

CREON   And make I not a third, equal with you?

OEDIPUS   Ay, there appears your friendship's falsity.

CREON   Not if you reason with yourself, as I.
            And note this first; if you can think that any

Would rather choose a sovereignty, with fears,
Than the same power, with undisturbed repose?
Neither am I, by nature, covetous
To be a king, rather than play the king,
Nor any man who has sagacity.
Now I have all things, without fear, from you;
Reigned I myself, I must do much I hated.
How were a throne, then, pleasanter for me
Than painless empire and authority?
I am not yet so blinded as to wish
For honour, other than is joined with gain.
Now am I hail-fellow-well-met with all;
Now every man gives me good-morrow; now
The waiters on your favour fawn on me;
For all their prospering depends thereby.
Then how should I exchange this lot for yours?
A mind well balanced cannot turn to crime.
I neither am in love with this design,
Nor, in a comrade, would I suffer it.
For proof of which, first, go to Pytho; ask
For the oracles, if I declared them truly;
Next, if you can detect me in the act
Of any conjuration with the seer,
Then, by a double vote, not one alone,
Mine and your own, take me, and take my life;
But do not, on a dubious argument,
Charge me beside the facts. For just it is not,
To hold bad men for good, good men for bad,
To no good end; nay, 'twere all one to me
To throw away a friend, a worthy one,
And one's own life, which most of all one values.
Ah well; in time, you will see these things plainly;
For time alone shews a man's honesty,
But in one day you may discern his guilt.

1 SENATOR   His words sound fair—to one who fears to fall;
             For swift in counsel is unsafe, my liege.

OEDIPUS   When he who plots against me in the dark

Comes swiftly on, I must be swift in turn.
If I stay quiet, his ends will have been gained,
And mine all missed.

CREON   What is it that you want?
To expel me from the country?

OEDIPUS   Not at all.
Your death I purpose, not your banishment.

CREON   Not without shewing, first, what a thing is jealousy!

OEDIPUS   You talk like one who will not yield, nor heed.

CREON   Because I see you mean injuriously.

OEDIPUS   Not to myself!

CREON   No more you ought to me!

OEDIPUS   You are a traitor!

CREON   What if you are no judge?

OEDIPUS   I must be ruler.

CREON   Not if you rule badly.

OEDIPUS   City, my city!

CREON   The city is mine too,
And not yours only.

1 SENATOR   Good my lords, have done,
Here is Jocasta; in good time, I see her
Come to you from the palace; with her aid
'Twere meet to appease your present difference.

Enter JOCASTA.

JOCASTA   Unhappy men, what was it made you raise
This senseless broil of words? Are you not both
Ashamed of stirring private grievances,
The land being thus afflicted? Get you in—
And, Creon, do you go home; push not mere nothing
On to some terrible calamity!

CREON   Sister, your husband Oedipus thinks fit
To treat me villainously; choosing for me
Of two bad things, one; to expatriate me,
Or seize and kill me.

OEDIPUS   I admit it, wife;

For I have found him out in an offence
Against my person, joined with treachery.

CREON   So may I never thrive, but perish, banned
Of Heaven, if I have done a thing to you
Of what you charge against me!

JOCASTA   Oedipus!
O in Heaven's name believe it! Above all
Revere this oath in heaven; secondly
Myself, and these, who stand before you here.

1 SENATOR   Hear her, my king! With wisdom and goodwill
I pray you hear!

OEDIPUS   What would you have me grant?

1 SENATOR   Respect his word; no bauble, heretofore;
And by this oath made weighty.

OEDIPUS   Do you know
For what you ask?

1 SENATOR   I do.

OEDIPUS   Say what you mean, then!

1 SENATOR   That you expel not, ever, with disgrace,
The friend, who has abjured it, on a charge
Void of clear proof.

OEDIPUS   Now, understand it well;
Seek this, you seek my death or exile!

1 SENATOR   Nay,
By the Sun-god, first of all Gods in heaven!
So may I perish, to the uttermost,
Cut off from Heaven, without the help of men,
If I have such a thought! But the land's waste
Will break my heart with grief—and that this woe,
Your strife, is added to its former woe.

OEDIPUS   Well, let him go, though I get slain outright,
Or thrust by force, dishonoured, from the land;
Your voice, not his, makes me compassionate,
Pleading for pity; he, where'er he be,
Shall have my hatred.

CREON   You display your spleen

In yielding; but, when your wrath passes bound,
Are formidable! Tempers such as yours
Most grievous are to their own selves to bear,
Not without justice.

OEDIPUS   Leave me; get you gone!

CREON   I go; you know me not; these know me honest.

[*Exit.*

1 SENATOR   Lady, what hinders you from taking him
  Into the house?

JOCASTA   I would know how this happened.

1 SENATOR   A blind surmise arose, out of mere babble;
  But even what is unjust inflicts a sting.

JOCASTA   On part of both?

1 SENATOR   Yes truly.

JOCASTA   And what was said?

1 SENATOR   Enough it seems, enough it seems to me,
  Under the former trouble of the land,
  To leave this where it lies.

OEDIPUS   Do you perceive
  How far you are carried—a well-meaning man!
  Slurring my anger thus, and blunting it?

1 SENATOR   I said it, O my king, not once alone—
  But be assured, I should have shewn myself
  Robbed of my wits, useless for work of wit,
  Renouncing thee! who didst impel the sails
  Of my dear land, baffled mid straits, right onward,
  And it may be, wilt waft her safely now!

JOCASTA   For Heaven's sake tell me too, my lord, what was it
  Caused you so deep an anger?

OEDIPUS   I will tell you;
  For I respect you, lady, more than these;
  'Twas Creon—at plots which he has laid for me.

JOCASTA   If you will charge the quarrel in plain terms,
  Why speak!

OEDIPUS   He says that I am Laius' slayer.

JOCASTA   Of his own knowledge, or on hearsay?

OEDIPUS   Nay,
    But by citation of a knavish seer;
    As for himself, he keeps his words blame-free.

JOCASTA   Now set you free from thought of that you talk of;
    Listen and learn, nothing in human life
    Turns on the soothsayer's art. Tokens of this
    I'll show you in few words. To Laius once
    There came an oracle, I do not say
    From Phoebus' self, but from his ministers,
    That so it should befall, that he should die
    By a son's hands, whom he should have by me.
    And him—the story goes—robbers abroad
    Have murdered, at a place where three roads meet;
    While from our son's birth not three days went by
    Before, with ankles pinned, he cast him out,
    By hands of others, on a pathless moor.
    And so Apollo did not bring about
    That he should be his father's murderer;
    Nor yet that Laius should endure the stroke
    At his son's hands, of which he was afraid.
    This is what came of soothsayers' oracles;
    Whereof take thou no heed. That which we lack,
    If a God seek, himself will soon reveal.

OEDIPUS   What perturbation and perplexity
    Take hold upon me, woman, hearing you!

JOCASTA   What stress of trouble is on you, that you say so?

OEDIPUS   I thought I heard you say Laius was slain
    Where three roads meet!

JOCASTA   Yes, so the rumour ran,
    And so runs still.

OEDIPUS   And where might be the spot
    Where this befell?

JOCASTA   Phocis the land is named;
    There are two separate roads converge in one
    From Daulia and Delphi.

OEDIPUS   And what time
    Has passed since then?

JOCASTA   It was but just before
    You were installed as ruler of the land,
    The tidings reached the city.
OEDIPUS   God of Heaven!
    What would'st thou do unto me!
JOCASTA   Oedipus,
    What is it on your mind?
OEDIPUS   Ask me not yet.
    But Laius—say, what was he like? what prime
    Of youth had he attained to?
JOCASTA   He was tall;
    The first white flowers had blossomed in his hair;
    His figure was not much unlike your own.
OEDIPUS   Me miserable! It seems I have but now
    Proffered myself to a tremendous curse
    Not knowing!
JOCASTA   How say you? I tremble, O my lord,
    To gaze upon you!
OEDIPUS   I am sore afraid
    The prophet was not blind; but you will make
    More certain, if you answer one thing more.
JOCASTA   Indeed I tremble; but the thing you ask
    I'll answer, when I know it.
OEDIPUS   Was he going
    Poorly attended, or with many spears
    About him, like a prince?
JOCASTA   But five in all;
    One was a herald; and one carriage held
    Laius himself,
OEDIPUS   O, it is plain already!
    Woman, who was it told this tale to you?
JOCASTA   A servant, who alone came safe away.
OEDIPUS   Is he perchance now present, in the house?
JOCASTA   Why no; for after he was come from thence,
    And saw you governing, and Laius dead,
    He came and touched my hand, and begged of me
    To send him to the fields and sheep-meadows,

So he might be as far as possible
From eyesight of the townsmen; and I sent him;
For he was worthy, for a slave, to obtain
Even greater favours.

OEDIPUS   Could we have him back
Quickly?

JOCASTA   We could. But why this order?

OEDIPUS   Wife,
I fear me I have spoken far too much;
Wherefore I wish to see him.

JOCASTA   He shall come!
But I am worthy, in my turn, to know
What weighs so heavily upon you, Sir?

OEDIPUS   And you shall know; since I have passed so far
The bounds of apprehension. For to whom
Could I impart, passing through such a need,
Greater in place—if that were all—than you?
—I am the son of Polybus of Corinth,
And of a Dorian mother, Merope.
And I was counted most preëminent
Among the townsmen there; up to the time
A circumstance befell me, of this fashion—
Worthy of wonder, though of my concern
Unworthy. At the board a drunken fellow
Over his cups called me a changeling;
And I, being indignant—all that day
Hardly refrained—but on the morrow went
And taxed my parents with it to their face;
Who took the scandal grievously, of him
Who launched the story. Well, with what they said
I was content; and yet the thing still galled me;
For it spread far. So without cognizance
Of sire or mother I set out to go
To Pytho.* Phoebus sent me of my quest

---

* The Pythian oracle at Delphi, as on page 3.

Bootless away; but other terrible
And strange and lamentable things revealed,
Saying I should wed my mother, and produce
A race intolerable for men to see,
And be my natural father's murderer.
When I heard that, measuring where Corinth stands
Even thereafter by the stars alone,
Where I might never think to see fulfilled
The scandals of ill prophecies of me,
I fled, an exile. As I journeyed on,
I found myself upon the self-same spot
Where, you say, this king perished. In your ears,
Wife, I will tell the whole. When in my travels
I was come near this place where three roads meet,
There met me a herald, and a man that rode
In a colt-carriage, as you tell of him,
And from the track the leader, by main force,
And the old man himself, would thrust me. I,
Being enraged, strike him who jostled me—
The driver—and the old man, when he saw it,
Watching as I was passing, from the car
With his goad's fork smote me upon the head.
He paid, though! duly I say not; but in brief,
Smitten by the staff in this right hand of mine,
Out of the middle of the carriage straight
He rolls down headlong; and I slay them all!
But if there be a semblance to connect
This nameless man with Laius, who is now
More miserable than I am? Who on earth
Could have been born with more of hate from heaven?
Whom never citizen or stranger may
Receive into their dwellings, or accost,
But must thrust out of doors; and 'tis no other
Laid all these curses on myself, than I!
Yea, with embraces of the arms whereby
He perished, I pollute my victim's bed!

Am I not vile? Am I not all unclean?
If I must fly, and flying, never can
See my own folk, or on my native land
Set foot, or else must with my mother wed,
And slay my father Polybus, who begat
And bred me? Would he not speak truly of me
Who judged these things sent by some barbarous Power?
Never, you sacred majesties of Heaven,
Never may I behold that day; but pass
Out of men's sight, ere I shall see myself
Touched by the stain of such a destiny!

1 SENATOR   My liege, these things affect us grievously;
Still, till you hear his story who was by,
Do not lose hope!

OEDIPUS   Yea, so much hope is left,
Merely to wait for him, the herdsman.

JOCASTA   Well,
Suppose him here, what do you want of him?

OEDIPUS   I'll tell you; if he should be found to say
Just what you said, I shall be clear from harm.

JOCASTA   What did you hear me say, that did not tally?

OEDIPUS   You were just telling me that he made mention
Of "robbers"—"men"—as Laius' murderers.
Now if he shall affirm their number still,
I did not slay him. One cannot be the same
As many. But if he shall speak of one—
One only, it is evident this deed
Already will have been brought home to me.

JOCASTA   But be assured, that was the word, quite plainly!
And now he cannot blot it out again.
Not I alone, but the whole city heard it.
Then, even if he shift from his first tale,
Not so, my lord, will he at all explain
The death of Laius, as it should have been,
Whom Loxias declared my son must slay!
And after all, the poor thing never killed him,

But died itself before! so that henceforth
I do not mean to look to left or right
For fear of soothsaying!

OEDIPUS   You are well advised.
Still, send and fetch the labourer; do not miss it.

JOCASTA   I will send quickly. Now let us go within.
I would do nothing that displeases you.

[*Exeunt* OEDIPUS *and* JOCASTA.

Chorus.

I. 1.

Let it be mine to keep
The holy purity of word and deed
    Foreguided all by mandates from on high
    Born in the ethereal region of the sky,
Their only sire Olympus; them nor seed
Of mortal man brought forth, nor Lethe cold
        Shall ever lay to sleep;
In them Deity is great, and grows not old.

I. 2.

Pride is the germ of kings;
Pride, when puffed up, vainly, with many things
    Unseasonable, unfitting, mounts the wall,
    Only to hurry to that fatal fall,
Where feet are vain to serve her. But the task
Propitious to the city GOD I ask
        Never to take away!
GOD I will never cease to hold my stay.

II. 1.

But if any man proceed
Insolently in word or deed,
    Without fear of right, or care

> For the seats where Virtues are,
> Him, for his ill-omened pride,
> Let an evil death betide!
> If honestly his gear he will not gain,
>   Nor keep himself from deeds unholy,
> Nor from inviolable things abstain,
>   Blinded by folly.
> In such a course, what mortal from his heart
>   Dart upon dart
> Can hope to avert of indignation?
> Yea, and if acts like these are held in estimation,
>   Why dance we here our part?

II. 2.

> Never to the inviolate hearth
> At the navel of the earth,*
> Nor to Abae's fane, in prayer,
> Nor the Olympian, will I fare,
> If it shall not so befall
> Manifestly unto all.
> But O our king—if thou art named aright—
>   Zeus, that art Lord of all things ever,
> Be this not hid from Thee, nor from Thy might
>   Which endeth never.
> For now already men invalidate
>   The dooms of Fate
>   Uttered for Laius, fading slowly;
> Apollo's name and rites are nowhere now kept holy;
>   Worship is out of date.

Enter JOCASTA, *attended.*

JOCASTA   Lords of the land, it came into my heart
                To approach the temples of the Deities,
                Taking in hand these garlands, and this incense;

---

* The oracle at Delphi.

For Oedipus lets his mind float too light
Upon the eddies of all kinds of grief;
Nor will he, like a man of soberness,
Measure the new by knowledge of the old,
But is at mercy of whoever speaks,
If he but speak the language of despair.
I can do nothing by exhorting him.
Wherefore, Lycean Phoebus, unto thee—
For thou art very near us—I am come,
Bringing these offerings, a petitioner
That thou afford us fair deliverance;
Since now we are all frighted, seeing him—
The vessel's pilot, as 'twere—panic-stricken.

Enter a Messenger.

MESSENGER   Sirs, might I learn of you, where is the palace
                Of Oedipus the King? or rather, where
                He is himself, if you know, tell me.
1 SENATOR   Stranger,
                This is his dwelling, and he is within;
                This lady is his children's mother, too.
MESSENGER   A blessing ever be on hers and her,
                Who is, in such a perfect sort, his wife!
JOCASTA   The like be with you too, as you deserve,
                Sir, for your compliment. But say what end
                You come for, and what news you wish to tell.
MESSENGER   Good to the house, and to your husband, lady.
JOCASTA   Of what sort? and from whom come you?
MESSENGER   From Corinth.
                In that which I am now about to say
                May you find pleasure! and why not? And yet
                Perhaps you may be sorry.
JOCASTA   But what is it?
                How can it carry such ambiguous force?
MESSENGER   The dwellers in the land of Isthmia,
                As was there said, intend to appoint him king.

JOCASTA   What! Is not Polybus, the old prince, still reigning?

MESSENGER   No, truly; he is Death's subject, in the grave.

JOCASTA   How say you, father? Is Polybus no more?

MESSENGER   I stake my life upon it, if I lie!

JOCASTA   Run, girl, and tell your master instantly.

[Exit an attendant.

O prophecies of Gods, where are you now!
Oedipus fled, long since, from this man's presence,
Fearing to kill him; and now he has died
A natural death, not by his means at all!

Enter OEDIPUS.

OEDIPUS   O my most dear Jocasta, wife of mine,
Why did you fetch me hither from the house?

JOCASTA   Hear this man speak! Listen and mark, to what
The dark responses of the God are come!

OEDIPUS   And who is this? What says he?

JOCASTA   He's from Corinth,
To tell us that your father Polybus
Lives no more, but is dead!

OEDIPUS   What say you, sir?
Tell your own tale yourself.

MESSENGER   If first of all
I must deliver this for certainty,
Know well, that he has gone the way of mortals.

OEDIPUS   Was it by treason, or some chance disease?

MESSENGER   A little shock prostrates an aged frame!

OEDIPUS   Sickness, you mean, was my poor father's end?

MESSENGER   Yes, and old age; his term of life was full.

OEDIPUS   Heigh ho! Why, wife! why should a man regard
The oracular hearth of Pytho, or the birds
Cawing above us, by whose canons I
Was to have slain my father? He is dead,
And buried out of sight; and here am I,
Laying no finger to the instrument,
(Unless, indeed, he pined for want of me,

And so, I killed him!) Well, Polybus is gone;
And with him all those oracles of ours
Bundled to Hades, for old songs, together!

JOCASTA   Did I not say so all along?

OEDIPUS   You did;
But I was led astray by fear.

JOCASTA   Well, now
Let none of these predictions any more
Weigh on your mind!

OEDIPUS   And how can I help dreading
My mother's bed?

JOCASTA   But why should men be fearful,
O'er whom Fortune is mistress, and foreknowledge
Of nothing sure? Best take life easily,
As a man may. For that maternal wedding,
Have you no fear; for many men ere now
Have dreamed as much; but he who by such dreams
Sets nothing, has the easiest life of it.

OEDIPUS   All these things would have been well said of you,
Were not my mother living still; but now,
She being alive, there is all need of dread;
Though you say well.

JOCASTA   And yet your father's burial
Lets in much daylight!

OEDIPUS   I acknowledge, much.
Still, her who lives I fear.

MESSENGER   But at what woman
Are you dismayed?

OEDIPUS   At Merope, old man,
The wife of Polybus.

MESSENGER   And what of her
Causes you terror?

OEDIPUS   A dark oracle,
Stranger, from heaven.

MESSENGER   May it be put in words?
Or is it wrong another man should know it?

OEDIPUS   No, not at all. Why, Loxias declared
        That I should one day marry my own mother,
        And with my own hands shed my father's blood.
        Wherefore from Corinth I have kept away
        Far, for long years; and prospered; none the less
        It is most sweet to see one's parents' face.

MESSENGER   And in this apprehension you became
        An emigrant from Corinth?

OEDIPUS   And, old man,
        Desiring not to be a parricide.

MESSENGER   Why should I not deliver you, my liege—
        Since my intent in coming here was good—
        Out of this fear?

OEDIPUS   Indeed you would obtain
        Good guerdon from me.

MESSENGER   And indeed for this
        Chiefest I came, that upon your return
        I might in some sort benefit.

OEDIPUS   But I
        Will never go, to meet my parents there!

MESSENGER   O son, 'tis plain you know not what you do!

OEDIPUS   How so, old man? in Heaven's name tell me!

MESSENGER   If
        On this account you shun the journey home!

OEDIPUS   Of course I fear lest Phoebus turn out true.

MESSENGER   Lest through your parents you incur foul stain?

OEDIPUS   Yes, father, yes; that is what always scares me.

MESSENGER   Now do you know you tremble, really, at nothing?

OEDIPUS   How can that be, if I was born their child?

MESSENGER   Because Polybus was nought akin to you!

OEDIPUS   What, did not Polybus beget me?

MESSENGER   No,
        No more than I did; just so much as I!

OEDIPUS   How, my own sire no more than—nobody?

MESSENGER   But neither he begat you, nor did I.

OEDIPUS   Then from what motive did he call me son?

MESSENGER   Look here; he had you as a gift from me.

OEDIPUS   And loved me then, so much, at second hand?

MESSENGER   Yes, his long childlessness prevailed on him.

OEDIPUS   And did you find or purchase me, to give him?

MESSENGER   I found you in Cithaeron's wooded dells.

OEDIPUS   How came you to be journeying in these parts?

MESSENGER   I tended flocks upon the mountains here.

OEDIPUS   You were a shepherd, and you ranged for hire?

MESSENGER   But at the same time your preserver, son!

OEDIPUS   You found me in distress? What was my trouble?

MESSENGER   Your ankle joints may witness.

OEDIPUS   O, why speak you
Of that old evil?

MESSENGER   I untied you, when
You had the soles of both your feet bored through.

OEDIPUS   A shameful sort of swaddling bands were mine.

MESSENGER   Such, that from them you had the name you bear.*

OEDIPUS   Tell me, by heaven! at sire's or mother's hand—

MESSENGER   I know not: he who gave you knows of that
Better than I.

OEDIPUS   You got me from another?
You did not find me?

MESSENGER   No, another shepherd
Gave you to me.

OEDIPUS   Who was he? are you able
To point him out?

MESSENGER   They said that he was one
Of those who followed Laius, whom you know.

OEDIPUS   Him who was once the monarch of this land?

MESSENGER   Precisely! This man was his herdsman.

OEDIPUS   Now
Is this man still alive for me to see?

MESSENGER   You must know best, the people of the place.

OEDIPUS   Is any here among you bystanders,

---

* By a folk etymology, the name Oedipus is taken to mean "swollen feet."

Who knows the herdsman whom he tells us of,
From seeing him, either in the fields or here?
Speak! it were time that this had been cleared up.

1 SENATOR   I think he is no other than that peasant
Whom you were taking pains to find, before;
But she could say as well as any one—
Jocasta.

OEDIPUS   Lady, you remember him
Whose coming we were wishing for but now;
Does he mean him?

JOCASTA   Why ask who 'twas he spoke of?
Nay, never mind—never remember it—
'Twas idly spoken!

OEDIPUS   Nay, it cannot be
That having such a clue I should refuse
To solve the mystery of my parentage!

JOCASTA   For Heaven's sake, if you care for your own life,
Don't seek it! I am sick, and that's enough!

OEDIPUS   Courage! At least, if I be thrice a slave,
Born so three-deep, it cannot injure you!

JOCASTA   But I beseech you, hearken! Do not do it!

OEDIPUS   I will not hearken—not to know the whole.

JOCASTA   I mean well; and I tell you for the best!

OEDIPUS   What you call best is an old sore of mine.

JOCASTA   Wretch, what thou art O might'st thou never know!

OEDIPUS   Will some one go and fetch the herdsman hither?
She is welcome to her gilded lineage!

JOCASTA   O
Woe, woe, unhappy! This is all I have
To say to thee, and no word more, for ever!

                                                    [*Exit.*

1 SENATOR   Why has the woman vanished, Oedipus,
Driven so wild with grief? I am afraid
Out of her silence will break forth some trouble.

OEDIPUS   Break out what will, I shall not hesitate,
Low though it be, to trace the source of me.

But she, perhaps, being, as a woman, proud,
Of my unfit extraction is ashamed.
—I deem myself the child of Fortune! I
Shall not be shamed of her, who favours me;
Seeing I have her for mother; and for kin
The limitary Moons, that found me small,
That fashioned me for great! Parented thus,
How could I ever in the issue prove
Other—that I should leave my birth unknown?

Chorus

1.

If I am a true seer,
My mind from error clear,
Tomorrow's moon shall not pass over us,
Ere, O Cithaeron, we
Shall magnify in thee
The land, the lap, the womb of Oedipus;
And we shall hymn thy praises, for good things
Of thy bestowing, done unto our kings.
Yea, Phoebus, if thou wilt, amen, so might it be!

2.

Who bare thee? Which, O child,
Over the mountain-wild
Sought to by Pan of the immortal Maids?
Or Loxias—was he
The sire who fathered thee?
For dear to him are all the upland glades.
Was it Cyllene's lord* acquired a son,
Or Bacchus, dweller on the heights, from one
Of those he liefest loves, Oreads** of Helicon?

* Hermes.
** Mountain nymphs.

Enter Attendants with an Old Man, a Shepherd.

OEDIPUS If I may guess, who never met with him,
    I think I see that herdsman, Senators,
    We have long been seeking; for his ripe old age
    Harmoniously accords with this man's measure;
    Besides, I recognize the men who bring him
    As of my household; but in certainty
    You can perhaps exceed me, who beheld
    The herdsman formerly.

1 SENATOR   Why, to be sure,
    I recognize him; for he was a man
    Trusty as any Laius ever had
    About his pastures.

OEDIPUS   You I ask the first,
    The Corinthian stranger; do you speak of him?

MESSENGER Yes, him you see:

OEDIPUS   Sirrah, old man, look here;
    Answer my questions. Were you Laius' man?

OLD MAN Truly his thrall; not bought, but bred at home.

OEDIPUS Minding what work, or in what character?

OLD MAN Most of my time I went after the flocks.

OEDIPUS In what directions, chiefly, were your folds?

OLD MAN There was Cithaeron; and a bit near by.

OEDIPUS Do you know this man, then? Did you see him there?

OLD MAN Him? After what? What man do you mean?

OEDIPUS   This fellow
    Here present; did you ever meet with him?

OLD MAN Not so to say off-hand, from memory.

MESSENGER And that's no wonder, sir; but beyond doubt
    I will remind him, though he has forgotten,
    I am quite sure he knows, once on a time,
    When in the bit about Cithaeron there—
    He with two flocks together, I with one—
    I was his neighbour for three whole half years
    From spring-tide onward to the Bear-ward's* day;

---

* The constellation Bootes.

And with the winter to my folds I drove,
And he to Laius' stables. Are these facts,
Or are they not—what I am saying?

OLD MAN   Yes,
You speak the truth; but it was long ago.

MESSENGER   Come, say now, don't you mind that you then gave me
A baby boy to bring up for my own?

OLD MAN   What do you mean? Why do you ask it me?

MESSENGER   This is the man, good fellow; who was then
A youngling!

OLD MAN   Out upon you! Hold your peace!

OEDIPUS   Nay, old man, do not chide him; for your words
Deserve a chiding rather than his own!

OLD MAN   O best of masters, what is my offence?

OEDIPUS   Not telling of that boy he asks about.

OLD MAN   He says he knows not what! He is all astray!

OEDIPUS   You will not speak of grace—you shall perforce!

OLD MAN   Do not for God's sake harm me, an old man!

OEDIPUS   Quick, some one, twist his hands behind him!

OLD MAN   Wretch,
What have I done? What do you want to know?

OEDIPUS   Did you give him that boy he asks about?

OLD MAN   I gave it him. Would I had died that day!

OEDIPUS   Tell the whole truth, or you will come to it!

OLD MAN   I am undone far more, though, if I speak!

OEDIPUS   The man is trifling with us, I believe.

OLD MAN   No, no; I said I gave it, long ago!

OEDIPUS   Where did you get it? At home, or from some other?

OLD MAN   It was not mine; another gave it me.

OEDIPUS   Which of these citizens? and from what roof?

OLD MAN   Don't, master, for God's sake, don't ask me more!

OEDIPUS   You are a dead man, if I speak again!

OLD MAN   Then—'twas a child—of Laius' household.

OEDIPUS   What,
Slave-born? or one of his own family?

OLD MAN   O, I am at the horror, now, to speak!

OEDIPUS   And I to hear. But I must hear—no less.

OLD MAN   Truly it was called his son; but she within,
     Your lady, could best tell you how it was.

OEDIPUS   Did she then give it you?

OLD MAN   My lord, even so.

OEDIPUS   For what?

OLD MAN   For me to make away with it.

OEDIPUS   Herself the mother? miserable!

OLD MAN   In dread
     Of evil prophecies—

OEDIPUS   What prophecies?

OLD MAN   That he should kill his parents, it was said.

OEDIPUS   How came you then to give it to this old man?

OLD MAN   For pity, O my master! thinking he
     Would carry it away to other soil,
     From whence he came; but he to the worst of harms
     Saved it! for if thou art the man he says,
     Sure thou wast born destined to misery!

OEDIPUS   Woe! woe! It is all plain, indeed! O Light,
     This be the last time I shall gaze on thee,
     Who am revealed to have been born of those
     Of whom I ought not—to have wedded whom
     I ought not—and slain whom I might not slay!

                                    [*Exit.*

Chorus.

I. 1.

    O generations of mankind!
        How do I find
       Your lives nought worth at all!
    For who is he—what state
    Is there, more fortunate
    Than only to seem great,
       And then, to fall?
    I having thee for pattern, and thy lot—
    Thine, O poor Oedipus—I envy not

Aught in mortality;
For this is he

I. 2.

Who, shooting far beyond the rest,
Won wealth all-blest,
Slaying, Zeus, thy monster-maid,
Crook-taloned, boding; and
Who did arise and stand
Betwixt death and our land,
A tower of aid;
Yea for this cause thou hast been named our king,
And honoured in the highest, governing
The city of Thebae great
In royal state.

II. 1.

And now, who lives more utterly undone?
Who with sad woes, who with mischances rude
Stands closer yoked by life's vicissitude?
O honoured head of Oedipus, for whom
Within the same wide haven there was room
To come—child, to the birth—
Sire, to the nuptial bower,
How could the furrows of thy parent earth—
How could they suffer thee, O hapless one,
In silence, to this hour?

II. 2.

Time found thee out—Time who sees everything—
Unwittingly guilty; and arraigns thee now
Consort ill-sorted, unto whom are bred
Sons of thy getting, in thine own birth-bed.
O scion of Laius' race,

Would I had never never seen thy face!
For I lament, even as from lips that sing
Pouring a dirge; yet verily it was thou
Gav'st me to rise
And breathe again, and close my watching eyes.

Enter a second MESSENGER.

2 MESSENGER   O you most honoured ever of this land,
What deeds have you to hear, what sights to see,
What sorrow to endure, if you still cherish
The house of Labdacus with loyalty?
For Ister* I suppose or Phasis'** wave
Never could purge this dwelling from the ills
It covers—or shall instantly reveal,
Invited, not inflicted; of all wounds,
Those that seem wilful are the worst to bear.

1 SENATOR   There was no lack, in what we knew before,
Of lamentable; what have you more to say?

2 MESSENGER   The speediest of all tales to hear and tell;
The illustrious Jocasta is no more.

1 SENATOR   Unhappy woman! From what cause?

2 MESSENGER   Self-slain.
Of what befell the saddest part is spared;
For you were not a witness. None the less
So far as I can tell it you shall hear
Her miserable story. When she passed
So frantically inside the vestibule,
She went straight onward to the bed-chamber,
With both her hands tearing her hair; the doors
She dashed to as she entered, crying out
On Laius, long since dead, calling to mind
His fore-begotten offspring, by whose hands
He, she said, died, and left to his own seed

---

* The Danube.
** A river emptying into the Black Sea.

Its mother's most unnatural bearing-bed.
Nor did she not bewail that nuptial-couch
Where she brought forth, unhappy, brood on brood,
Spouse to her spouse, and children to her child.
And then—I know no further how she perished;
For Oedipus brake in, crying aloud;
For whom it was impossible to watch
The ending of her misery; but on him
We gazed, as he went raging all about,
Beseeching us to furnish him a sword
And say where he could find his wife—no wife,
Rather the mother-soil both of himself
And children; and, as he raved thus, some Power
Shews him—at least, none of us present did.
Then, shouting loud, he sprang upon the doors
As following some guide, and burst the bars
Out of their sockets, and alights within.
There we beheld his wife hanging, entwined
In a twined noose. He seeing her, with a groan
Looses the halter; then, when on the ground
Lay the poor wretch, dreadful it was to see
What followed; snatching from her dress gold pins
Wherewith she was adorned, he lifted them,
And smote the nerves of his own eyeballs, saying
Something like this—that they should see no more
Evils like those he had endured or wrought;
Darkling, thereafter, let them gaze on forms
He might not see, and fail to recognize
The faces he desired! Chanting this burden,
Not once, but many times, he raised his hand
And stabbed his eyes; so that from both of them
The blood ran down his face, not drop by drop,
But all at once, in a dark shower of gore.
—These are the ills that from a two-fold source,
Not one alone, but in both wife and spouse,
Mingled together, have burst forth at once.

Their former pristine happiness indeed
Was happiness before; but in this hour
Shame—lamentation—Atè*—death—of all
That has a name of evil, nought's away!

1 SENATOR   And does he stand in any respite now
Of misery, poor soul?

2 MESSENGER   He calls aloud
For some one to undo the bolts, and shew
To all the Cadmeans him, his father's slayer—
His mother's—uttering words unhallowed—words
I may not speak; that he will cast himself
Forth of the land, abide no more at home
Under the curse of his own cursing. Nay,
But he lacks force, and guidance; for his sickness
Is more than man can bear. See for yourself;
For these gates open, and you will straight behold
A sight—such as even he that loathes must pity!

Enter OEDIPUS *blind*.

Chorus.

O sorrow, lamentable for eyes to see!
Sorest of all past ills encountering me!
What frenzy, O wretch, is this, that came on thee?

What Deity was it that with a leap so great—
Farther than farthest—sprang on thy sad fate?
Woe is me, woe is me for thee—unfortunate!

Fain would I gaze at thee, would ask thee much,
Many things learn of thee, wert thou not such
As I may not even behold, as I shudder to touch.

OEDIPUS   Me miserable! Whither must I go?
Ah whither flits my voice, borne to and fro?
Thou Power unseen, how hast thou brought me low!

* Doom caused by guilt and ignorance.

1 SENATOR   To ills, intolerable to hear or see.

OEDIPUS   Thou horror of thick darkness overspread,
        Thou shadow of unutterable dread
        Not to be stemmed or stayed, fallen on my head—

        Woe's me once more! How crowd upon my heart
          Stings of these wounds, and memories of woe!

1 SENATOR   No marvel if thou bear a double smart
        And writhe, so stricken, with a two-fold throe!

OEDIPUS   Still art thou near me—ready still to tend
        And to endure me, faithful to the end,
        Blind as I am, with kindness, O my friend!

        For strange thou art not; but full well I know
          That voice of thine, all darkling though I be.

1 SENATOR   Rash man, how could'st thou bear to outrage so
        Thine eyes? What Power was it, that wrought on thee?

OEDIPUS   Apollo, Apollo fulfils,
        O friends, my measure of ills—
        Fills my measure of woe;
        Author was none, but I,
        None other, of the blow;
        For why was I to see,
          When to descry
    No sight on earth could have a charm for me?

1 SENATOR   It was even as thou sayest.

OEDIPUS   What was there left for sight?
        What, that could give delight?
          Or whose address,
    O friends, could I still hear with happiness?
        Lead me to exile straight;
        Lead me, O my friends, the worst

Of murderers, of mortals most accurst,
    Yea and to Gods chief object of their hate.

1 SENATOR   Of cunning hapless, as of hapless fate,
    I would that I had never known thy name!

OEDIPUS   May he perish, whoe'er 'twas drew me
            Out of the cruel gyve
            That bound my feet, on the lea!
            He who saved me alive,
            Who rescued me from fate,
            Shewing no kindness to me!
               Sorrow so great,
  Had I died then, had spared both mine and me.

1 SENATOR   Fain were I too it had been so.

OEDIPUS   Not then had I become
            My father's murderer,
      Nor wedded her I have my being from:
            Whom now no God will bless,
            Child of incestuousness
    In her that bare me, being the spouse of her;
    Yea if aught ill worse than all ill be there,
           That Oedipus must bear.

1 SENATOR   I know not how to say thou hast done well;
    For it were better for thee now to die,
    Than to live on in blindness.

OEDIPUS   Tell me not—
    Give me no counsel now, that what is done
    Has not been done thus best. I know not how
    With seeing eyes I could have looked upon
    My father—coming to the under-world,
    Or my poor mother, when against them both
    I have sinned sins, worse than a halter's meed.
    Or do you think that children were a sight
    Delectable for me to gaze at, born

As they were born? Never with eyes of mine!
No, nor the city, nor the citadel,
Nor consecrated shrines of deities,
From which, to my most utter misery,
I, of all other men in Thebes the man
Most bravely nurtured, cut myself away,
And of my own mouth dictated to all
To thrust out me, the impious—me, declared
Abominable of Heaven, and Laius' son.
Was I, who in myself made evident
So dark a stain, with unaverted eyes
To look on these? That least of all! Nay rather,
If there were any way to choke the fount
Of hearing, through my ears, I would have tried
To seal up all this miserable frame
And live blind, deaf to all things; sweet it were
To dwell in fancy, out of reach of pain.
—Cithaeron! wherefore didst thou harbour me!
Why not at once have slain me? Never then
Had I displayed before the face of men
Who and from whom I am! O Polybus,
And Corinth, and the old paternal roof
I once called mine, with what thin film of honour,
Corruption over-skinned, you fostered me,
Found ill myself, and from ill parents, now!
O you, the three roads, and the lonely brake,
The copse, and pass at the divided way,
Which at my hands drank blood that was my own—
My father's—do you keep in memory
What in your sight I did, and how again
I wrought, when I came hither? Wedlock, wedlock,
You gave me being, you raised up seed again
To the same lineage, and exhibited
In one incestuous flesh son—brother—sire,
Bride, wife and mother; and all ghastliest deeds
Wrought among men! But O, ill done, ill worded!

In Heaven's name hide me with all speed away,
Or slay me, or send adrift upon some sea
Where you may look on me no longer! Come,
Touch, if you will, a miserable man;
Pray you, fear nothing; for my misery
No mortal but myself can underbear.

1 SENATOR Creon is at hand; he is the man you need,
Who must decide and do; being, after you,
The sole protector left us, for the land.

OEDIPUS Ah Heaven, what language shall I hold to him?
What rightful credit will appear in me?
For I have been found wholly in the wrong
In all that passed between us heretofore!

Enter CREON.

CREON Not as a mocker come I, Oedipus,
Nor to reproach for any former pain.
But you—even if you reverence no more
Children of men,—at least so far revere
The royal Sun-god's all-sustaining fire,
Not to parade, thus flagrant, such a sore
As neither earth nor day can tolerate,
Nor dew from Heaven! Take him in instantly!
That kindred only should behold and hear
The griefs of kin, fits best with decency.

OEDIPUS In Heaven's name, seeing that you transported me
Beyond all hope, coming, the first of men,
To me the last of men, grant me one boon!
'Tis for your good, not for my own, I say it.

CREON What is it that you crave so eagerly?

OEDIPUS Out of this country cast me with all speed,
Where I may pass without accost of men.

CREON So had I done, be sure, had I not wished
To learn our duty, first, at the God's mouth.

OEDIPUS Surely his oracle was all made plain,
Me, the profane, the parricide, to slay!

CREON   So was it said; but in our present need
         'Tis better to enquire what we must do.
OEDIPUS   Will ye seek answer for a wretch like me?
CREON   Even you might trust what the God answers, now.
OEDIPUS   Ay, and I charge thee, and will beg of thee,
         Order thyself such burial as thou wilt,
         For her who lies within; seeing it is meet
         Thou do so, for thine own. But never more
         Be this my native town burdened with me
         For living inmate; rather suffer me
         To haunt the mountains—where my mountain is,
         Cithaeron, which my mother and my sire,
         Living, appointed for my sepulchre,
         That as they meant, my slayers, I may expire.
         Howbeit this much I know, neither disease
         Nor aught beside can kill me; never else
         Had I been rescued from the brink of death,
         But for some dire calamity. Ah well,
         Let our own fate wag onward as it may;
         And for my sons, Creon, take thou no care
         Upon thee; they are men, so that they never
         Can lack the means to live, where'er they be;
         But my two girls, wretched and pitiable,
         For whose repast was never board of mine
         Ordered apart, without me, but in all
         That I partook they always shared with me,
         Take care of them; and let me, above all else,
         Touch them with hands, and weep away my troubles!
         Pardon, my lord; pardon, illustrious sir;
         If but my hands could feel them, I might seem
         To have them still, as when I still could see.

ANTIGONE *and* ISMENE *are brought in.*

         —What do I say? In Heaven's name, do I not
         Hear my two darlings, somewhere shedding tears?
         And can it be that Creon, pitying me,

                Sends me my dearest, my two daughters, hither?
                Is it so indeed?

CREON   Yes, it is I vouchsafed this boon, aware
                What joy you have and long have had of them.

OEDIPUS   Why then, good luck go with thee, and Providence
                Be guardian to thee, better than to me,
                In payment for their coming!—Children dear,
                Where are you? Come, come hither to my arms—
                To these brotherly arms—procurers that
                The eyes—that were your sire's—once bright—should see
                Thus! who am shewn, O children, to have been
                Author of you—unseeing—unknowing—in
                Her bed, whence I derived my being! You
                I weep for; for I cannot gaze on you;
                Knowing what is left of bitter in the life
                Which at men's hands you needs must henceforth live.
                For to what gatherings of the citizens
                Will you resort, or to what festivals,
                Whence you will not, in place of holiday,
                Come home in tears? Or when you shall have grown
                To years of marriage, who—ah, who will be
                The man to abide the hazard of disgrace
                Such as must be the bane, both of my sons,
                And you as well? For what reproach is lacking?
                Your father slew his father, and became
                Father of you—by her who bare him. So
                Will they reproach you; who will wed you then?
                No one, my children; but you needs must wither,
                Barren—unwed. But thou, Menoeceus' son,
                Since thou art all the father these have left them,
                For we, the two that were their parents, now
                Are both undone, do not thou suffer them
                To wander, vagabond and husband-less,
                Being of thy kin; nor let them fall so low
                As are my fortunes; but have pity on them,
                Seeing them so tender, and so desolate

Of all friends, but for thee. Give me thy hand,
Good sir, and promise this.—To you, my girls,
If you were old enough to understand,
I should have much to say; but as it is,
This be your prayer; in some permitted place
That you may breathe; and have your lot in life
Happier than his, who did engender you.

CREON   Get thee in; thou hast bewailed thee enough, in reason.

OEDIPUS   Though it be bitter, I must do it.

CREON   All's good, in good season.

OEDIPUS   Do you know how to make me?

CREON   Say on, and I shall know.

OEDIPUS   Banish me from this country.

CREON   That must the God bestow.

OEDIPUS   But to Gods, above all men, I am a mark for hate.

CREON   And for that same reason you will obtain it straight.

OEDIPUS   Say you so?

CREON   Yes truly, and I mean what I say.

OEDIPUS   Lead me hence then, quickly.

CREON   Go; but let the children stay.

OEDIPUS   Do not take them from me!

CREON   Think not to have all at thy pleasure;
For what thou didst attain to far outwent thy measure.

CREON, *the Children, etc. retire.*   OEDIPUS *is led in.*

Chorus.

Dwellers in Thebes, behold this Oedipus,
The man who solved the riddle marvellous,
A prince of men,
Whose lot what citizen
Did not with envy see,
How deep the billows of calamity
    Above him roll.

Watch therefore and regard that supreme day;
And of no mortal say
"That man is happy," till
Vexed by no grievous ill
    He pass Life's goal.

[*Exeunt omnes.*

Electra

SOPHOCLES

Characters

ORESTES, *son of Agamemnon, the late king of Argos and Mycenæ, and of Clytæmnestra.*

PYLADES, *friend to Orestes.*

An old Attendant, Guardian to Orestes.

ELECTRA,
CHRYSOTHEMIS, } *daughters of Agamemnon and Clytæmnestra.*

CLYTÆMNESTRA, *queen of Argos and Mycenæ.*

ÆGISTHUS, *cousin to Agamemnon, and in his lifetime the paramour of Clytæmnestra.*

The Chorus is composed of Ladies of Mycenæ, friends to Electra.

Attendants on Clytæmnestra.

ELECTRA

Scene, before the Palace at Mycenæ.

Enter ORESTES, PYLADES *and Guardian.*

GUARDIAN.   Son of our Captain in the wars of Troy,
  Great Agamemnon, it is given thee now
  With thine own eyes, Orestes, to behold
  Those scenes thou hast ever longed for. Here it lies,
  Argos, the ancient land of thy desire;
  The sacred glade of her the gadfly drave,
  Inachus' daughter;* that's the Agora
  They call Lycean, from the wolf-slaying God;
  This, on the left, Hera's renowned fane;
  And from the point we are reaching you can swear
  You see Mycenæ's Golden City, and this,
  The death-fraught house of Pelops' family;
  Whence I received you at your sister's hands,
  And saved you from the slaughter of your sire,
  And carried you away, and fostered you
  So far toward manhood, ready to revenge
  A father's blood. Wherefore, Orestes, now —
  And Pylades, thou dearest of allies —
  Take we brief counsel what is right to do;

---

* Io, daughter of the river god Inachus, became attractive to Zeus, thereby incurring the wrath of Hera, who changed her into a cow, and set a stinging insect upon her which drove her out of Argos.

For see, already the bright gleam of day
Calls up the birds to sing their matins clear
Above us, and the sable star-lit night
Has passed away. Now, before any man
Comes forth abroad, join you in conference;
For where we stand, it is no season more
To hesitate; the hour is come for action.

ORESTES.   My faithfullest of followers, what clear signs
You manifest of your good will to us!
For as a generous steed, though he be old,
Beset with difficulties, pricks his ears
And bates not of his courage, you impart
Spirit to us, and lag no whit behind.
As you desire, I will unfold my scheme;
Do you the while mark my words heedfully,
And if I miss the target, mend my aim.
Late, when I sought the Pythian oracle,
To learn how I might execute revenge
Upon my father's murderers, Phœbus gave me
Answer in this sort; I will tell it you;
I by myself unarmed with shields and martial bands
By craft held condign slaughter hidden in my hands.
Well, with this answer sounding in our ears,
Go you, as opportunity may lead,
Into the house, and gather all that passes,
And bring us word of all; for in old age,
And so long after, they will never know
Now, nor suspect you, frosted thus by time.
Tell your tale thus; you are a citizen
Of Phocis, and you come from Phanoteus,
Who is their best ally; tell them (and swear it)
Orestes has been killed by accident,
By a fall from his chariot, at the Pythian games;
Let it stand so. We, as He bade, the while,
First with libations and shorn curls of hair
Will deck my father's grave; then back again
Return, carrying an urn of beaten brass,

(The same, you know, that in the brake lies hidden,)
That in feigned words we may convey to them
Glad tidings — how my body is destroyed,
Burnt up already and made embers of!
For where's the harm to be called dead, when really
I am alive, and gather praise thereby?
No word that profits us can hurt, I fancy.
Why, I have seen men often, who were wise,
Falsely pretending death; then, when again
They came back home, they have been more prized than ever;
So I expect yet, out of this report,
To blaze forth, star-like, living, on my foes.
But O my native land! Gods of the soil!
Welcome me with good fortune in these ways;
And thou, paternal Home! for I thy cleanser
Come here of right, the ambassador of Heaven;
Send me not with dishonour from this land,
But grant me to inherit and set up
The old estate. — I have spoken. Now, old friend,
Be it your care to guard your post; go forward;
And let us forth. It is the season; this,
In every action, is men's best ally.

ELECTRA (*within*). Ah woe is me!

GUARDIAN.   Hark!
    I thought I heard some handmaiden cry faintly
    Inside the doors, my son!

ORESTES.   Is it perhaps
    The wronged Electra? Shall we stay awhile
    And listen to her sorrowing?

GUARDIAN.   By no means.
    Do nothing ere performing what is bidden
    Of Loxias,* and initiate all from thence,

---

* Epithet of Apollo, meaning either *the Ambiguous* or *the Speaker*.

Pouring lustrations on your father's grave.
This wafts us victory, and nerves our doings.   [*Exeunt.*

Enter ELECTRA.

ELECTRA.   Holy Light, with Earth, and Sky,
　　Whom thou fillest equally,
　　Ah how many a note of woe,
　　Many a self-inflicted blow
　　On my scarred breast might'st thou mark,
　　Ever as recedes the dark;
　　Known, too, all my nightlong cheer
　　To bitter bed and chamber drear,
　　How I mourn my father lost,
　　Whom on no barbarian coast
　　　　Did red Ares greet amain,
　　But as woodmen cleave an oak
　　My mother's axe dealt murderous stroke,
　　Backed by the partner of her bed,
　　Fell Ægisthus, on his head;
　　Whence no pity, save from me,
　　O my father, flows for thee,
　　　　So falsely, foully slain.
　　Yet I will not cease from sighing,
　　Cease to pour my bitter crying,
　　While I see this light of day,
　　Or the stars' resplendent play,
　　Uttering forth a sound of wail,
　　Like the child-slayer, the nightingale,*
　　Here before my father's door
　　Crying to all men evermore.
　　O Furies dark, of birth divine!
　　O Hades wide, and Proserpine!
　　　　Thou nether Hermes! Ara great!†

---

* Philomela, who, with Procne, killed Tereus' son Itys, cooked him and served him to his
father.
† Ara: goddess of destruction and revenge.

Ye who regard the untimely dead,
The dupes of an adulterous bed,
Come ye, help me, and require
The foul murder of our sire;
And send my brother back again;
Else I may no more sustain
    Grief's overmastering weight.

Enter Chorus of Ladies of Mycenæ.

CHORUS. O child, Electra, child
    Of one too fatally bold,
    How sighest thou, unsatisfied yet,
    Evermore wasting away,
    For him, Agamemnon, beguiled
    By thy crafty mother of old,
    Spite of all Gods, in her net,
    To base hands given for a prey?
    Accurst be the author of this!
        If I pray not amiss.

ELECTRA. O women of noble strain,
    Ye are come to solace my pain;
    I know it, I well perceive;
    It escapes me not at all;
    Howbeit I will not leave
    To lament my father's fall.
    Ye my love who repay
    With all love ever gave,
    Ah let me be, I pray,
        Leave me to rave.

CHORUS. But not from Hades below,
    Not from the all-welcoming shore,
    Even with strong crying and prayer
    Canst thou raise thy father again.
    Past all measure in woe
    Thou art perishing evermore,

Sinking deep in despair,
Where no release is from pain;
Ah why so bent upon grief,
    Too sore for relief?

ELECTRA. None but fools could forget
    Their fathers' wrongs, who are gone.
    But on her my fancy is set,
    The bird, Heaven's messenger,
    Wildly bemoaning her
    For Itys, Itys alone!
    O forlorn Niobe,*
    As one godlike I deem of thee,
    Alas! that abidest, weeping,
        In a rock-tomb's keeping!

CHORUS. Not first of mortals with thee,
    Daughter, did sorrow begin;
    Whereas thou passest the rest,
    Thy kith and kindred within,
    The life Chrysothemis lives,
    And Iphianassa, and he
    In the flower of his youth who grieves,
    Hid, but not all unblest,
    Whom the land, Mycenæ fair,
    Will receive, her princes' heir,
    When he, Orestes, shall come
        By Heaven's guidance home.

ELECTRA. Whom I wait for, and go
    Ceaselessly wet with tears,
    Unespoused, childless, forlorn,
    Bearing still, as I must,
    The unending burden of woe;
    But he forgets with the years

---

* Boastful, blasphemous woman whose fourteen children were wiped out by Apollo and Artemis. She had claimed to be more fertile than their mother Leto. Niobe herself was turned to stone.

All he has heard and borne;
For what message comes I can trust?
Ever he longs to be here —
    He will not appear!

CHORUS.   Nay cheer thee, cheer thee, my child;
    God in the Heavens is yet great,
    Who surveys all else and commands.
    Leave thou then in his hands
    Anger — the excess of regret,
    Nor chide overmuch — nor forget
    Those whom thou needs must hate.
    For Time is a God right mild;
    Nor can Agamemnon's son
    By Crisa's pastoral shore,
    Nor the monarch of Acheron,
        Be deaf evermore.

ELECTRA.   But already most of my day,
    Hopeless, has faded away;
    I can do no longer withal;
    Without parents to cherish me I waste,
    Without husband's love, to defend;
    Yea alien-like, disgraced,
    I inhabit my father's hall,
    And in this guise attend
    At a board with no feast laid,
        Uncomely arrayed.

CHORUS.   At his return arose
    A burden of woes — of woes
    To thy father's resting-place,
    What time was darted a thrust,
    From fangs all brass, at his face.
    Fraud was deviser — Lust
    Was slayer — embodying the shade
    Of a fell deed foully planned,

Yea, whether by heavenly aid
  Or a mortal's hand.

ELECTRA.   O day that far beyond all
  Dawned most hateful to see!
  O night—O sorrows abhorred
  Of that ghastly festival—
  Murder done villainously
  On my sire, by the hands of twain
  Who took my life as a prey,
  Who annihilated me!
  Whom may God with rightful reward,
  The Olympian Power, again
  For their deeds amply repay,
  Nor let them compass their bliss
    By an act like this!

CHORUS.   Take heed; say no more.
  Hast thou no consciousness
  Out of what wealth before
  Thou fall'st thus miserably
  Into ills that abide with thee?
  Thou hast wrought thee woes in excess,
  Bringing forth strife on strife
  To the heaviness of thy life;
  And is it so easy a thing
    To contend with a king?

ELECTRA.   Hard is my fate, full hard;
  I know it; I am mad, I confess;
  Yet not for the fates that oppress
  Will I keep this wrath under guard,
  The while my life shall endure!
  For from whom, companions dear,
  Should I submissively hear
  Reason, or from whom, that is wise,
  Counsel, fit for mine ear?
  Let me be; cease to advise;

All this must pass without cure;
I shall never be free from distress,
 And laments numberless.

CHORUS. Yet I bid thee, faithful still,
As a mother, and in good will,
Do not add new ill unto ill.

ELECTRA. And where should a limit be set
 For evil to spread?
Or how is it well, to forget
 The cause of the dead?
In what man's heart
 Could a plant like this find place?
Be mine no part
 In such men's favour or grace!
Nor, if with any good things
 My fortune is blent,
Be it mine to rest in content,
 And fetter the wings
Of piercing cries, or tire,
 Praising my sire.
For if in the earth, as nought,
 The dead must lie,
And these, in return, who ought,
 The slayers, not die,
Then farewell honour, and fall
 Men's reverence, all!

I LADY. I came, my daughter, zealous for your good
As for my own; but if I say not well,
Have it your way; for we will follow you.

ELECTRA. I am ashamed, dear ladies, if to you
Through frequent lamentations I appear
Too sorely oppressed; but, for necessity
Obliges me to do so, pardon me.
For how should any woman gently born,
Viewing the sorrows of her father's house,

Do otherwise than I, who witness them
For ever day by day and night by night
Rather increase than lessen? to whom, first,
The mother's face who bare me has become
Most hostile; next, I must be companied
In my own home with my sire's murderers,
By them be ruled, take at their hands, or else
At their hands hunger! Then, what sort of days
Do you suppose I lead, when I behold
Ægisthus seated on my father's throne,
Wearing the selfsame garments which he wore,
And pouring out libations on the hearth
By which he slew him? When I witness, too,
The consummation of their impudence,
The homicide lying in my father's bed
With that abandoned mother—if it be right
To call her mother, who consorts with him!
And she—so profligate that she lives on
With her blood-guilty mate—fearing no vengeance—
Rather, as if exulting in her doings—
Looks out the day on which by cunning erst
She slew my father, and each month on it
Sets dances going, and sacrifices sheep
In offering to her guardian deities!
I see it, I, ill-fated one! At home
I weep and waste and sorrow as I survey
The unblest feast that bears my father's name,
In private; for I cannot even weep
So freely as my heart would have me do;
For this tongue-valiant woman with vile words
Upbraids me, crying "Thou God-forsaken thing,
Has no man's father died, save only thine?
Is nobody in mourning, except thee?
Ill death betide thee, and the nether Gods
Give thee no end to these thy sorrowings!"
So she reviles; save when she hears it said
Orestes is at hand; then instantly

She is possest, and comes and screams at me—
"Is it not you who are the cause of this?
Pray is not this your doing, who stole Orestes
Out of my hands, and conjured him away?
But mind you, you shall pay me well for it!"
So snarling, there joins with her and stands by
And hounds her forward her illustrious groom,
The all unmanly, all injurious pest,
Who fights no battles without women! I,
Waiting and waiting, till Orestes come
And end it, miserably daily die.
For always meaning, never doing, he
Has utterly confounded all my hopes
Remote or present. Friends, in such a case,
There is no room—no, not for soberness
Or piety; but, beneath injuries,
There is deep need we prove injurious, too!

I LADY.   Stay, tell me, is it with Ægisthus near
You talk thus to us, or is he gone from home?

ELECTRA.   That is he. Never think, if he were by,
I could roam forth; but he is abroad just now.

I LADY.   Then I might come with better confidence
To speech of you, that being so.

ELECTRA.   Oh, ask freely;
He is not here. What do you want to know?

I LADY.   And so I will. What of your brother say you?
I would fain know, will he come soon, or tarry?

ELECTRA.   He says he will. He does not keep his word.

I LADY.   A man is backward, when on some great exploit.

ELECTRA.   I was not backward, when I rescued him!

I LADY.   Take courage, he is of a worthy stock;
He will not fail his friends.

ELECTRA.   I trust so. Else
    I never should have been alive so long.

1 LADY.   Hush, say no more just now; for I perceive
    Chrysothemis your sister, who was born
    Of the same mother and same sire as you,
    Come from the palace, carrying in her hands
    Oblations customary to the dead.

Enter CHRYSOTHEMIS.

CHRYSOTHEMIS.   Sister, what talk is this, you come and cry
    Aloud, abroad, before the outer gate,
    Nor will not learn, taught by long years, to cease
    Vainly indulging unavailing rage?
    I for myself can say as much as this—
    I chafe at those I live with, in such fashion
    As, if I could get power, I would make plain
    The sort of temper that I bear towards them;
    But in these dangers it seems good to sail
    Close-reefed, and not pretend to be at work,
    But effect nothing harmful; and I wish
    You too would do the like; and yet, the right
    Is not as I declare, but as you judge it;
    Still, if I am to live at liberty,
    I must in all things heed my governors.

ELECTRA.   Well, it is strange that you, being his child
    Who was your sire, should have regard for her,
    Your mother, and have quite forgotten him!
    All this good counsel you bestow on me
    Is of her teaching; and of your own self
    You can say nothing. Therefore take your choice;
    Either to be of evil mind, or else
    Well minded to forget those dear to you;
    Who said but now, if you could get the power,
    You would shew plain the hate you have for them;

And yet, while I am doing everything
To avenge our father, do not take your part,
And seek to turn me from it, who take mine!
Danger! Is there not cowardice as well?
Come, answer me, what should it profit me
To cease my mourning? Or else hear me speak;
Do I not live? unprosperously I know,
But well enough for me; to them, the while,
I am a torment, and so render honour
To him that's gone, if there be service there!
You — madam hatress — you pretend you hate,
But really take your father's murderers' side!
For my part, I will never bend to them;
Not though a man should come and offer me
These gauds of yours, in which you glory now!
Yours be the full-spread board, the cup o'erflowing;
For me — be it my only sustenance
Not to offend against my conscience. Thus,
I do not ask to share your dignities,
And were you well-advised, no more would you!
But now, though it be in your power to be called
Your father's child — the foremost of mankind,
Be called — your mother's! So you shall appear
In most men's eyes unmeritoriously,
False to your friends, and to your father's shade.

1 LADY.   Now in Heaven's name, no chiding! There is good
            In what you both have said, if you would learn
            Something from her, and she, in turn, from you.

CHRYSOTHEMIS.   Oh, I am quite accustomed to her talk;
            Nor, ladies, had I ever said one word,
            Had I not heard a very great mishap
            Was coming on her, which will make her cease
            From her long sorrowing.

ELECTRA.   Come, your bug-bear, tell it!

If you can mention any greater grief
Than these I have, I will reply no more.

CHRYSOTHEMIS.   Well, I will tell you everything I know.
They are going, if you will not cease this mourning,
To send you where you will not any more
See daylight, but sing sorrow underground,
Buried alive, out of this territory.
Wherefore take heed, or by and by, in trouble
Never blame me. Prudence is easy, now.

ELECTRA.   Ay? have they purposed to do so to me?

CHRYSOTHEMIS.   Most surely, when Ægisthus shall come home.

ELECTRA.   Why as for that, let him come speedily!

CHRYSOTHEMIS.   What was it that you prayed for, silly one?

ELECTRA.   For him to come; if he is that way minded.

CHRYSOTHEMIS.   So you may get—what treatment? Are you mad?

ELECTRA.   So I may get—farthest away from you!

CHRYSOTHEMIS.   And of life present have you no regard?

ELECTRA.   Living like mine is choice, to marvel at!

CHRYSOTHEMIS.   It might be, had you sense to be discreet.

ELECTRA.   Do not instruct me to be treacherous.

CHRYSOTHEMIS.   I do not; but to yield to those who govern.

ELECTRA.   Well, gloze it so; you do not speak my language.

CHRYSOTHEMIS.   Yet it were well not to be ruined through folly.

ELECTRA.   Come ruin, if needful, in a father's quarrel!

CHRYSOTHEMIS.   I am sure our father pardons us for this.

ELECTRA.   That is the speech a villain might approve.

CHRYSOTHEMIS.   You will not hearken and agree with me?

ELECTRA.   I trust I am not yet so senseless. No!

CHRYSOTHEMIS.   Then I will go on whither I was sent.

ELECTRA.   Where are you going? To whom bear you these offerings?

CHRYSOTHEMIS.   My mother sends me, to strew my father's grave.

ELECTRA.   How say you? To the most detested foe —

CHRYSOTHEMIS.   Yes — "whom she murdered!" That is what you mean?

ELECTRA.   By whom, of all friends, bidden? At whose desire?

CHRYSOTHEMIS.   Through some nocturnal panic, to my thinking.

ELECTRA.   God of my fathers, only aid me now!

CHRYSOTHEMIS.   Do you gain any courage from her scare?

ELECTRA.   Tell me about the dream, and I could say.

CHRYSOTHEMIS.   Only I do not know it; except just
In brief, the story.

ELECTRA.   Well, but tell me that;
Brief words ere now have often led astray —
And righted mortals.

CHRYSOTHEMIS.   It is said she saw
An apparition of your sire and mine
Come back again to daylight; and he took
The sceptre which he sometime bore himself,
But now Ægisthus bears, and planted it
Upon the hearth, and out of it a shoot
Budded and grew, till all Mycenæ's land
Was covered with its shadow. So I heard
Related by a fellow who was by,
While to the Sun-God she disclosed her dream.
But more than this I know not; only that
She sends me on account of this alarm.
Now I beseech you, by our country's Gods,

Listen to me, and be not ruined by folly;
For though you should repulse me, by and by
In trouble you will turn to me again.

ELECTRA.   Nay but let nothing of your fardel, dear,
Light on the tomb! for it were shame — were sin
From an abominable spouse to bring
Lustrations near, or perform obsequies
To a sire's shade. Let the winds have them, rather!
Or hide them deep in dust, where none of them
Shall ever touch our father's resting-place;
Let them be kept, stored underground, for her
When she is dead! Why, if she were not grown
The most abandoned of all womankind,
She never would have dreamt of smothering
With her unfriendly strewments him she murdered!
Why look you, think you the entombed dead
Will take these gifts in kindness, at her hands
Who slew him foully, like an enemy,
Lopped of the extremities, the stains of blood
Smeared off, for lustral washings, on his head!
Do you imagine what you bear can purge
Her from her murder? Never! Let it be!
Cut from your head the longest locks of hair —
And mine, unhappy — small the gift, indeed,
But what I have — and give it him, this hair
Untended, and my girdle, unadorned
With broiderings! Fall upon your knees, and pray him
In favour come and help us, from the earth,
Against our enemies; and that his boy
Orestes may set foot, before he die,
Superior, on the bodies of his foes,
That we may crown him afterward with hands
Larger in gift than we can proffer now!
Yea I believe, I do believe, that he
Had part in sending her this ugly dream;
But still, sister, do this, for your own good,

And mine, and his, the man of all mankind
Dearest, our sire, who in the grave lies dead.

1 LADY.   The princess speaks religiously, my friend;
And you, if you are wise, will heed her.

CHRYSOTHEMIS.   Yes.
It stands to reason, not that two should quarrel
Over their duty, but be quick and do it.
Only while I essay this business, friends,
Do you keep secret, in the name of Heaven!
For if my mother hears it, to my cost,
Methinks, I shall attempt this venture, yet.

[*Exit* CHRYSOTHEMIS.

CHORUS.

I.

If I be seer
Not wholly erring and unpolicied,
Self-prophesying Justice means to appear,
Bringing large succour to the righteous side,
And following on, my child, with no long waiting-tide.
Courage springs up within me, as I hear
The voice of dreams, breathing sweet music near;
He who begat thee, the Hellenian King,
Forgets not ever; nor that Ancient Thing,
The two-edged brazen fang, by which he foully died.

2.

Lo, this is she,
Erinys,* hiding her dread ambushed bands,
Sandalled with brass, with myriad feet and hands.
Yea time hath been, when they who should not, plied
A blood-stained spousal-work, unmeet for bed or bride.
Whence it comes o'er me, I shall never see

* Collective name for the Eumenides, or Furies.

On doer and accomplice harmlessly
This portent fall; and nothing future can
By good or ill dream be revealed to man,
If this night-vision speed not, landward, on the tide.

O chariot-race weary
    Of Pelops of old,
How fateful, how dreary,
    Thou hast proved to this land!
For since Myrtilus slumbered,
    From the chariot, all gold,
Torn, silenced for ever,
    Flung far from the strand,
From thenceforth never
    The weary disgrace
Of troubles unnumbered
    Hath passed from the race.

Enter CLYTÆMNESTRA, *attended.*

CLYTÆMNESTRA.   You gad abroad, then, masterless again,
    Ægisthus absent; who did hinder you
    From bringing scandal on your family
    By brawling at the doors! Now he is gone,
    You pay no heed to me; though many a time,
    In many people's ears, you have proclaimed —
    I, without shame or warrant, violate
    Your rights and honours! I meanwhile commit
    No violence; I but repay with scorn
    The scorn you heap on me. Your father, though —
    This and no other — is your pretext still,
    How by my hand he died! By mine; I know it;
    There's no denial of the deed in me.
    But Justice slew him; I was not alone;
    And had you sense, you ought to take her side;
    Since he, this father whom you still bewail,

Alone of all the Argives had the heart
To offer to the Gods your sister's life —
Whose pains in her begetting equalled not
My travail-pangs, who bare her! Be it so;
Now tell me for what cause, and for whose sake,
He offered her? For the Argives, will you say?
They had no right to kill a child of mine!
If for his brother Menelaus' sake
He slew my daughter, was not he to pay
Forfeit for that? Were there not children twain
Born to that father, who, had right been done,
Ought rather to have died, whose sire and dam
Themselves had caused that voyage? Had the Grave
Some fancy for my offspring, for its feast,
Rather than hers? Or had all natural love
Expired in that pernicious father's heart
For children born of me, but not for children
Of Menelaus? Was it not the act
Of a perverse insensate sire? I think it,
Though you deny; and so would that dead girl
Say, could she speak. For what my hands have done
I do not feel remorse; but if to you
I seem of evil mind, censure your folk,
When you yourself are just!

ELECTRA.   You cannot say
    Now, that I crossed you and you answered me!
    Yet if you gave me scope, I would speak fairly
    For him that's dead, and for my sister too.

CLYTÆMNÈSTRA.   I give it you! If you addressed me thus
    Always, it would not chafe me so to hear.

ELECTRA.   Then listen! You avow my father's death;
    What could more ill become your mouth than this,
    Whether he were unjustly slain or nò?

But let me tell you that you slew him not
For Justice, but perverted by the lure
Of a base wretch, who is your consort now.
What! Question of the Huntress Artemis
On whose account she held the various winds
Spell-bound in Aulis! Rather, I will tell;
For 'tis not given you to learn of her.
My father once, as I have heard the tale,
While sporting in a sacred wood of hers,
Roused as he went a dappled antlered roe,
And with some careless vaunt of slaughtering it
Shoots at and hits it; wherefore Leto's maid,
Wrathful at this, kept back the Achaian host,
Till he should render up for sacrifice,
In payment for the beast, his daughter dear—
And therefore was she offered; since escape
There was none other for the armament,
Either toward Ilium, or backward home.
Whence much enforced, and much resisting it,
Not for the sake of Menelaus, he
Unwillingly gave her to the knife at last.
But what an if (for I will take your story)
He did it through benevolence for him?
Was it thereafter just that he should perish,
And at your hand? Under what law? Beware
You do not, while you set this law to others,
Lay up repentance for yourself, and pain.
If we begin to exchange life for life,
You should die next, if you received your due.
But look you do not proffer for excuse
That which is not; for tell me, if you will,
Why you are now doing things most execrable,
Consorting with the branded murderer
By whose connivance erst you slew my sire,
And bearing children, to the extrusion of
Your honest first-born, born in honesty?
How should I pardon this? Or will you claim

In this, too, to be trying to avenge
Your daughter? It sounds vilely, if you do;
For 'twere unseemly in a daughter's quarrel
To couple with an enemy! Ay truly,
It's an offence even to admonish you,
Who let your tongue run freely, when you say
That I speak evil of my mother! I
A slave-mistress account you, over us,
As much as mother; for a servile life
Is that I lead, compassed with many griefs,
Wrought by yourself and by your paramour.
And poor Orestes is an exile, too,
Hardly delivered from your violence,
And living on in wretchedness — the same
You have so oft charged me with nurturing
To take revenge on you; and so I would —
Never doubt that — if I were strong enough.
Now, for that treason, publish me to all
Shameless — perverse — abusive — what you will;
And if I be an adept in the same,
I do bare justice to your blood in me!

I LADY.   I see her breathing fury! Right or wrong,
Now, 'tis all one, for any thought she gives it!

CLYTÆMNESTRA.   What sort of thought, then, must I give to her,
Who in this fashion dares insult her mother,
And at her years? Do you suppose she means
To exceed all measure in her shamelessness?

ELECTRA.   Now understand, I do feel shame at this,
Although to you I may not seem to feel it.
I do perceive that I am doing things
Unseasonable, and unbefitting me.
Only your acts and your hostility
Force me to this behaviour. Infamy
Is got by contact with the infamous.

CLYTÆMNESTRA.   Insolent creature! I, my words and acts,
    Make you so loudly over-eloquent?

ÆLECTRA.   It is your fault, not mine; you are the doer,
    And deeds find names.

CLYTÆMNESTRA.   Now not by Artemis,
    Who is my mistress, when Ægisthus comes
    Shall you escape, for this audacity!

ELECTRA.   See, now you fly into a frenzy! First
    You let me speak my mind — then, you'll not listen!

CLYTÆMNESTRA.   Will you not let me sacrifice, without
    Words of ill omen, after suffering you
    To say all that you can?

ELECTRA.   Go, sacrifice!
    I let you! Nay, I bid you! Censure not
    My mouth again, for I shall say no more.

CLYTÆMNESTRA.   Take up the offerings, you that wait on me,
    The fruits of earth, that unto this my Lord
    I may prefer petitions for release
    Out of my present terrors. — Hear thou now,
    Protector Phœbus, my unuttered vow!
    For what I say I say not among friends,
    Nor is it meet to uncover all my ends
    Here, in her presence, to the open sky,
    Lest she with malice and loud clamorous cry
    Scatter vain babblings to the city round;
    But softly list, and soft my words shall sound.
    The ambiguous visions, whose dim shadowing
    Last night I witnessed, O Lycean King,
    If they portended good, give them like close;
    If evil, turn them backward on my foes,
    And do not thou, if any would by stealth,
    Let them disturb me from my present wealth;
    Let me live on securely, as to-day,

Holding the Atridæ's palace, and their sway,
Abiding with the friends I bide withal
Now, in good case; and with my children, all
Through whom no bitter pang is made to strike
Their mother's heart, nor shudder of dislike.
Hear, great Apollo, what I pray for thus,
And, as we ask, in grace give all of us.
—The rest, I think, thou, being divine, perceiv'st,
Though I be silent; for it cannot be
But all is open to the sons of Jove.

Enter Guardian.

GUARDIAN.   Ladies, to whom I am a foreigner,
Pray how might I discover if this palace
Be that of King Ægisthus?

I LADY.   Sir, it is;
Your guess is right.

GUARDIAN.   And am I further right
In guessing that this lady is his wife?
She bears a queenly presence.

I LADY.   Certainly:
You see her there before you.

GUARDIAN.   Madam, hail!
I bring you pleasant tidings from a friend;
You, and Ægisthus also.

CLYTÆMNESTRA.   They are welcome.
But I would hear first, who he was that sent you.

GUARDIAN.   Phanoteus of Phocis, with a weighty charge.

CLYTÆMNESTRA.   Of what sort, stranger, say? for I am sure,
Being from a friend, that you will speak us friendly.

GUARDIAN.   Briefly I speak. Orestes is no more.

ELECTRA.   O I am lost, unhappy!

CLYTÆMNESTRA.   What sir, what?
Never mind her!

GUARDIAN.   I say as I have said.
Orestes is dead.

ELECTRA.   O me, I am undone!
Now I am nothing!

CLYTÆMNESTRA.   Yea, see thou to that.
How came he by his death, sir? Tell me truly.

GUARDIAN.   I will tell all; for to that end I came.
The man had gone to the great festival —
The glory of Hellas — for the Delphian games;
And when he heard the shouting of the crier
Calling the foot-race, which is first adjudged,
He entered for it, comely to behold,
The worship of the eyes of all men there;
And having reached the limit of the course
Whence they were started, he came out of it
With the all-honoured prize of victory.
To say but little out of much I might,
I never saw before the acts and prowess
Of such a man as he; but take one statement;
In every heat for which the judges set
The customary courses, out and home,
He brought off all the honours of the day,
And was congratulated, and proclaimed
"An Argive, named Orestes" — and "the son
Of Agamemnon," him who mustered once
The illustrious host of Hellas. So far well.
But if some Deity is bent on harm,
It is not even a strong man can escape.
For he, another day at sunrise, when
Owners of horses met to try their speed,
With many other charioteers, went in.

One was Achaian, one from Sparta, two
Libyans, skilled masters of the yoke and car;
He among these, with mares of Thessaly,
Came fifth; the sixth was from Ætolia,
With bright bay colts; the seventh Magnesian;
The eighth of Ænian birth, his horses white;
The ninth from Athens the divinely builded;
Last, a Bœotian's car made up the ten.
These, stationed where the judges of the course
Cast each his lot, and ranked his driving-board,
Forth started at the brazen bugle's note,
And cheering to their horses all at once
Shook the grasped reins; then the whole course was filled
With rattle of the chariot metal-work;
The dust rose high; crowded together, all
Spared not the goad — so might some one of them
Fore-reach on snorting steed and axle-tree;
While evermore alike on back and wheel,
Foaming and quick, the coursers' panting came.
But he kept close under the endmost mark,
Sweeping his axle round continuously,
And, giving rein to the right-handmost steed,
Pulled back the inner goer. And at first
The driving-boards all held themselves upright;
But afterwards the Ænian's hard-mouthed colts
Bolt violently; and coming from the turn,
After the sixth, just in the seventh round,
Dash all their fronts against the Barca car;
Then, in an instant, from one accident,
Car upon car began to crash and fall,
And the whole plain of Crisa became filled
With wreck of steeds and tackling. At the sight
That crafty driver, he from Athens, draws
Out of the way, and slackens, passing by
The surge of chariots eddying in the midst.
Last came Orestes, trusting to the close,
Keeping his fillies back; but seeing him

Left in alone, he launches a shrill whoop
Through his fleet coursers' ears, and races him,
And yoke and yoke the couple drove along,
Now one and now the other shewing head
Out in the front, over their carriages.
Well, all his rounds, poor fellow, till the last,
He stood up straight, and kept his chariot straight,
And drove straight through; then, slackening the left rein
As his horse turns, he struck unwittingly
The corner of the mark, and snapped the nave
Short from the axle, and slipped instantly
Over the rail, and in the cloven reins
Was tangled; as upon the plain he fell,
His steeds into the middle of the course
Ran all astray. Then the whole host, that saw him
Precipitated from the driving-board,
Lifted their voices to bewail the youth
Who did such feats, and met with such hard fate,
Now dashed upon the ground, now seen with limbs
All upward flung to heaven; till chariot-men
Hardly restrained the steeds in their career,
And loosed him, bathed in blood, so that no friend,
Seeing the poor body, could have known 'twas he.
Then certain Phocians, ordered for the task,
Straightway consumed it on a funeral pile,
And hither in a little urn they bring
That mighty stature, in poor embers now,
To win a tomb in his own fathers' land.
Such is my tale; right piteous in the telling;
But in the sight of us, who witnessed it,
The saddest thing of all I ever saw.

1 LADY.   Alack, the lineage of our lords of old
Is all, too plainly, ruined from the root.

CLYTÆMNESTRA.   O God, this fortune — shall I call it fair,
Or black, though profitable? yet is it hard

That I should save my own life, through misfortunes
Which are my own!

GUARDIAN.   Why thus regretful, lady,
At what I have just told you?

CLYTÆMNESTRA.   It is strange —
This motherhood; for sons of one's own bearing,
However ill entreated at their hands,
One cannot muster hatred.

GUARDIAN.   I am come,
It seems, in vain.

CLYTÆMNESTRA.   Nay indeed, not in vain.
Why should you say in vain? if you are come
With a sure token that the man is dead,
Who was indeed the offspring of my being,
But from this bosom and maternal care
Revolted, and became as one estranged,
An exile; never, from the day he left
This country, saw me more; but, laying to me
His father's death, was ever threatening me,
So that sweet sleep by neither night nor day
Would cover me, but the impending hour
Held me continually in fear of death;
While now, since I am this day freed from terror
Of him, and of her too — for she dwelt with me
A far worse canker, ever draining deep
My very life-blood — now, for all her menaces,
I shall dwell tranquil!

ELECTRA.   O me miserable!
Why now, Orestes, there is room enough
To groan for thy misfortune, when, being thus,
Thou art scorned by this thy mother! Is it well?

CLYTÆMNESTRA.   Not thou — but he being as he is, is well.

ELECTRA.   Hear, Nemesis* of him who is no more!

CLYTÆMNESTRA.   Those she should hear Nemesis did hear, and well
   Did she perform!

ELECTRA.   Triumph! you are happy now.

CLYTÆMNESTRA.   You and Orestes cannot hinder me.

ELECTRA.   'Tis we are hindered; far from hindering you.

CLYTÆMNESTRA.   I were beholden to your coming, friend,
   If you could hinder her from her loud clamour.

GUARDIAN.   Well then, I will be going — if all is well.

CLYTÆMNESTRA.   Nay, for it were unworthy both of me
   And of the friend who sent you, did you meet
   Such entertainment. Please you enter in?
   Leave her alone, to sorrow out of doors
   For her dear friends' misfortunes, and her own.
                       [*Exeunt* CLYTÆMNESTRA *and Guardian.*

ELECTRA.   Seems it to you as if, in grief and pain,
   She was lamenting, weeping sore — the wretch!
   Over her son, thus lost? She is gone smiling!
   O me unhappy! Orestes, O my darling,
   How has thy death undone me! Parting thus,
   Thou tearest all the hopes out of my heart —
   All I had left — that thou would'st come, some day,
   Living, avenger of thy father's death,
   And of my wrongs. Now, whither should I turn?
   I am alone; I have no father; now
   I have not thee. Must I be slave once more
   Among the most detested of mankind,
   My father's murderers? Is it well·with me?
   Nay, for the future never more at all
   Shall one roof hold us; rather, on this door-stone, friendless
   I will sink down and wear away and die!
   For this if any of the tribe within

* Another, more famous, goddess of revenge.

Is angered, let him kill me; death were welcome;
Life is but pain, and I am sick of it.

I. I.

I LADY.   Where be Jove's thunders, where the flaming Day,
    If, seeing these things, they hide them, and are still?

ELECTRA.   Ah, welaway!

I LADY.   My child, why weepest thou?

ELECTRA.   Fie then —

I LADY.   Speak gently.

ELECTRA.   Thou wilt slay me.

I LADY.   How?

ELECTRA.   Yea, in my wasting, thou wilt trample more
    Upon me, if thou wilt suggest a hope
    For those who manifestly are dead and gone.

I. 2.

I LADY.   I know that women's gold-bound toils ensnared
    The king Amphiaraus;* and now beneath —

ELECTRA.   Ah well a day!

I LADY.   He reigns, with all his powers.

ELECTRA.   Ah, woe!

I LADY.   Woe, for the murderess —

ELECTRA.   Slain?

I LADY.   Ay, slain.

ELECTRA.   I know it, I know it; a champion was revealed
    For him, in trouble; none is left, for me;

---

* A reluctant participant in the mission of the Seven Against Thebes who was tricked by his
wife Eriphyle into joining up. Departing, he put a curse upon her which his own son later
fulfilled by killing her.

He who yet was is taken from me, and gone.

II.   I.

1 LADY.   Thou art meet for pity; piteous is thy lot.

ELECTRA.   That know I well, too well; my life is full
With month on month, with surge on surge of woes,
Hateful and fearful.

1 LADY.   All thy groans we know.

ELECTRA.   Therefore no more dissuade me, since not one —

1 LADY.   How say'st thou?

ELECTRA.   Is left of all my hopes of aid,
From him, the heir, born of one birth with me.

II.   2.

1 LADY.   All have their fate.

ELECTRA.   Meet all such fate as his,
Dragged in a cleft of the reins, poor hapless one,
Among fleet emulous hoofs?

1 LADY.   Strange, the mishap!

ELECTRA.   How otherwise, when without care of mine,
A stranger —

1 LADY.   Out, alas!

ELECTRA.   He passed away,
Meeting no burial, no lament, from me.

Enter CHRYSOTHEMIS.

CHRYSOTHEMIS.   My dearest, I am driven, for delight,
To throw decorum to the winds, and run!
For I bring pleasure, and an end of ills
You suffered from before, and sorrowed for.

ELECTRA.   Whence would you fetch assistance for my woes,
Whereof all healing is impossible?

CHRYSOTHEMIS.   Orestes is at hand! I tell you so!
He's here, in sight, plainly as you see me!

ELECTRA.   Fie, are you frantic, wretch, and do you jest
At your own sorrows, and at mine?

CHRYSOTHEMIS.   Not I,
By the house-altar! I do not say this
For wantonness; but he is come, indeed!

ELECTRA.   O wretched that I am! and from whose mouth
Did you receive this tale, that you believe
So over fondly?

CHRYSOTHEMIS.   It is proved to me
By my own eyes, none other; for I see
Clear evidence.

ELECTRA.   See proof? O wretch, what proof?
What did you see, to inflame you all at once
With this mad fever?

CHRYSOTHEMIS.   Listen, in Heaven's name,
That you may learn; and call me, afterwards,
Crazed, if you like, or sober.

ELECTRA.   Say your say,
If it affords you any pleasure.

CHRYSOTHEMIS.   I
Am telling you exactly what I saw.
As I approached our sire's ancestral grave,
I observed streams upon the pillar's top
Of milk fresh-running, and the sepulchre
Circled with garlands of all flowers in bloom.
I was surprised to see it, and looked round,
To see that no one near laid hand on me.
But when I found all quiet about the place,

I crept up to the tombstone, and perceived,
Upon the very corner of the pile,
A severed ringlet of a young man's hair.
No sooner did I see it, than there darts
Into my heart an image — ah! well known,
This that I was beholding was the token
Of my most dear Orestes! No light word
I uttered; but I took it in my hands,
And my eyes filled with tears at once, for joy.
And well I know, and well I knew it then,
How from no other came that ornament.
For whose work should it be, save yours or mine?
And I at least, I am certain, did it not,
Nor yet did you; how could you? when you know
You cannot even with impunity
Go out of doors to worship at a shrine;
Nor can it be our mother who would care
To do it, or have done it unperceived.
No, 'twas Orestes made those offerings.
But O dear heart, take courage! The same Power
Succours not always the same side alike;
And on us twain it has frowned hitherto;
But none the less, this morning shall be fraught
With many things for good.

ELECTRA.   Alack the while!
How I pity you for your folly!

CHRYSOTHEMIS.   But what is it?
Do I not speak to please you now?

ELECTRA.   You know not
Whither you are borne — how far you are astray!

CHRYSOTHEMIS.   But how can I not know, what I saw plainly?

ELECTRA.   O wretched girl, he's dead! his saving us
Is done and ended; never look to him!

CHRYSOTHEMIS.   Alas for pity! Who was it told you so?

ELECTRA. One that was present with him, when he perished.

CHRYSOTHEMIS. 'Tis very strange. Where is he?

ELECTRA.   In the house;
   Welcome, not odious, in our mother's eyes.

CHRYSOTHEMIS. Alas for pity! But from whom, then, came
   All those oblations to our father's grave?

ELECTRA. I think most likely some one put them there
   In memory of Orestes, who was dead.

CHRYSOTHEMIS. O miserable! and I was hastening hither,
   Joyful to have such tidings, unaware
   What mischief was upon us! Now, arrived,
   I find the old sorrows still, with others new.

ELECTRA. 'Tis so indeed; but if you list to me,
   You can relieve the burden of the woe
   Weighing on us now.

CHRYSOTHEMIS.   What, can I raise the dead?

ELECTRA. That is not what I said; I am not so senseless!

CHRYSOTHEMIS. What do you bid me, that is in my power?

ELECTRA. Dare to do that which I shall urge on you!

CHRYSOTHEMIS. If it will aid us, I shall not refuse.

ELECTRA. Look, without effort nothing thrives.

CHRYSOTHEMIS.   I know it.
   All I have strength for I will help to bear.

ELECTRA. Hear, then, the course I am resolved upon.
   Friends to stand by us even you must know
   That none are left us; but the Grave has taken
   And reft them; and we two remain alone.
   I, while I heard my brother was alive
   And well, had hopes that he would come, one day,

To the requiting of his father's death;
But since he is no more, to you I look
Not to refuse, with me, your sister here,
To slay the author of that father's murder,
Ægisthus; (we need have no secrets, now.)
For whither — to what still surviving hope
Do you yet look, and suffer patiently?
Who for the loss of your ancestral wealth
Have cause for grieving, and have cause for pain
At all the time that passes over you,
Growing so old, a maiden and unwed.
And these delights no longer hope to gain
At any time; Ægisthus is too prudent
To suffer that your progeny or mine
Should see the light, to his own clear undoing!
While, if you will be guided by my counsels,
First, you shall have the praise of piety
From your dead sire and brother in the grave,
Next, shall be called hereafter, as at first,
Free, and obtain a marriage worthy of you
For all men pay regard to honesty.
And as for glory — see you not what glory
You will confer upon yourself and me,
If you should heed me? For what citizen
Or stranger, who beholds us, will not greet
Our passing steps with praises such as these:
"Friends, look at those two sisters, who redeemed
Their fathers' house; who, prodigal of life,
Were ministers of slaughter to their foes
Who prospered well before; to them be worship,
To them the love of all men; at high feasts,
In general concourse, for their fortitude,
That pair let all men honour." Of us two
Such are the things that every man will say,
So that our glory shall not cease from us,
Living or dead. O, be persuaded, dear!
Succour your father's, aid your brother's cause,

Liberate me from evils, and yourself,
Remembering this, that a dishonoured life
Is shame to those who have been born in honour.

1 LADY.   In work like this forethought is serviceable
Both to the speaker and the listener.

CHRYSOTHEMIS.   And if she were not mentally perverse,
She would have had some thought of prudence, ladies,
Before she ever spake — which now she has not.
Why, in what prospect do you arm yourself
With such a valour, and call me to aid?
Can you not see, you are not man, but woman?
Your hand is weaker than your enemies'.
Heaven sends good fortune daily upon them,
Which runs from us, and comes to nothingness.
Who, then, that schemed the death of one so mighty,
Could scape uninjured by calamity?
Look that we do not happen on worse ills,
Ill as we fare, if some one hears these sayings.
Death, with disgrace, though we obtain some credit,
Is no advantage and no help to us;
For death is not the worst; rather, in vain
To wish for death, and not to compass it.
But I beseech you, ere we are destroyed
With a complete destruction utterly,
Ere you abolish our whole family,
Set bounds on passion! What you said just now
I will keep close, unspoken, unensued;
Only be wise enough to yield at length
To stronger power, having yourself no strength.

1 LADY.   Let her persuade you; there is no good thing
Better than foresight and sobriety.

ELECTRA.   You have said nought I did not look for. Well
I knew, you would reject my instances.
Yes, I must do it by myself alone;
At least, without one blow, we will not leave it.

CHRYSOTHEMIS. Ah, would you had been so minded, when our sire
    Was murdered! Then you would have ended all!

ELECTRA. I was, in temper; I lacked wisdom then.

CHRYSOTHEMIS. Try and remain as wise for evermore!

ELECTRA. Now that you preach, I know you will not help me!

CHRYSOTHEMIS. And any man would come to harm who did!

ELECTRA. I envy you your prudence; for your cowardice,
    I hate you!

CHRYSOTHEMIS. I will bear it, when you praise.

ELECTRA. Only you never will get praise of me!

CHRYSOTHEMIS. It will be long, yet, before that is settled.

ELECTRA. There is no service in you; get you gone.

CHRYSOTHEMIS. There is! With you there is no towardness.

ELECTRA. Go to your mother; tell it all to her.

CHRYSOTHEMIS. Nay, I am not so much your enemy.

ELECTRA. Do not forget, though, to what shame you drag me.

CHRYSOTHEMIS. Shame not at all; but forethought for your good.

ELECTRA. So I must follow what you think is just?

CHRYSOTHEMIS. When you are prudent, you shall guide us both.

ELECTRA. Pity that you should speak so well, and miss it!

CHRYSOTHEMIS. You have named right the fault on your own side.

ELECTRA. How can that be? Do you deny the justice
    Of what I say?

CHRYSOTHEMIS. Justice sometimes brings damage.

ELECTRA. Under those laws I do not choose to live

CHRYSOTHEMIS. Well, you will find me right, if you will do it.

ELECTRA. Ay and I will! You cannot frighten me.

CHRYSOTHEMIS. Is't really so? Will you not change your mind?

ELECTRA. Nothing's more odious than an evil mind.

CHRYSOTHEMIS. You seem to care for nothing I can say.

ELECTRA. I have resolved to do it of old time,
Not newly.

CHRYSOTHEMIS. I am going. Neither you
Deign to approve my words, nor I your ways.

ELECTRA. Go in, then! I shall never follow you;
Not though you come to wish it earnestly;
There were small sense in running after — folly!

CHRYSOTHEMIS. And if you think that reason is with you,
So reason still! for, when your footsteps light
In evil ways, then you will find me right.

[*Exit* CHRYSOTHEMIS.

CHORUS.

I. 1.

We that regard
The excellent wisdom of the birds of air,
Who for the nurture care
Of those they spring from — those who gave them food,
Why is it hard
For us, like them, to render good for good?
But, by the thunderbolt of sovereign Jove,
And Themis, throned above,
We scape not long!
Thou, who to mortals in the realms of death
Passest through earth, send forth thy voice, O Fame,
With piteous cry, to Atreus' sons beneath,
Bearing thy tale of shame
Unmeet for song.

I. 2.

How first of all
Corruption dwells within their palace hall,
    And, with their children, strife;
The dissonant watchword harmonized no more
      Now, as before,
By sweet endearments of their household life.
Electra, left alone, by rude waves tossed,
    Mourns for her father lost
      With ceaseless wail,
Even as the ever-sorrowing nightingale,
Careless for death, so she might end them too,
The accursed pair—yea, ready for the gloom;
    What woman lives as true
      This side the tomb?

II. 1.

For none among the great
    Would court oblivion,
Darkening his honour by a life of pain,
    As thou, my child, hast done,
    Choosing to share a fate
Full of all tears, not caring to obtain
At once, in the same breath, the twofold prize
Of daughter perfect, and of maiden wise.

II. 2.

Live thou—in wealth and force
    Above thy foes as far
As now thou dwellest underneath their might!
    For under no good star
    Have I held the course
Lying, of thy life; yet in the paths of Right

Most sovereign — thou, I say, in these hast trod
The foremost, through thy piety to God.

Enter ORESTES *and* PYLADES, *with an urn.*

ORESTES.   Were we told right, and are we tending right,
As we desire, fair ladies?

I LADY.   And what seek you?
What are you here for?

ORESTES.   I was asking where
Ægisthus lodged.

I LADY.   Then you are well arrived,
And your informant blameless.

ORESTES.   Which of you
Would kindly carry word to those within
Of the long-looked-for presence of us twain?

I LADY.   If the most near ought to announce it, she will.

ORESTES.   Lady, go in and tell them certain Phocians
Seek for Ægisthus.

ELECTRA.   O me miserable!
Are you not bringing tokens to confirm
The tale we heard?

ORESTES.   I do not know your story;
But my old master, Strophius, gave me charge
To tell about Orestes.

ELECTRA.   O sir, what?
How terror creeps upon me!

ORESTES.   We bring home
Poor relics of him, in a narrow urn,
Dead, as you see.

ELECTRA.   Unhappy that I am!

Here is the thing already evident.
I see your burden, I suppose, at hand.

ORESTES.   If you are grieving for Orestes' ills,
Know, that this vessel holds the dust of him.

ELECTRA.   O sir, in Heaven's name give it — if this urn
Hides him indeed — into my hands, to hold,
That I may weep and mourn to the uttermost
For my own self, and my whole race, at once,
Over these ashes!

ORESTES.   Bring it here, and give her,
Whoever she may be; for I am sure
She does not ask it out of enmity,
But as some friend, or blood-relation born.

ELECTRA.   Ah thou memorial of my best-beloved,
All that is left me of Orestes, how
Do I receive thee back — not as I hoped,
When I first sped thee on thy way! For now
I bear thee in my hands, and thou art nothing;
But O my child, I sent thee forth from home
Glorious with life! Would that I first had died,
Before I sent thee to a foreign land,
Stolen by these hands and out of slaughter saved;
So had that day beheld thee lying dead,
Partaking with me in thy father's grave.
But now thou hast perished — perished miserably,
An exile in a strange land, far from home,
Far from thy sister; nor with loving hands
Bathed I thy body, and laid it out — woe's me!
Nor, as was fitting, from the blazing pyre
Took up the poor remains. But cared for — ah,
By unfamiliar hands thou art come hither,
A little burden, in a little urn.
Ah me unhappy for my ancient care
Made fruitless, for the pleasing toil I spent,
Often, on thee! for not at any time

Wert thou thy mother's darling, more than mine;
I was thy nurse; no houselings fostered thee;
I was thy "sister," ever, too, by name.
But now all this has vanished in a day,
Even with thy death. For thou hast gathered all
Together, like a whirlwind, and art gone;
My father is no more; I too am dead
In thee; thyself art dead, and gone from me;
And our foes laugh; and that disnatured mother,
Of whom thou hast often sent word privily
Thou would'st thyself appear to punish her,
Raves with delight! This the ill Destiny
Of thee and me wrested away; who sent thee
On to me thus — not the dear form I loved,
But embers, and an unavailing shade.
— Woe's me! O piteous sight! Alas, alas,
A terrible journey hast thou gone, my dear;
Woe's me! and without thee I am undone;
I am undone without thee, O my brother!
Receive me then into this house of thine,
Nought unto nought, to dwell with thee below
For evermore. For when thou wast on earth,
All that I had on earth I shared with thee;
And — for I see no grieving in the dead —
I would die now, so I might share thy tomb.

I LADY.   Your sire, Electra, was a mortal man;
So was Orestes; wherefore do not grieve
Beyond all bounds; we all owe Heaven a death.

ORESTES.   O Heavens, what shall I say? whither shall I turn
For lack of words? for I have lost the power
Of speech!

ELECTRA.   What ails you? Wherefore do you say it?

ORESTES.   Is this the illustrious Electra — you?

ELECTRA.   That is it, and in case right miserable.

ORESTES.   Alack therefore, for this thy wretched lot!

ELECTRA.   Sir, you are not lamenting thus for me?

ORESTES.   O beauty foully — impiously destroyed!

ELECTRA.   The wretch you speak of is no other, sir,
   Than I.

ORESTES.   Alas for thy estate, unwed,
   Unfortunate!

ELECTRA.   Why do you groan, sir, thus,
   Gazing on me!

ORESTES.   How did I nothing know
   Of my own woes!

ELECTRA.   By what, that has been said,
   Did you discover that?

ORESTES.   By seeing you,
   Preëminent in multitude of griefs.

ELECTRA.   And yet you see but little of my woes.

ORESTES.   How could there be worse things than these to see?

ELECTRA.   That I am sorted with the murderers.

ORESTES.   Whose murderers? Whence is this hint of crime?

ELECTRA.   My father's. Next, I am perforce their slave.

ORESTES.   Who is it bends you to this exigence?

ELECTRA.   My mother — in name — but nothing mother-like.

ORESTES.   And how? by force, or wearing injury?

ELECTRA.   By force, by wearing, and all ills that be.

ORESTES.   And was none by to help or hinder it?

ELECTRA.   No; him I had you have brought here in ashes.

ORESTES.   Ill-fated one, how has the sight of you
    Moved my compassion!

ELECTRA.   Know, you are the first
    Who ever had compassion upon me.

ORESTES.   Because I am the first to come, who feel
    With your misfortunes.

ELECTRA.   It can never be
    You are some kinsman, who have come — whence could you?

ORESTES.   If these are friends about us, I will tell.

ELECTRA.   Yes, they are friends; you parley to safe ears.

ORESTES.   Put down this vessel, now, and learn the whole.

ELECTRA.   Ah sir, for Heaven's sake urge not this on me!

ORESTES.   Do as I tell you, and you shall not err.

ELECTRA.   Now, I adjure you, do not take away
    My greatest treasure!

ORESTES.   I will not let you hold it.

ELECTRA.   O my Orestes! Woe is me for thee,
    If I must be deprived of burying thee!

ORESTES.   Do not speak rashly. You do wrong to mourn.

ELECTRA.   How wrong, in mourning for my brother dead?

ORESTES.   It is not meet that you should call him so.

ELECTRA.   Am I then so disdained of him that's dead?

ORESTES.   Disdained of none; but you have no part here.

ELECTRA.   Not when I bear Orestes' ashes?

ORESTES.   Not
    Orestes' ashes; only his in feigning.

ELECTRA.   Then where is that poor body's sepulchre?

ORESTES.   No where. The living have no sepulchre!

ELECTRA.   What say you, fellow?

ORESTES.   What I say is true.

ELECTRA.   Is he alive?

ORESTES.   Yes, unless I am dead!

ELECTRA.   What, are you he?

ORESTES.   See here, my father's seal!
    Look at it well, and learn if I speak truly.

ELECTRA.   O happy day!

ORESTES.   Most happy; even so.

ELECTRA.   O art thou come, dear voice?

ORESTES.   No more to sound
    From alien lips.

ELECTRA.   What, have I got you?

ORESTES.   Yes,
    For you to keep, in future, evermore.

ELECTRA.   O dearest friends! O ladies, neighbours! Look,
    Here is Orestes, only dead in craft,
    And by that craft alive and safe at home!

I LADY.   Daughter, we see it; and the tears of joy
    Steal from our eyes, at what has come to pass:

ELECTRA.   O son, dear seed
                        Of one most dear to me!
                            And art thou come indeed?
    Thou hast found—hast come, hast seen those thou didst
        seek to see!

ORESTES.   Yes, I am here; but hush, keep silence.

ELECTRA.   Why?

ORESTES. Best to keep close, lest some one hear indoors.

ELECTRA. Nay but, by the ever-virgin Artemis,
    I never think to quail again at this,
    The cumbering plague of numbers feminine,
        That ever swarm within!

ORESTES. O but remember that in women too
    There lives a spirit of war; and thou hast proved it.

ELECTRA. Ah well a day!
    Thou makest the memory plain —
    That will not pass away —
        That cannot be forgotten — of my pain.

ORESTES. Sister, I know it; but, when occasion speaks,
    Then is it we should call to mind these doings.

ELECTRA. All day, all night,
    Were not too much for me
    To speak of them aright;
        Now that my lips at last are set at liberty.

ORESTES. I say not nay; therefore take heed.

ELECTRA.   Of what?

ORESTES. Now 'tis no time for talk, be sparing of it.

ELECTRA. Who, after thy appearing, would exchange
    Language for silence? That were dearly bought,
    Now I have found thee, in a manner strange
        Beyond all hope or thought!

ORESTES. You saw me then, when the Gods urged my coming.

ELECTRA. O grace, far more
    Than that thou first didst tell!
    If to thy kinsmen's door
        God sent thee safe, that count I miracle!

ORESTES. I am unwilling to restrain your joy,
    But fear you are too much overcome with rapture.

ELECTRA.   Oh, if after years of waiting
 I have found thee condescending
 By a way full fraught with blessing
  Here before me to appear,
 Seeing me so full of troubles,
 Spare, O spare—

ORESTES.   What should I spare thee?

ELECTRA.   Be not thou so much my wronger
 As to make me lose the pleasure
 Of thy presence!

ORESTES.   Nay,
 I should be very wroth with other men
 If I beheld them—

ELECTRA.   Do you say so?

ORESTES.   How
 Could I forbear?

ELECTRA.   Hark, the voice, women dear,
 I had never hoped to hear!
 Listening, how could I have heard,
 And held my peace, without one word,
 Sorrowing? But I have thee, now!
 With most sweet face there standest thou,
 Face, that even in misery
 Could not pass away from me.

ORESTES.   Pass what need not be said; spare me the telling
 How base our mother; how Ægisthus drains
 The family substance, giving largess here,
 There scattering without purpose; for the tale
 Would keep you from the occasion time has given.
 But what will fit the present urgency,
 Where, either visible or from ambushment,
 We may give pause in this day's enterprise

To foes who mock, explain; be careful, too,
That as we enter at the palace door
Your mother do not spy your secret out
In your glad aspect; but be sighing, still,
As at that fiction of calamity;
For when we are successful, we shall be
Free to rejoice and laugh ungrudgingly.

ELECTRA.   Well, brother, as it pleases you in this,
So too shall be my pleasure; for from you
I have derived the blessings I enjoy —
Blessings not mine; and I could never bear,
By causing you annoy, ever so brief,
To reap great gain myself; for ill should I
So minister to the Providence at hand.
You know, no doubt, all that is passing here;
You heard Ægisthus was away from home,
My mother in the palace; and for her,
Fear not she will perceive my countenance
Radiant with smiles; for my long-standing hate
Is well worn in; and, having seen thy face,
I shall not leave off weeping now, for joy.
How should I leave it? who in this day's work
Saw thee first dead, then living! Yea, thou hast wrought
Very strangely with me; so that if my sire
Were to come here in life, I should not now
Deem it a marvel, but believe I saw him.
Since then by such a road thou art come hither
Lead on, as thou art minded; for alone
One of two things I had not failed to achieve —
Bravely to right myself, or bravely perish.

1 LADY.   Peace, I advise you; for of those within
I hear one coming outward.

ELECTRA.   Enter, sirs;
The rather that you bring — what none would drive
Far from their doors — or willingly receive!

Enter Guardian.

GUARDIAN. O most unwise and impotent of mind,
 Have you no longer any care to live,
 Or is no natural prudence bred in you,
 When in the very midst of ills most great,
 Not on their verge, you stand, and do not see it?
 If I had not been keeping, all along,
 Watch at the door-posts, all your business here
 Would have forestalled your presence in the house;
 But as it is, I took good heed of that.
 Now make an end of your long conference,
 And this insatiate crying out for joy,
 And pass within; for in such work as this
 Delay is loss, and it is time to finish.

ORESTES. What will the issue be, if I go in?

GUARDIAN. All's well so far, that you are quite unknown.

ORESTES. You told them, I suppose, that I was dead?

GUARDIAN. You'd think you were in Hades, though alive,
 To hear them talk!

ORESTES.   Do they rejoice at that?
 What are they saying?

GUARDIAN.   When the time is ripe
 I will inform you; but as things are now,
 All they are doing, however ill, goes well.

ELECTRA. Brother, who is this man? For Heaven's sake, tell me!

ORESTES. Do you not know him?

ELECTRA.   I cannot even guess.

ORESTES. Not him, to whom you once delivered me?

ELECTRA. What man? what do you mean?

ORESTES.   Him, in whose hands

I was made off with to the Phocians' land
By your providing?

ELECTRA.   What, is this the man
Whom only I found faithful out of many
When our sire perished?

ORESTES.   Once for all, 'tis he.

ELECTRA. O happy day! O only saviour
Of Agamemnon's house! How art thou come hither!
Art thou the man who out of many woes
Didst save both him and me? O hands most dear!
O feet, most grateful for your ministry!
How could'st thou so long hide thee in my presence,
And kill me with false words, and shew me not,
Knowing all the while, the sweet reality?
O welcome, father! in thee I seem to see
A father! Welcome! Surely of all men thee
Within one day I have hated most — and love!

GUARDIAN.   Enough, I say; the story of all since then
Many revolving nights and days as many
Shall make to pass before Electra's eyes. —
But now I warn you both, you who stand by,
This is the time to act; now Clytæmnestra
Is left alone; now no one of the men
Is within doors; but if you will delay,
Consider, you will have to cope with these,
And more besides, and of more wit, than they.

ORESTES.   This need not be a matter to us now
For any long discoursing, Pylades!
Rather, first worshipping the ancestral shrines
Of all the Gods who keep this vestibule,
As quickly as we may, let us pass in.
                    [*Exeunt* ORESTES, PYLADES *and Guardian.*

ELECTRA.   O King Apollo, hear them graciously,
And me as well; me, who have come to thee

Right often, with persistent hand, that gave
Of all I had; so now with all I have,
Apollo, King Lycean, I implore,
I supplicate, I pray thee — go before,
And help us to our ends; and make mankind confess
How the Gods quit them, for their wickedness!   [*Retires.*

CHORUS.

I.

Behold where Ares, breathing forth the breath
    Of strife and carnage, paces — paces on.
The inevitable hounds of death,
    Hunters upon the track of guilt, are gone.
They stand the roof beneath;
And now not long the vision of my prayer
Shall tarry, floating in the fields of air.

2.

For now within these walls, with stealthy pace,
    The aider of the kingdoms of the dead
To his ancestral dwelling-place,
    Bearing keen slaughter in his hands, is led.
Hermes, of Maia's race,
Hiding his toils in darkness, leads the way
Straight to the goal, and makes no more delay.

ELECTRA (*advancing*).   O dearest women, 'tis the moment, now,
    For them to do the deed; but hush, keep still.

1 LADY.   How then? What are they doing?

ELECTRA.   She is dressing
    The urn for burial; and the Pair stand by.

1 LADY.   And what did you rush out for?

ELECTRA.   To take care

Ægisthus come not in without our knowing.

CLYTÆMNESTRA (*within*).   Woe's me! Alack, the house—
Empty of friends, and filled with murderers!

ELECTRA.   A cry within! O friends, do not you hear it?

I LADY.   I heard, unhappy, sounds I might not hear;
And I am chill with horror.

CLYTÆMNESTRA (*within*).   Woe is me!
Ægisthus, O where are you?

I LADY.   Hark again,
Some one is shrieking loud.

CLYTÆMNESTRA (*within*).   O child, my child,
Have mercy on your mother!

ELECTRA.   Thou hadst none
On him, or on his father who begat him.

CHORUS.

O city, O race ill-starred!
The curse is ever on thee, day by day,
To fade, and fade!

CLYTÆMNESTRA (*within*).   O, I am smitten!

ELECTRA.   If thou beëst a man,
Strike twice!

CLYTÆMNESTRA (*within*).   Again!

ELECTRA.   O for Ægisthus too!

CHORUS.

The curse is fulfilled.
They live, who lie in the grave.

Slain long since, they drink, at last,
The blood of their slayers, in turn.

1 LADY.   See, they come forth! Their fingers drip with gore
Poured out on Ares' altar. I am dumb.

Enter ORESTES *and* PYLADES.

ELECTRA.   How is it with you, Orestes?

ORESTES.   In the house
Well; if Apollo's oracle be well.

ELECTRA.   Is the wretch dead?

ORESTES.   No longer be afraid
Thy mother's pride shall trample on thee more.

1 LADY.   Cease, for I see Ægisthus full in view!

ELECTRA.   Back, boys!

ORESTES.   Where do you see the man?

ELECTRA.   He comes
Towards us from the precincts, gay at heart.

CHORUS.

Make for the entrance, quick!
Now, as ye have well achieved the former task,
Finish this too!

ORESTES.   Be easy; we will do it.

ELECTRA.   Go your ways.

ORESTES.   I am gone.

ELECTRA.   I will provide for matters here.
                              [*Exeunt* ORESTES *and* PYLADES.

CHORUS.

'Twere well to pronounce
Brief words in this man's ear,
Mildly couched, that he may rush
On the hidden struggle of doom.

Enter ÆGISTHUS.

ÆGISTHUS.   Which of you knows, where are those Phocian strangers
They say have brought us tidings that Orestes
Has lost his life, by shipwreck of his team?
You there, my question is of you, yes, you
That used before to be so malapert;
For it concerns you most, I think, to know,
And more than all, it is for you to say.

ELECTRA.   I know. How could I help it? Otherwise
I should be ignorant of calamity
Nearest to me — of mine.

ÆGISTHUS.   And where may be
The strangers? tell me, pray.

ELECTRA.   They are within.
They — fell on a kind hostess!

ÆGISTHUS.   Did they say
That he is dead in very earnest?

ELECTRA.   Nay,
They brought and shewed it us — not merely told us.

ÆGISTHUS.   Is it hard by, that I may see, and know?

ELECTRA.   You may, indeed — a very sorry sight.

ÆGISTHUS.   Your words have pleased me much; which is not usual.

ELECTRA.   If they can give you pleasure, pray be pleased.

ÆGISTHUS.   Now hold your peace, and open wide the gates,
For Myceneans, Argives — all to see,
So that, if any of them heretofore
Were buoyed by empty hopes of such an one,
Seeing him now dead, they may accept my curb,
And, having me for chastener, may not need
To be compelled to bring forth fruits of wisdom!

ELECTRA.   It is all done, on my part; for at last
I have the wit to choose the stronger side.

The scene opens, disclosing the body of CLYTÆMNESTRA, *veiled;*
ORESTES *and* PYLADES *standing by.*

ÆGISTHUS.   Zeus, I behold a thing — that hath not fallen,
But by the jealousy of Heaven! — Nay,
If there is yet a Nemesis, I unsay it!
Loosen all coverings from before my face,
That of me too my kindred may obtain
The meed of mourning.

ELECTRA.   Take them off yourself.
To see this corpse, and speak with amity,
Is not my work, but yours.

ÆGISTHUS.   Well, you say true,
And I will do your bidding; in mean while,
If she is in the house, call Clytæmnestra.

He raises the veil.

ORESTES.   Seek her no further; she is at your side.

ÆGISTHUS.   O what is this?

ORESTES.   Who is it, whom you fear?
Who is it, whom you do not recognize?

ÆGISTHUS.   Who are the men into whose very toils
I have fallen, unhappy?

ORESTES.   Did you never dream
    They were alive, whom you miscall as dead?

ÆGISTHUS.   O me, I understand you! It must be
    No other than Orestes speaks to me.

ORESTES.   Excellent seer! and yet so long deceived!

ÆGISTHUS.   I am lost, miserably! But suffer me
    To speak a little —

ELECTRA.   Brother, in Heaven's name let him
    No further parley, and prolong discourse.
    Once overtaken by calamity,
    What profit should a man who is to die
    Draw from delay? Nay, kill him on the spot,
    And cast him forth, slain, to such buriers
    As it is fitting he should meet withal,
    Out of our eye-sight! This alone can be
    An expiation for my wrongs of old.

ORESTES.   Go thou within, with speed. The contest now
    Lies not in words, but for thy life-blood.

ÆGISTHUS.   Nay,
    Why do you drag me to the house? What need
    Of darkness, if the deed is honourable?
    Why are you backward to despatch me here?

ORESTES.   Prescribe not thou! Pass, where thou slew'st my father,
    And perish there.

ÆGISTHUS.   Is it fated that this roof
    Must witness all the ills of Pelops' race,
    That are, or shall be?

ORESTES.   Thine, at any rate.
    I am soothsayer good enough to tell thee that!

ÆGISTHUS.   The craft you boast was not inherited, then!

ORESTES.   Thou prat'st, and prat'st; and the way lengthens out;
    Move on.

ÆGISTHUS.   Lead forward.

ORESTES.   Thou must foot it first.

ÆGISTHUS.   Lest I escape thee?

ORESTES.   Rather, that thy soul
    May not pass easily; this bitterness
    I must reserve for thee. And well it were
    If this quick justice could be dealt on all—
    Whoever will transgress the bounds of right,
    To strike him dead.   [*Kills* ÆGISTHUS.
              So should not villainy thrive.

CHORUS.

    O Atreus' seed!
How hardly, after many labours past,
Art thou come forth to liberty at last,
    Through this new trial perfected indeed!
              [*Exeunt omnes.*

Medea

EURIPIDES

Characters

MEDEA, *princess of Colchis and wife of*

JASON, *son of* AESON, *king of Iolcus*

Two children of MEDEA *and* JASON

CREON, *king of Corinth*

AEGEUS, *king of Athens*

NURSE *to* MEDEA

TUTOR *to* MEDEA's *children*

MESSENGER

CHORUS *of Corinthian Women*

SCENE: *In front of Medea's house in Corinth. Enter from the house Medea's nurse.*

NURSE   How I wish the Argo* never had reached the land
         Of Colchis, skimming through the blue Symplegades,
         Nor ever had fallen in the glades of Pelion
         The smitten fir-tree to furnish oars for the hands
         Of heroes who in Pelias' name attempted
         The Golden Fleece! For then my mistress Medea
         Would not have sailed for the towers of the land of Iolcus,
         Her heart on fire with passionate love for Jason;
         Nor would she have persuaded the daughters of Pelias
         To kill their father, and now be living here
         In Corinth with her husband and children. She gave
         Pleasure to the people of her land of exile,
         And she herself helped Jason in every way.
         This is indeed the greatest salvation of all—
         For the wife not to stand apart from the husband.
         But now there's hatred everywhere, Love is diseased.
         For, deserting his own children and my mistress,
         Jason has taken a royal wife to his bed,
         The daughter of the ruler of this land, Creon.
         And poor Medea is slighted, and cries aloud on the
         Vows they made to each other, the right hands clasped

---

* Jason's ship on the expedition of the Argonauts, sent by Pelias, king of Iolcus in Thessaly (Jason's uncle, who had usurped the throne), to Colchis on the Black Sea. The Symplegades were clashing rocks, one of the obstacles along the way. Pelion is a mountain in Thessaly. Medea was a princess of Colchis who fell in love with Jason and followed him back to Greece.

175

In eternal promise. She calls upon the gods to witness
What sort of return Jason has made to her love.
She lies without food and gives herself up to suffering,
Wasting away every moment of the day in tears.
So it has gone since she knew herself slighted by him.
Not stirring an eye, not moving her face from the ground,
No more than either a rock or surging sea water
She listens when she is given friendly advice.
Except that sometimes she twists back her white neck and
Moans to herself, calling out on her father's name,
And her land, and her home betrayed when she came away
    with
A man who now is determined to dishonor her.
Poor creature, she has discovered by her sufferings
What it means to one not to have lost one's own country.
She has turned from the children and does not like to see
    them.
I am afraid she may think of some dreadful thing,
For her heart is violent. She will never put up with
The treatment she is getting. I know and fear her
Lest she may sharpen a sword and thrust to the heart,
Stealing into the palace where the bed is made,
Or even kill the king and the new-wedded groom,
And thus bring a greater misfortune on herself.
She's a strange woman. I know it won't be easy
To make an enemy of her and come off best.
But here the children come. They have finished playing.
They have no thought at all of their mother's trouble.
Indeed it is not usual for the young to grieve.

> (*Enter from the right the slave who is the tutor to
> Medea's two small children. The children follow him.*)

TUTOR   You old retainer of my mistress' household,
        Why are you standing here all alone in front of the
        Gates and moaning to yourself over your misfortune?
        Medea could not wish you to leave her alone.

NURSE   Old man, and guardian of the children of Jason,
          If one is a good servant, it's a terrible thing
          When one's master's luck is out; it goes to one's heart.
          So I myself have got into such a state of grief
          That a longing stole over me to come outside here
          And tell the earth and air of my mistress' sorrows.

TUTOR   Has the poor lady not yet given up her crying?

NURSE   Given up? She's at the start, not halfway through her tears.

TUTOR   Poor fool—if I may call my mistress such a name—
          How ignorant she is of trouble more to come.

NURSE   What do you mean, old man? You needn't fear to speak.

TUTOR   Nothing. I take back the words which I used just now.

NURSE   Don't, by your beard, hide this from me, your fellow-
              servant.
          If need be, I'll keep quiet about what you tell me.

TUTOR   I heard a person saying, while I myself seemed
          Not to be paying attention, when I was at the place
          Where the old draught-players sit, by the holy fountain,
          That Creon, ruler of the land, intends to drive
          These children and their mother in exile from Corinth.
          But whether what he said is really true or not
          I do not know. I pray that it may not be true.

NURSE   And will Jason put up with it that his children
          Should suffer so, though he's no friend to their mother?

TUTOR   Old ties give place to new ones. As for Jason, he
          No longer has a feeling for this house of ours.

NURSE   It's black indeed for us, when we add new to old
          Sorrows before even the present sky has cleared.

TUTOR   But you be silent, and keep all this to yourself.
          It is not the right time to tell our mistress of it.

NURSE   Do you hear, children, what a father he is to you?
         I wish he were dead—but no, he is still my master.
         Yet certainly he has proved unkind to his dear ones.

TUTOR   What's strange in that? Have you only just discovered
         That everyone loves himself more than his neighbor?
         Some have good reason, others get something out of it.
         So Jason neglects his children for the new bride.

NURSE   Go indoors, children. That will be the best thing.
         And you, keep them to themselves as much as pos-
         sible.
         Don't bring them near their mother in her angry mood.
         For I've seen her already blazing her eyes at them
         As though she meant some mischief and I am sure that
         She'll not stop raging until she has struck at someone.
         May it be an enemy and not a friend she hurts!

                                    (*Medea is heard inside the house.*)

MEDEA   Ah, wretch! Ah, lost in my sufferings,
         I wish, I wish I might die.

NURSE   What did I say, dear children? Your mother
         Frets her heart and frets it to anger.
         Run away quickly into the house,
         And keep well out of her sight.
         Don't go anywhere near, but be careful
         Of the wildness and bitter nature
         Of that proud mind.
         Go now! Run quickly indoors.
         It is clear that she soon will put lightning
         In that cloud of her cries that is rising
         With a passion increasing. O, what will she do,
         Proud-hearted and not to be checked on her course,
         A soul bitten into with wrong?

                            (*The Tutor takes the children into the house.*)

MEDEA   Ah, I have suffered
        What should be wept for bitterly. I hate you,
        Children of a hateful mother. I curse you
        And your father. Let the whole house crash.

NURSE   Ah, I pity you, you poor creature.
        How can your children share in their father's
        Wickedness? Why do you hate them? Oh children,
        How much I fear that something may happen!
        Great people's tempers are terrible, always
        Having their own way, seldom checked,
        Dangerous they shift from mood to mood.
        How much better to have been accustomed
        To live on equal terms with one's neighbors.
        I would like to be safe and grow old in a
        Humble way. What is moderate sounds best,
        Also in practice is best for everyone.
        Greatness brings no profit to people.
        God indeed, when in anger, brings
        Greater ruin to great men's houses.

                    (*Enter, on the right, a Chorus of Corinthian women.
                    They have come to inquire about Medea and to at-
                    tempt to console her.*)

CHORUS I heard the voice, I heard the cry
        Of Colchis' wretched daughter.
        Tell me, mother, is she not yet
        At rest? Within the double gates
        Of the court I heard her cry. I am sorry
        For the sorrow of this home. O, say, what has happened?

NURSE   There is no home. It's over and done with.
        Her husband holds fast to his royal wedding,
        While she, my mistress, cries out her eyes
        There in her room, and takes no warmth from
        Any word of any friend.

MEDEA   Oh, I wish
           That lightning from heaven would split my head open.
           Oh, what use have I now for life?
           I would find my release in death
           And leave hateful existence behind me.

CHORUS   O God and Earth and Heaven!
           Did you hear what a cry was that
           Which the sad wife sings?
           Poor foolish one, why should you long
           For that appalling rest?
           The final end of death comes fast.
           No need to pray for that.
           Suppose your man gives honor
           To another woman's bed.
           It often happens. Don't be hurt.
           God will be your friend in this.
           You must not waste away
           Grieving too much for him who shared your bed.

MEDEA   Great Themis, lady Artemis,* behold
           The things I suffer, though I made him promise,
           My hateful husband. I pray that I may see him,
           Him and his bride and all their palace shattered
           For the wrong they dare to do me without cause.
           Oh, my father! Oh, my country! In what dishonor
           I left you, killing my own brother for it.**

NURSE   Do you hear what she says, and how she cries
           On Themis, the goddess of Promises, and on Zeus,
           Whom we believe to be the Keeper of Oaths?
           Of this I am sure, that no small thing
           Will appease my mistress' anger.

---

* Goddesses: Themis was the goddess of justice, the virgin Artemis would be sensitive to the
plight of women.

** During the escape from Colchis, to delay her father's pursuit.

CHORUS   Will she come into our presence?
         Will she listen when we are speaking
         To the words we say?
         I wish she might relax her rage
         And temper of her heart.
         My willingness to help will never
         Be wanting to my friends.
         But go inside and bring her
         Out of the house to us,
         And speak kindly to her: hurry,
         Before she wrongs her own.
         This passion of hers moves to something great.

NURSE   I will, but I doubt if I'll manage
         To win my mistress over.
         But still I'll attempt it to please you.
         Such a look she will flash on her servants
         If any comes near with a message,
         Like a lioness guarding her cubs.
         It is right, I think, to consider
         Both stupid and lacking in foresight
         Those poets of old who wrote songs
         For revels and dinners and banquets,
         Pleasant sounds for men living at ease;
         But none of them all has discovered
         How to put to an end with their singing
         Or musical instruments grief,
         Bitter grief, from which death and disaster
         Cheat the hopes of a house. Yet how good
         If music could cure men of this! But why raise
         To no purpose the voice at a banquet? For *there* is
         Already abundance of pleasure for men
         With a joy of its own.

                                   (*The Nurse goes into the house.*)

CHORUS   I heard a shriek that is laden with sorrow.
         Shrilling out her hard grief she cries out
         Upon him who betrayed both her bed and her marriage.
         Wronged, she calls on the gods,
         On the justice of Zeus, the oath sworn,
         Which brought her away
         To the opposite shore of the Greeks
         Through the gloomy salt straits to the gateway
         Of the salty unlimited sea.

         (Medea, attended by servants, comes out of the house.)

MEDEA   Women of Corinth, I have come outside to you
         Lest you should be indignant with me; for I know
         That many people are overproud, some when alone,
         And others when in company. And those who live
         Quietly, as I do, get a bad reputation.
         For a just judgment is not evident in the eyes
         When a man at first sight hates another, before
         Learning his character, being in no way injured;
         And a foreigner especially must adapt himself.
         I'd not approve of even a fellow-countryman
         Who by pride and want of manners offends his neighbors.
         But on me this thing has fallen so unexpectedly,
         It has broken my heart. I am finished. I let go
         All my life's joy. My friends, I only want to die.
         It was everything to me to think well of one man,
         And he, my own husband, has turned out wholly vile.
         Of all things which are living and can form a judgment
         We women are the most unfortunate creatures.
         Firstly, with an excess of wealth it is required
         For us to buy a husband and take for our bodies
         A master; for not to take one is even worse.
         And now the question is serious whether we take
         A good or bad one; for there is no easy escape
         For a woman, nor can she say no to her marriage.
         She arrives among new modes of behavior and manners,

And needs prophetic power, unless she has learned at
    home,
How best to manage him who shares the bed with her.
And if we work out all this well and carefully,
And the husband lives with us and lightly bears his yoke,
Then life is enviable. If not, I'd rather die.
A man, when he's tired of the company in his home,
Goes out of the house and puts an end to his boredom
And turns to a friend or companion of his own age.
But we are forced to keep our eyes on one alone.
What they say of us is that we have a peaceful time
Living at home, while they do the fighting in war.
How wrong they are! I would very much rather stand
Three times in the front of battle than bear one child.
Yet what applies to me does not apply to you.
You have a country. Your family home is here.
You enjoy life and the company of your friends.
But I am deserted, a refugee, thought nothing of
By my husband—something he won in a foreign land.
I have no mother or brother, nor any relation
With whom I can take refuge in this sea of woe.
This much then is the service I would beg from you:
If I can find the means or devise any scheme
To pay my husband back for what he has done to me—
Him and his father-in-law and the girl who married him—
Just to keep silent. For in other ways a woman
Is full of fear, defenseless, dreads the sight of cold
Steel; but, when once she is wronged in the matter of love,
No other soul can hold so many thoughts of blood.

CHORUS   This I will promise. You are in the right, Medea,
In paying your husband back. I am not surprised at you
For being sad.
                But look! I see our King Creon
Approaching. He will tell us of some new plan.

(Enter, from the right, Creon, with attendants.)

CREON   You, with that angry look, so set against your husband,
          Medea, I order you to leave my territories
          An exile, and take along with you your two children,
          And not to waste time doing it. It is my decree,
          And I will see it done. I will not return home
          Until you are cast from the boundaries of my land.

MEDEA   Oh, this is the end for me. I am utterly lost.
          Now I am in the full force of the storm of hate
          And have no harbor from ruin to reach easily.
          Yet still, in spite of it all, I'll ask the question:
          What is your reason, Creon, for banishing me?

CREON   I am afraid of you—why should I dissemble it?—
          Afraid that you may injure my daughter mortally.
          Many things accumulate to support my feeling.
          You are a clever woman, versed in evil arts,
          And are angry at having lost your husband's love.
          I hear that you are threatening, so they tell me,
          To do something against my daughter and Jason
          And me, too. I shall take my precautions first.
          I tell you, I prefer to earn your hatred now
          Than to be soft-hearted and afterward regret it.

MEDEA   This is not the first time, Creon. Often previously
          Through being considered clever I have suffered much.
          A person of sense ought never to have his children
          Brought up to be more clever than the average.
          For, apart from cleverness bringing them no profit,
          It will make them objects of envy and ill-will.
          If you put new ideas before the eyes of fools
          They'll think you foolish and worthless into the bargain;
          And if you are thought superior to those who have
          Some reputation for learning, you will become hated.
          I have some knowledge myself of how this happens;
          For being clever, I find that some will envy me,
          Others object to me. Yet all my cleverness

Is not so much.

               Well, then, are you frightened, Creon,
That I should harm you? There is no need. It is not
My way to transgress the authority of a king.
How have you injured me? You gave your daughter away
To the man you wanted. Oh, certainly I hate
My husband, but you, I think, have acted wisely;
Nor do I grudge it you that your affairs go well.
May the marriage be a lucky one! Only let me
Live in this land. For even though I have been wronged,
I will not raise my voice, but submit to my betters.

CREON   What you say sounds gentle enough. Still in my heart
I greatly dread that you are plotting some evil,
And therefore I trust you even less than before.
A sharp-tempered woman, or, for that matter, a man,
Is easier to deal with than the clever type
Who holds her tongue. No. You must go. No need for more
Speeches. The thing is fixed. By no manner of means
Shall you, an enemy of mine, stay in my country.

MEDEA   I beg you. By your knees, by your new-wedded girl.

CREON   Your words are wasted. You will never persuade me.

MEDEA   Will you drive me out, and give no heed to my prayers?

CREON   I will, for I love my family more than you.

MEDEA   O my country! How bitterly now I remember you!

CREON   I love my country too—next after my children.

MEDEA   Oh what an evil to men is passionate love!

CREON   That would depend on the luck that goes along with it.

MEDEA   O God, do not forget who is the cause of this!

CREON   Go. It is no use. Spare me the pain of forcing you.

MEDEA   I'm spared no pain. I lack no pain to be spared me.

CREON   Then you'll be removed by force by one of my men.

MEDEA   No, Creon, not that! But do listen, I beg you.

CREON   Woman, you seem to want to create a disturbance.

MEDEA   I *will* go into exile. *This* is not what I beg for.

CREON   Why then this violence and clinging to my hand?

MEDEA   Allow me to remain here just for this one day,
          So I may consider where to live in my exile,
          And look for support for my children, since their father
          Chooses to make no kind of provision for them.
          Have pity on them! You have children of your own.
          It is natural for you to look kindly on them.
          For myself I do not mind if I go into exile.
          It is the children being in trouble that I mind.

CREON   There is nothing tyrannical about my nature,
          And by showing mercy I have often been the loser.
          Even now I know that I am making a mistake.
          All the same you shall have your will. But this I tell you,
          That if the light of heaven tomorrow shall see you,
          You and your children in the confines of my land,
          You die. This word I have spoken is firmly fixed.
          But now, if you must stay, stay for this day alone.
          For in it you can do none of the things I fear.

                                        (*Exit Creon with his attendants.*)

CHORUS   Oh, unfortunate one! Oh, cruel!
          Where will you turn? Who will help you?
          What house or what land to preserve you
          From ill can you find?
          Medea, a god has thrown suffering
          Upon you in waves of despair.

MEDEA   Things have gone badly every way. No doubt of that.
          But not these things this far, and don't imagine so.
          There are still trials to come for the new-wedded pair,
          And for their relations pain that will mean something.
          Do you think that I would ever have fawned on that man

Unless I had some end to gain or profit in it?
I would not even have spoken or touched him with my
    hands.
But he has got to such a pitch of foolishness
That, though he could have made nothing of all my plans
By exiling me, he has given me this one day
To stay here, and in this I will make dead bodies
Of three of my enemies—father, the girl, and my husband.
I have many ways of death which I might suit to them,
And do not know, friends, which one to take in hand;
Whether to set fire underneath their bridal mansion,
Or sharpen a sword and thrust it to the heart,
Stealing into the palace where the bed is made.
There is just one obstacle to this. If I am caught
Breaking into the house and scheming against it,
I shall die, and give my enemies cause for laughter.
It is best to go by the straight road, the one in which
I am most skilled, and make away with them by poison.
So be it then.
And now suppose them dead. What town will receive me?
What friend will offer me a refuge in his land,
Or the guaranty of his house and save my own life?
There is none. So I must wait a little time yet,
And if some sure defense should then appear for me,
In craft and silence I will set about this murder.
But if my fate should drive me on without help,
Even though death is certain, I will take the sword
Myself and kill, and steadfastly advance to crime.
It shall not be—I swear it by her, my mistress,
Whom most I honor and have chosen as partner,
Hecate,* who dwells in the recesses of my hearth—
That any man shall be glad to have injured me.
Bitter I will make their marriage for them and mournful,
Bitter the alliance and the driving me out of the land.

* A goddess of the night.

Ah, come, Medea, in your plotting and scheming
Leave nothing untried of all those things which you know.
Go forward to the dreadful act. The test has come
For resolution. You see how you are treated. Never
Shall you be mocked by Jason's Corinthian wedding,
Whose father was noble, whose grandfather Helius. *
You have the skill. What is more, you were born a woman,
And women, though most helpless in doing good deeds,
Are of every evil the cleverest of contrivers.

CHORUS Flow backward to your sources, sacred rivers,
And let the world's great order be reversed.
It is the thoughts of *men* that are deceitful,
Their pledges that are loose.
Story shall now turn my condition to a fair one,
Women are paid their due.
No more shall evil-sounding fame be theirs.

Cease now, you muses of the ancient singers,
To tell the tale of my unfaithfulness;
For not on us did Phoebus, lord of music, **
Bestow the lyre's divine
Power, for otherwise I should have sung an answer
To the other sex. Long time
Has much to tell of us, and much of them.

You sailed away from your father's home,
With a heart on fire you passed
The double rocks of the sea.
And now in a foreign country
You have lost your rest in a widowed bed,
And are driven forth, a refugee
In dishonor from the land.

Good faith has gone, and no more remains
In great Greece a sense of shame.

* Sun god.
** Apollo.

It has flown away to the sky.
No father's house for a haven
Is at hand for you now, and another queen
Of your bed has dispossessed you and
Is mistress of your home.

(Enter Jason, with attendants.)

JASON   This is not the first occasion that I have noticed
How hopeless it is to deal with a stubborn temper.
For, with reasonable submission to our ruler's will,
You might have lived in this land and kept your home.
As it is you are going to be exiled for your loose speaking.
Not that I mind myself. You are free to continue
Telling everyone that Jason is a worthless man.
But as to your talk about the king, consider
Yourself most lucky that exile is your punishment.
I, for my part, have always tried to calm down
The anger of the king, and wished you to remain.
But you will not give up your folly, continually
Speaking ill of him, and so you are going to be banished.
All the same, and in spite of your conduct, I'll not desert
My friends, but have come to make some provision for you,
So that you and the children may not be penniless
Or in need of anything in exile. Certainly
Exile brings many troubles with it. And even
If you hate me, I cannot think badly of you.

MEDEA   O coward in every way—that is what I call you,
With bitterest reproach for your lack of manliness,
You have come, you, my worst enemy, have come to me!
It is not an example of overconfidence
Or of boldness thus to look your friends in the face,
Friends you have injured—no, it is the worst of all
Human diseases, shamelessness. But you did well
To come, for I can speak ill of you and lighten
My heart, and you will suffer while you are listening.
And first I will begin from what happened first.

I saved your life, and every Greek knows I saved it,
Who was a shipmate of yours aboard the Argo,
When you were sent to control the bulls that breathed fire
And yoke them, and when you would sow that deadly field.
Also that snake, who encircled with his many folds
The Golden Fleece and guarded it and never slept,
I killed, and so gave you the safety of the light.
And I myself betrayed my father and my home,
And came with you to Pelias' land of Iolcus.
And then, showing more willingness to help than wisdom,
I killed him, Pelias, with a most dreadful death
At his own daughters' hands, and took away your fear.
This is how I behaved to you, you wretched man,
And you forsook me, took another bride to bed,
Though you had children; for, if that had not been,
You would have had an excuse for another wedding.
Faith in your word has gone. Indeed, I cannot tell
Whether you think the gods whose names you swore by
      then
Have ceased to rule and that new standards are set up,
Since you must know you have broken your word to me.
O my right hand, and the knees which you often clasped
In supplication, how senselessly I am treated
By this bad man, and how my hopes have missed their
      mark!
Come, I will share my thoughts as though you were a
      friend—
You! Can I think that you would ever treat me well?
But I will do it, and these questions will make you
Appear the baser. Where am I to go? To my father's?
Him I betrayed and his land when I came with you.
To Pelias' wretched daughters? What a fine welcome
They would prepare for me who murdered their father!
For this is my position—hated by my friends
At home, I have, in kindness to you, made enemies
Of others whom there was no need to have injured.

And how happy among Greek women you have made me
On your side for all this! A distinguished husband
I have—for breaking promises. When in misery
I am cast out of the land and go into exile,
Quite without friends and all alone with my children,
That will be a fine shame for the new-wedded groom,
For his children to wander as beggars and she who saved
   him.
O God, you have given to mortals a sure method
Of telling the gold that is pure from the counterfeit;
Why is there no mark engraved upon men's bodies,
By which we could know the true ones from the false ones?

CHORUS   It is a strange form of anger, difficult to cure,
When two friends turn upon each other in hatred.

JASON   As for me, it seems I must be no bad speaker.
But, like a man who has a good grip of the tiller,
Reef up his sail, and so run away from under
This mouthing tempest, woman, of your bitter tongue.
Since you insist on building up your kindness to me,
My view is that Cypris* was alone responsible
Of men and gods for the preserving of my life.
You are clever enough—but really I need not enter
Into the story of how it was love's inescapable
Power that compelled you to keep my person safe.
On this I will not go into too much detail.
In so far as you helped me, you did well enough.
But on this question of saving me, I can prove
You have certainly got from me more than you gave.
Firstly, instead of living among barbarians,
You inhabit a Greek land and understand our ways,
How to live by law instead of the sweet will of force.
And all the Greeks considered you a clever woman.
You were honored for it; while, if you were living at

* Aphrodite, goddess of love.

The ends of the earth, nobody would have heard of you.
For my part, rather than stores of gold in my house
Or power to sing even sweeter songs than Orpheus,
I'd choose the fate that made me a distinguished man.
There is my reply to your story of my labors.
Remember it was you who started the argument.
Next for your attack on my wedding with the princess:
Here I will prove that, first, it was a clever move,
Secondly, a wise one, and, finally, that I made it
In your best interests and the children's. Please keep
    calm.
When I arrived here from the land of Iolcus,
Involved, as I was, in every kind of difficulty,
What luckier chance could I have come across than this,
An exile to marry the daughter of the king?
It was not—the point that seems to upset you—that I
Grew tired of your bed and felt the need of a new bride;
Nor with any wish to outdo your number of children.
We have enough already. I am quite content.
But—this was the main reason—that we might live well,
And not be short of anything. I know that all
A man's friends leave him stone-cold if he becomes poor.
Also that I might bring my children up worthily
Of my position, and, by producing more of them
To be brothers of yours, we would draw the families
Together and all be happy. You need no children.
And it pays me to do good to those I have now
By having others. Do you think this a bad plan?
You wouldn't if the love question hadn't upset you.
But you women have got into such a state of mind
That, if your life at night is good, you think you have
Everything; but, if in that quarter things go wrong,
You will consider your best and truest interests
Most hateful. It would have been better far for men
To have got their children in some other way, and women
Not to have existed. Then life would have been good.

CHORUS   Jason, though you have made this speech of yours look
          well,
          Still I think, even though others do not agree,
          You have betrayed your wife and are acting badly.

MEDEA   Surely in many ways I hold different views
          From others, for I think that the plausible speaker
          Who is a villain deserves the greatest punishment.
          Confident in his tongue's power to adorn evil,
          He stops at nothing. Yet he is not really wise.
          As in your case. There is no need to put on the airs
          Of a clever speaker, for one word will lay you flat.
          If you were not a coward, you would not have married
          Behind my back, but discussed it with me first.

JASON   And you, no doubt, would have furthered the proposal,
          If I had told you of it, you who even now
          Are incapable of controlling your bitter temper.

MEDEA   It was not that. No, you thought it was not respectable
          As you got on in years to have a foreign wife.

JASON   Make sure of this: it was not because of a woman
          I made the royal alliance in which I now live,
          But, as I said before, I wished to preserve you
          And breed a royal progeny to be brothers
          To the children I have now, a sure defense to us.

MEDEA   Let me have no happy fortune that brings pain with it,
          Or prosperity which is upsetting to the mind!

JASON   Change your ideas of what you want, and show more sense.
          Do not consider painful what is good for you,
          Nor, when you are lucky, think yourself unfortunate.

MEDEA   You can insult me. You have somewhere to turn to.
          But I shall go from this land into exile, friendless.

JASON   It was what you chose yourself. Don't blame others for it.

MEDEA   And how did I choose it? Did I betray my husband?

JASON   You called down wicked curses on the king's family.

MEDEA   . A curse, that is what I am become to your house too.

JASON·   I do not propose to go into all the rest of it;
           But, if you wish for the children or for yourself
           In exile to have some of my money to help you,
           Say so, for I am prepared to give with open hand,
           Or to provide you with introductions to my friends
           Who will treat you well. You are a fool if you do not
           Accept this. Cease your anger and you will profit.

MEDEA   I shall never accept the favors of friends of yours,
           Nor take a thing from you, so you need not offer it.
           There is no benefit in the gifts of a bad man.

JASON   Then, in any case, I call the gods to witness that
           I wish to help you and the children in every way,
           But you refuse what is good for you. Obstinately
           You push away your friends. You are sure to suffer for it.

MEDEA   Go! No doubt you hanker for your virginal bride,
           And are guilty of lingering too long out of her house.
           Enjoy your wedding. But perhaps—with the help of
               God—
           You will make the kind of marriage that you will regret.

                                        (*Jason goes out with his attendants.*)

CHORUS   When love is in excess
           It brings a man no honor
           Nor any worthiness.
           But if in moderation Cypris comes,
           There is no other power at all so gracious.
           O goddess, never on me let loose the unerring
           Shaft of your bow in the poison of desire.

           Let my heart be wise.
           It is the gods' best gift.

On me let mighty Cypris
Inflict no wordy wars or restless anger
To urge my passion to a different love.
But with discernment may she guide women's weddings,
Honoring most what is peaceful in the bed.

O country and home,
Never, never may I be without you,
Living the hopeless life,
Hard to pass through and painful,
Most pitiable of all.
Let death first lay me low and death
Free me from this daylight.
There is no sorrow above
The loss of a native land.

I have seen it myself,
Do not tell of a secondhand story.
Neither city nor friend
Pitied you when you suffered
The worst of sufferings.
O let him die ungraced whose heart
Will not reward his friends,
Who cannot open an honest mind
No friend will he be of mine.

(*Enter Aegeus, king of Athens, an old friend of Medea.*)

AEGEUS   Medea, greeting! This is the best introduction
         Of which men know for conversation between friends.

MEDEA   Greeting to you too, Aegeus, son of King Pandion.
         Where have you come from to visit this country's soil?

AEGEUS   I have just left the ancient oracle of Phoebus.

MEDEA   And why did you go to earth's prophetic center?

AEGEUS   I went to inquire how children might be born to me.

MEDEA   Is it so? Your life still up to this point is childless?

AEGEUS   Yes. By the fate of some power we have no children.

MEDEA   Have you a wife, or is there none to share your bed?

AEGEUS   There is. Yes, I am joined to my wife in marriage.

MEDEA   And what did Phoebus say to you about children?

AEGEUS   Words too wise for a mere man to guess their meaning.

MEDEA   Is it proper for me to be told the god's reply?

AEGEUS   It is. For sure what is needed is cleverness.

MEDEA   Then what was his message? Tell me, if I may hear.

AEGEUS   I am not to loosen the hanging foot of the wine-skin . . .

MEDEA   Until you have done something, or reached some country?

AEGEUS   Until I return again to my hearth and house.

MEDEA   And for what purpose have you journeyed to this land?

AEGEUS   There is a man called Pittheus, king of Troezen.

MEDEA   A son of Pelops, they say, a most righteous man.

AEGEUS   With him I wish to discuss the reply of the god.

MEDEA   Yes. He is wise and experienced in such matters.

AEGEUS   And to me also the dearest of all my spear-friends.

MEDEA   Well, I hope you have good luck, and achieve your will.

AEGEUS   But why this downcast eye of yours, and this pale cheek?

MEDEA   O Aegeus, my husband has been the worst of all to me.

AEGEUS   What do you mean? Say clearly what has caused this grief.

MEDEA   Jason wrongs me, though I have never injured him.

AEGEUS   What has he done? Tell me about it in clearer words.

MEDEA   He has taken a wife to his house, supplanting me.

AEGEUS   Surely he would not dare to do a thing like that.

MEDEA   Be sure he has. Once dear, I now am slighted by him.

AEGEUS   Did he fall in love? Or is he tired of your love?

MEDEA   He was greatly in love, this traitor to his friends.

AEGEUS   Then let him go, if, as you say, he is so bad.

MEDEA   A passionate love—for an alliance with the king.

AEGEUS   And who gave him his wife? Tell me the rest of it.

MEDEA   It was Creon, he who rules this land of Corinth.

AEGEUS   Indeed, Medea, your grief was understandable.

MEDEA   I am ruined. And there is more to come: I am banished.

AEGEUS   Banished? By whom? Here you tell me of a new wrong.

MEDEA   Creon drives me an exile from the land of Corinth.

AEGEUS   Does Jason consent? I cannot approve of this.

MEDEA   He pretends not to, but he will put up with it.
         Ah, Aegeus, I beg and beseech you, by your beard
         And by your knees I am making myself your suppliant,
         Have pity on me, have pity on your poor friend,
         And do not let me go into exile desolate,
         But receive me in your land and at your very hearth.
         So may your love, with God's help, lead to the bearing
         Of children, and so may you yourself die happy.
         You do not know what a chance you have come on here.
         I will end your childlessness, and I will make you able
         To beget children. The drugs I know can do this.

AEGEUS   For many reasons, woman, I am anxious to do
         This favor for you. First, for the sake of the gods,
         And then for the birth of children which you promise,

For in that respect I am entirely at my wits' end.
But this is my position: if you reach my land,
I, being in my rights, will try to befriend you.
But this much I must warn you of beforehand:
I shall not agree to take you out of this country;
But if you by yourself can reach my house, then you
Shall stay there safely. To none will I give you up
But from this land you must make your escape yourself,
For I do not wish to incur blame from my friends.

MEDEA   It shall be so. But, if I might have a pledge from you
For this, then I would have from you all I desire.

AEGEUS   Do you not trust me? What is it rankles with you?

MEDEA   I trust you, yes. But the house of Pelias hates me,
And so does Creon. If you are bound by this oath,
When they try to drag me from your land, you will not
Abandon me; but if our pact is only words,
With no oath to the gods, you will be lightly armed,
Unable to resist their summons. I am weak,
While they have wealth to help them and a royal house.

AEGEUS   You show much foresight for such negotiations.
Well, if you will have it so, I will not refuse.
For, both on my side this will be the safest way
To have some excuse to put forward to your enemies,
And for you it is more certain. You may name the gods.

MEDEA   Swear by the plain of Earth, and Helius, father
Of my father, and name together all the gods . . .

AEGEUS   That I will act or not act in what way? Speak.

MEDEA   That you yourself will never cast me from your land,
Nor, if any of my enemies should demand me,
Will you, in your life, willingly hand me over.

AEGEUS   ·I swear by the Earth, by the holy light of Helius,
By all the gods, I will abide by this you say.

MEDEA   Enough. And, if you fail, what shall happen to you?

AEGEUS   What comes to those who have no regard for heaven.

MEDEA   Go on your way. Farewell. For I am satisfied.
         And I will reach your city as soon as I can,
         Having done the deed I have to do and gained my end.

                                              (*Aegeus goes out.*)

CHORUS   May Hermes, god of travelers,
         Escort you, Aegeus, to your home!
         And may you have the things you wish
         So eagerly; for you
         Appear to me to be a generous man.

MEDEA   God, and God's daughter, justice, and light of Helius!
         Now, friends, has come the time of my triumph over
         My enemies, and now my foot is on the road.
         Now I am confident they will pay the penalty.
         For this man, Aegeus, has been like a harbor to me
         In all my plans just where I was most distressed.
         To him I can fasten the cable of my safety
         When I have reached the town and fortress of Pallas. *
         And now I shall tell to you the whole of my plan.
         Listen to these words that are not spoken idly.
         I shall send one of my servants to find Jason
         And request him to come once more into my sight.
         And when he comes, the words I'll say will be soft ones.
         I'll say that I agree with him, that I approve
         The royal wedding he has made, betraying me.
         I'll say it was profitable, an excellent idea.
         But I shall beg that my children may remain here:
         Not that I would leave in a country that hates me
         Children of mine to feel their enemies' insults,
         But that by a trick I may kill the king's daughter.

* Athens, the town of Athena.

For I will send the children with gifts in their hands
To carry to the bride, so as not to be banished—
A finely woven dress and a golden diadem.
And if she takes them and wears them upon her skin
She and all who touch the girl will die in agony;
Such poison will I lay upon the gifts I send.
But there, however, I must leave that account paid.
I weep to think of what a deed I have to do
Next after that; for I shall kill my own children.
My children, there is none who can give them safety.
And when I have ruined the whole of Jason's house,
I shall leave the land and flee from the murder of my
Dear children, and I shall have done a dreadful deed.
For it is not bearable to be mocked by enemies.
So it must happen. What profit have I in life?
I have no land, no home, no refuge from my pain.
My mistake was made the time I left behind me
My father's house, and trusted the words of a Greek,
Who, with heaven's help, will pay me the price for that.
For those children he had from me he will never
See alive again, nor will he on his new bride
Beget another child, for she is to be forced
To die a most terrible death by these my poisons.
Let no one think me a weak one, feeble-spirited,
A stay-at-home, but rather just the opposite,
One who can hurt my enemies and help my friends;
For the lives of such persons are most remembered.

CHORUS   Since you have shared the knowledge of your plan with us,
I both wish to help you and support the normal
Ways of mankind, and tell you not to do this thing.

MEDEA   I can do no other thing. It is understandable
For you to speak thus. You have not suffered as I have.

CHORUS   But can you have the heart to kill your flesh and blood?

MEDEA   Yes, for this is the best way to wound my husband.

CHORUS   And you, too. Of women you will be most unhappy.

MEDEA   So it must be. No compromise is possible.

(She turns to the Nurse.)

Go, you, at once, and tell Jason to come to me.
You I employ on all affairs of greatest trust.
Say nothing of these decisions which I have made,
If you love your mistress, if you were born a woman.

CHORUS   From of old the children of Erechtheus* are
Splendid, the sons of blessed gods. They dwell
In Athens' holy and unconquered land,
Where famous Wisdom feeds them and they pass gaily
Always through that most brilliant air where once, they say,
That golden Harmony gave birth to the nine
Pure Muses of Pieria.

And beside the sweet flow of Cephisus' stream,**
Where Cypris sailed, they say, to draw the water,
And mild soft breezes breathed along her path,
And on her hair were flung the sweet-smelling garlands
Of flowers of roses by the Lovers, the companions
Of Wisdom, her escort, the helpers of men
In every kind of excellence.

How then can these holy rivers
Or this holy land love you,
Or the city find you a home,
You, who will kill your children,
You, not pure with the rest?
O think of the blow at your children
And think of the blood that you shed.
O, over and over I beg you,
By your knees I beg you do not
Be the murderess of your babes!

* The Athenians.
** At Athens.

O where will you find the courage
Or the skill of hand and heart,
When you set yourself to attempt
A deed so dreadful to do?
How, when you look upon them,
Can you tearlessly hold the decision
For murder? You will not be able,
When your children fall down and implore you,
You will not be able to dip
Steadfast your hand in their blood.

(Enter Jason with attendants.)

JASON   I have come at your request. Indeed, although you are
Bitter against me, this you shall have: I will listen
To what new thing you want, woman, to get from me.

MEDEA   Jason, I beg you to be forgiving toward me
For what I said. It is natural for you to bear with
My temper, since we have had much love together.
I have talked with myself about this and I have
Reproached myself. "Fool," I said, "why am I so mad?
Why am I set against those who have planned wisely?
Why make myself an enemy of the authorities
And of my husband, who does the best thing for me
By marrying royalty and having children who
Will be as brothers to my own? What is wrong with me?
Let me give up anger, for the gods are kind to me.
Have I not children, and do I not know that we
In exile from our country must be short of friends?"
When I considered this I saw that I had shown
Great lack of sense, and that my anger was foolish.
Now I agree with you. I think that you are wise
In having this other wife as well as me, and I
Was mad. I should have helped you in these plans of yours,
Have joined in the wedding, stood by the marriage bed,
Have taken pleasure in attendance on your bride.

But we women are what we are—perhaps a little
Worthless; and you men must not be like us in this,
Nor be foolish in return when we are foolish.
Now, I give in, and admit that then I was wrong.
I have come to a better understanding now.

(She turns toward the house.)

Children, come here, my children, come outdoors to us!
Welcome your father with me, and say goodbye to him,
And with your mother, who just now was his enemy,
Join again in making friends with him who loves us.

(Enter the children, attended by the Tutor.)

We have made peace, and all our anger is over.
Take hold of his right hand—O God, I am thinking
Of something which may happen in the secret future.
O children, will you just so, after a long life,
Hold out your loving arms at the grave? O children,
How ready to cry I am, how full of foreboding!
I am ending at last this quarrel with your father,
And look, my soft eyes have suddenly filled with tears.

CHORUS   And the pale tears have started also in my eyes.
O may the trouble not grow worse than now it is!

JASON   I approve of what you say. And I cannot blame you
Even for what you said before. It is natural
For a woman to be wild with her husband when he
Goes in for secret love. But now your mind has turned
To better reasoning. In the end you have come to
The right decision, like the clever woman you are.
And of you, children, your father is taking care.
He has made, with God's help, ample provision for you.
For I think that a time will come when you will be
The leading people in Corinth with your brothers.
You must grow up. As to the future, your father
And those of the gods who love him will deal with that.
I want to see you, when you have become young men,

Healthy and strong, better men than my enemies.
Medea, why are your eyes all wet with pale tears?
Why is your cheek so white and turned away from me?
Are not these words of mine pleasing for you to hear?

MEDEA   It is nothing. I was thinking about these children.

JASON   You must be cheerful. I shall look after them well.

MEDEA   I will be. It is not that I distrust your words,
But a woman is a frail thing, prone to crying.

JASON   But why then should you grieve so much for these children?

MEDEA   I am their mother. When you prayed that they might live
I felt unhappy to think that these things will be.
But come, I have said something of the things I meant
To say to you, and now I will tell you the rest.
Since it is the king's will to banish me from here—
And for me, too, I know that this is the best thing,
Not to be in your way by living here or in
The king's way, since they think me ill-disposed to them—
I then am going into exile from this land;
But do you, so that you may have the care of them,
Beg Creon that the children may not be banished.

JASON   I doubt if I'll succeed, but still I'll attempt it.

MEDEA   Then you must tell your wife to beg from her father
That the children may be reprieved from banishment.

JASON   I will, and with her I shall certainly succeed.

MEDEA   If she is like the rest of us women, you will.
And I, too, will take a hand with you in this business,
For I will send her some gifts which are far fairer,
I am sure of it, than those which now are in fashion,
A finely woven dress and a golden diadem,
And the children shall present them. Quick, let one of you
Servants bring here to me that beautiful dress.

(*One of her attendants goes into the house.*)

She will be happy not in one way, but in a hundred,
Having so fine a man as you to share her bed,
And with this beautiful dress which Helius of old,
My father's father, bestowed on his descendants.

(*Enter attendant carrying the poisoned dress and diadem.*)

There, children, take these wedding presents in your hands.
Take them to the royal princess, the happy bride,
And give them to her. She will not think little of them.

JASON   No, don't be foolish, and empty your hands of these.
Do you think the palace is short of dresses to wear?
Do you think there is no gold there? Keep them, don't give them
Away. If my wife considers me of any value,
She will think more of me than money, I am sure of it.

MEDEA   No, let me have my way. They say the gods themselves
Are moved by gifts, and gold does more with men than words.
Hers is the luck, her fortune that which god blesses;
She is young and a princess; but for my children's reprieve
I would give my very life, and not gold only.
Go children, go together to that rich palace,
Be suppliants to the new wife of your father,
My lady, beg her not to let you be banished.
And give her the dress—for this is of great importance,
That she should take the gift into her hand from yours.
Go, quick as you can. And bring your mother good news
By your success of those things which she longs to gain.

(*Jason goes out with his attendants, followed by the Tutor and the children carrying the poisoned gifts.*)

CHORUS   Now there is no hope left for the children's lives.
Now there is none. They are walking already to murder.

The bride, poor bride, will accept the curse of the gold,
Will accept the bright diadem.
Around her yellow hair she will set that dress
Of death with her own hands.

The grace and the perfume and glow of the golden robe
Will charm her to put them upon her and wear the wreath,
And now her wedding will be with the dead below,
Into such a trap she will fall,
Poor thing, into such a fate of death and never
Escape from under that curse.
You, too, O wretched bridegroom, making your match
     with kings,
You do not see that you bring
Destruction on your children and on her,
Your wife, a fearful death.
Poor soul, what a fall is yours!

In your grief, too, I weep, mother of little children,
You who will murder your own,
In vengeance for the loss of married love
Which Jason has betrayed
As he lives with another wife.

                              (*Enter the Tutor with the children.*)

TUTOR   Mistress, I tell you that these children are reprieved,
        And the royal bride has been pleased to take in her hands
        Your gifts. In that quarter the children are secure.
        But come,
        Why do you stand confused when you are fortunate?
        Why have you turned round with your cheek away
             from me?
        Are not these words of mine pleasing for you to hear?

MEDEA   Oh! I am lost!

TUTOR   That word is not in harmony with my tidings.

MEDEA   I am lost, I am lost!

TUTOR   Am I in ignorance telling you
         Of some disaster, and not the good news I thought?

MEDEA   You have told what you have told. I do not blame you.

TUTOR   Why then this downcast eye, and this weeping of tears?

MEDEA   Oh, I am forced to weep, old man. The gods and I,
         I in a kind of madness, have contrived all this.

TUTOR   Courage! You, too, will be brought home by your children.

MEDEA   Ah, before that happens I shall bring others home.

TUTOR   Others before you have been parted from their children.
         Mortals must bear in resignation their ill luck.

MEDEA   That is what I shall do. But go inside the house,
         And do for the children your usual daily work.

         (The Tutor goes into the house. Medea turns to her children.)

         O children, O my children, you have a city,
         You have a home, and you can leave me behind you,
         And without your mother you may live there forever.
         But I am going in exile to another land
         Before I have seen you happy and taken pleasure in you,
         Before I have dressed your brides and made your marriage
             beds
         And held up the torch at the ceremony of wedding.
         Oh, what a wretch I am in this my self-willed thought!
         What was the purpose, children, for which I reared you?
         For all my travail and wearing myself away?
         They were sterile, those pains I had in the bearing of you.
         Oh surely once the hopes in you I had, poor me,
         Were high ones: you would look after me in old age,
         And when I died would deck me well with your own hands;
         A thing which all would have done. Oh but now it is gone,

That lovely thought. For, once I am left without you,
Sad will be the life I'll lead and sorrowful for me.
And you will never see your mother again with
Your dear eyes, gone to another mode of living.
Why, children, do you look upon me with your eyes?
Why do you smile so sweetly that last smile of all?
Oh, Oh, what can I do? My spirit has gone from me,
Friends, when I saw that bright look in the children's eyes.
I cannot bear to do it. I renounce my plans
I had before. I'll take my children away from
This land. Why should I hurt their father with the pain
They feel, and suffer twice as much of pain myself?
No, no, I will not do it. I renounce my plans.
Ah, what is wrong with me? Do I want to let go
My enemies unhurt and be laughed at for it?
I must face this thing. Oh, but what a weak woman
Even to admit to my mind these soft arguments.
Children, go into the house. And he whom law forbids
To stand in attendance at my sacrifices,
Let him see to it. I shall not mar my handiwork.
Oh! Oh!
Do not, O my heart, you must not do these things!
Poor heart, let them go, have pity upon the children.
If they live with you in Athens they will cheer you.
No! By Hell's avenging furies it shall not be—
This shall never be, that I should suffer my children
To be the prey of my enemies' insolence.
Every way is it fixed. The bride will not escape.
No, the diadem is now upon her head, and she,
The royal princess, is dying in the dress, I know it.
But—for it is the most dreadful of roads for me
To tread, and them I shall send on a more dreadful still—
I wish to speak to the children.

(*She calls the children to her.*)

Come, children, give
Me your hands, give your mother your hands to kiss them.
Oh the dear hands, and oh how dear are these lips to me,
And the generous eyes and the bearing of my children!
I wish you happiness, but not here in this world.
What is here your father took. Oh how good to hold you!
How delicate the skin, how sweet the breath of children!
Go, go! I am no longer able, no longer
To look upon you. I am overcome by sorrow.

(The children go into the house.)

I know indeed what evil I intend to do,
But stronger than all my afterthoughts is my fury,
Fury that brings upon mortals the greatest evils.

(She goes out to the right, toward the royal palace.)

CHORUS Often before
I have gone through more subtle reasons,
And have come upon questionings greater
Than a woman should strive to search out.
But we too have a goddess to help us
And accompany us into wisdom.
Not all of us. Still you will find
Among many women a few,
And our sex is not without learning.
This I say, that those who have never
Had children, who know nothing of it,
In happiness have the advantage
Over those who are parents.
The childless, who never discover
Whether children turn out as a good thing
Or as something to cause pain, are spared
Many troubles in lacking this knowledge.
And those who have in their homes
The sweet presence of children, I see that their lives

Are all wasted away by their worries.
First they must think how to bring them up well and
How to leave them something to live on.
And then after this whether all their toil
Is for those who will turn out good or bad,
Is still an unanswered question.
And of one more trouble, the last of all,
That is common to mortals I tell.
For suppose you have found them enough for their living,
Suppose that the children have grown into youth
And have turned out good, still, if God so wills it,
Death will away with your children's bodies,
And carry them off into Hades.
What is our profit, then, that for the sake of
Children the gods should pile upon mortals
After all else
This most terrible grief of all?

> (*Enter Medea, from the spectators' right.*)

MEDEA   Friends, I can tell you that for long I have waited
          For the event. I stare toward the place from where
          The news will come. And now, see one of Jason's servants
          Is on his way here, and that labored breath of his
          Shows he has tidings for us, and evil tidings.

> (*Enter, also from the right, the Messenger.*)

MESSENGER   Medea, you who have done such a dreadful thing,
              So outrageous, run for your life, take what you can,
              A ship to bear you hence or chariot on land.

MEDEA   And what is the reason deserves such flight as this?

MESSENGER   She is dead, only just now, the royal princess,
              And Creon dead, too, her father, by your poisons.

MEDEA   The finest words you have spoken. Now and hereafter
          I shall count you among my benefactors and friends.

MESSENGER   What! Are you right in the mind? Are you not mad,
Woman? The house of the king is outraged by you.
Do you enjoy it? Not afraid of such doings?

MEDEA   To what you say I on my side have something too
To say in answer. Do not be in a hurry, friend,
But speak. How did they die? You will delight me twice
As much again if you say they died in agony.

MESSENGER   When those two children, born of you, had entered in,
Their father with them, and passed into the bride's house,
We were pleased, we slaves who were distressed by your
wrongs.
All through the house we were talking of but one thing,
How you and your husband had made up your quarrel.
Some kissed the children's hands and some their yellow
hair,
And I myself was so full of my joy that I
Followed the children into the women's quarters.
Our mistress, whom we honor now instead of you,
Before she noticed that your two children were there,
Was keeping her eye fixed eagerly on Jason.
Afterwards, however, she covered up her eyes,
Her cheek paled, and she turned herself away from him,
So disgusted was she at the children's coming there.
But your husband tried to end the girl's bad temper,
And said, "You must not look unkindly on your friends.
Cease to be angry. Turn your head to me again.
Have as your friends the same ones as your husband has.
And take these gifts, and beg your father to reprieve
These children from their exile. Do it for my sake."
She, when she saw the dress, could not restrain herself.
She agreed with all her husband said, and before
He and the children had gone far from the palace,
She took the gorgeous robe and dressed herself in it,
And put the golden crown around her curly locks,

And arranged the set of the hair in a shining mirror,
And smiled at the lifeless image of herself in it.
Then she rose from her chair and walked about the room,
With her gleaming feet stepping most soft and delicate,
All overjoyed with the present. Often and often
She would stretch her foot out straight and look along it.
But after that it was a fearful thing to see.
The color of her face changed, and she staggered back,
She ran, and her legs trembled, and she only just
Managed to reach a chair without falling flat down.
An aged woman servant who, I take it, thought
This was some seizure of Pan or another god,
Cried out, "God bless us," but that was before she saw
The white foam breaking through her lips and her rolling
The pupils of her eyes and her face all bloodless.
Then she raised a different cry from that "God bless us,"
A huge shriek, and the women ran, one to the king,
One to the newly wedded husband to tell him
What had happened to his bride; and with frequent sound
The whole of the palace rang as they went running.
One walking quickly round the course of a race-track
Would now have turned the bend and be close to the goal,
When she, poor girl, opened her shut and speechless eye,
And with a terrible groan she came to herself.
For a twofold pain was moving up against her.
The wreath of gold that was resting around her head
Let forth a fearful stream of all-devouring fire,
And the finely woven dress your children gave to her,
Was fastening on the unhappy girl's fine flesh.
She leapt up from the chair, and all on fire she ran,
Shaking her hair now this way and now that, trying
To hurl the diadem away; but fixedly
The gold preserved its grip, and, when she shook her hair,
Then more and twice as fiercely the fire blazed out.
Till, beaten by her fate, she fell down to the ground,

Hard to be recognized except by a parent.
Neither the setting of her eyes was plain to see,
Nor the shapeliness of her face. From the top of
Her head there oozed out blood and fire mixed together.
Like the drops on pine-bark, so the flesh from her bones
Dropped away, torn by the hidden fang of the poison.
It was a fearful sight; and terror held us all
From touching the corpse. We had learned from what had
  happened.
But her wretched father, knowing nothing of the event,
Came suddenly to the house, and fell upon the corpse,
And at once cried out and folded his arms about her,
And kissed her and spoke to her, saying, "O my poor child,
What heavenly power has so shamefully destroyed you?
And who has set me here like an ancient sepulcher,
Deprived of you? O let me die with you, my child!"
And when he had made an end of his wailing and crying,
Then the old man wished to raise himself to his feet;
But, as the ivy clings to the twigs of the laurel,
So he stuck to the fine dress, and he struggled fearfully.
For he was trying to lift himself to his knee,
And she was pulling him down, and when he tugged hard
He would be ripping his aged flesh from his bones.
At last his life was quenched, and the unhappy man
Gave up the ghost, no longer could hold up his head.
There they lie close, the daughter and the old father,
Dead bodies, an event he prayed for in his tears.
As for your interests, I will say nothing of them,
For you will find your own escape from punishment.
Our human life I think and have thought a shadow,
And I do not fear to say that those who are held
Wise among men and who search the reasons of things
Are those who bring the most sorrow on themselves.
For of mortals there is no one who is happy.
If wealth flows in upon one, one may be perhaps

Luckier than one's neighbor, but still not happy.

(*Exit.*)

CHORUS   Heaven, it seems, on this day has fastened many
Evils on Jason, and Jason has deserved them.
Poor girl, the daughter of Creon, how I pity you
And your misfortunes, you who have gone quite away
To the house of Hades because of marrying Jason.

MEDEA   Women, my task is fixed: as quickly as I may
To kill my children, and start away from this land,
And not, by wasting time, to suffer my children
To be slain by another hand less kindly to them.
Force every way will have it they must die, and since
This must be so, then I, their mother, shall kill them.
Oh, arm yourself in steel, my heart! Do not hang back
From doing this fearful and necessary wrong.
Oh, come, my hand, poor wretched hand, and take the
    sword,
Take it, step forward to this bitter starting point,
And do not be a coward, do not think of them,
How sweet they are, and how you are their mother. Just for
This one short day be forgetful of your children,
Afterward weep; for even though you will kill them,
They were very dear—Oh, I am an unhappy woman!

(*With a cry she rushes into the house.*)

CHORUS   O Earth, and the far shining
Ray of the Sun, look down, look down upon
This poor lost woman, look, before she raises
The hand of murder against her flesh and blood.
Yours was the golden birth from which
She sprang, and now I fear divine
Blood may be shed by men.
O heavenly light, hold back her hand,

Check her, and drive from out the house
The bloody Fury raised by fiends of Hell.

Vain waste, your care of children;
Was it in vain you bore the babes you loved,
After you passed the inhospitable strait
Between the dark blue rocks, Symplegades?
O wretched one, how has it come,
This heavy anger on your heart,
This cruel bloody mind?
For God from mortals asks a stern
Price for the stain of kindred blood
In like disaster falling on their homes.

(A cry from one of the children is heard.)

CHORUS Do you hear the cry, do you hear the children's cry?
O you hard heart, O woman fated for evil!

ONE OF THE CHILDREN (from within) What can I do and how
escape my mother's hands?

ANOTHER CHILD (from within) O my dear brother, I cannot tell. We
are lost.

CHORUS Shall I enter the house? Oh, surely I should
Defend the children from murder.

A CHILD (from within) O help us, in God's name, for now we need
your help.
Now, now we are close to it. We are trapped by the sword.

CHORUS O your heart must have been made of rock or steel,
You who can kill
With your own hand the fruit of your own womb.
Of one alone I have heard, one woman alone
Of those of old who laid her hands on her children,
Ino, sent mad by heaven when the wife of Zeus
Drove her out from her home and made her wander;

And because of the wicked shedding of blood
Of her own children she threw
Herself, poor wretch, into the sea and stepped away
Over the sea-cliff to die with her two children.
What horror more can be? O women's love,
So full of trouble,
How many evils have you caused already!

(*Enter Jason, with attendants.*)

JASON   You women, standing close in front of this dwelling,
Is she, Medea, she who did this dreadful deed,
Still in the house, or has she run away in flight?
For she will have to hide herself beneath the earth,
Or raise herself on wings into the height of air,
If she wishes to escape the royal vengeance.
Does she imagine that, having killed our rulers,
She will herself escape uninjured from this house?
But I am thinking not so much of her as for
The children—her the king's friends will make to suffer
For what she did. So I have come to save the lives
Of my boys, in case the royal house should harm them
While taking vengeance for their mother's wicked deed.

CHORUS   O Jason, if you but knew how deeply you are
Involved in sorrow, you would not have spoken so.

JASON   What is it? That she is planning to kill me also?

CHORUS   Your children are dead, and by their own mother's hand.

JASON   What! That is it? O woman, you have destroyed me!

CHORUS   You must make up your mind your children are no more.

JASON   Where did she kill them? Was it here or in the house?

CHORUS   Open the gates and there you will see them murdered.

JASON   Quick as you can unlock the doors, men, and undo
        The fastenings and let me see this double evil,
        My children dead and her—Oh her I will repay.

        (*His attendants rush to the door. Medea appears above
        the house in a chariot drawn by dragons. She has the
        dead bodies of the children with her.*)

MEDEA   Why do you batter these gates and try to unbar them,
        Seeking the corpses and for me who did the deed?
        You may cease your trouble, and, if you have need of me,
        Speak, if you wish. You will never touch me with your
            hand,
        Such a chariot has Helius, my father's father,
        Given me to defend me from my enemies.

JASON   You hateful thing, you woman most utterly loathed
        By the gods and me and by all the race of mankind,
        You who have had the heart to raise a sword against
        Your children, you, their mother, and left me childless—
        You have done this, and do you still look at the sun
        And at the earth, after these most fearful doings?
        I wish you dead. Now I see it plain, though at that time
        I did not, when I took you from your foreign home
        And brought you to a Greek house, you, an evil thing,
        A traitress to your father and your native land.
        The gods hurled the avenging curse of yours on me.
        For your own brother you slew at your own hearthside,
        And then came aboard that beautiful ship, the Argo.
        And that was your beginning. When you were married
        To me, your husband, and had borne children to me,
        For the sake of pleasure in the bed you killed them.
        There is no Greek woman who would have dared such
            deeds,
        Out of all those whom I passed over and chose you
        To marry instead, a bitter destructive match,

A monster, not a woman, having a nature
Wilder than that of Scylla in the Tuscan sea.*
Ah! no, not if I had ten thousand words of shame
Could I sting you. You are naturally so brazen.
Go, worker in evil, stained with your children's blood.
For me remains to cry aloud upon my fate,
Who will get no pleasure from my newly wedded love,
And the boys whom I begot and brought up, never
Shall I speak to them alive. Oh, my life is over!

MEDEA   Long would be the answer which I might have made to
These words of yours, if Zeus the father did not know
How I have treated you and what you did to me.
No, it was not to be that you should scorn my love,
And pleasantly live your life through, laughing at me;
Nor would the princess, nor he who offered the match,
Creon, drive me away without paying for it.
So now you may call me a monster, if you wish,
A Scylla housed in the caves of the Tuscan sea.
I too, as I had to, have taken hold of your heart.

JASON   You feel the pain yourself. You share in my sorrow.

MEDEA   Yes, and my grief is gain when you cannot mock it.

JASON   O children, what a wicked mother she was to you!

MEDEA   They died from a disease they caught from their father.

JASON   I tell you it was not my hand that destroyed them.

MEDEA   But it was your insolence, and your virgin wedding.

JASON   And just for the sake of that you chose to kill them.

MEDEA   Is love so small a pain, do you think, for a woman?

JASON   For a wise one, certainly. But you are wholly evil.

---

* A monster in the *Odyssey*.

MEDEA   The children are dead. I say this to make you suffer.

JASON   The children, I think, will bring down curses on you.

MEDEA   The gods know who was the author of this sorrow.

JASON   Yes, the gods know indeed, they know your loathsome
         heart.

MEDEA   Hate me. But I tire of your barking bitterness.

JASON   And I of yours. It is easier to leave you.

MEDEA   How then? What shall I do? I long to leave you too.

JASON   Give me the bodies to bury and to mourn them.

MEDEA   No, that I will not. I will bury them myself,
         Bearing them to Hera's temple on the promontory;
         So that no enemy may evilly treat them
         By tearing up their grave. In this land of Corinth
         I shall establish a holy feast and sacrifice
         Each year for ever to atone for the blood guilt.
         And I myself go to the land of Erechtheus
         To dwell in Aegeus' house, the son of Pandion.
         While you, as is right, will die without distinction,
         Struck on the head by a piece of the Argo's timber,
         And you will have seen the bitter end of my love.

JASON   May a Fury for the children's sake destroy you,
         And justice, Requitor of blood.

MEDEA   What heavenly power lends an ear
         To a breaker of oaths, a deceiver?

JASON   Oh, I hate you, murderess of children.

MEDEA   Go to your palace. Bury your bride.

JASON   I go, with two children to mourn for.

MEDEA   Not yet do you feel it. Wait for the future.

JASON   Oh, children I loved!

MEDEA   I loved them, you did not.

JASON   You loved them, and killed them.

MEDEA   To make you feel pain.

JASON   Oh, wretch that I am, how I long
         To kiss the dear lips of my children!

MEDEA   Now you would speak to them, now you would kiss them.
         Then you rejected them.

JASON   Let me, I beg you,
         Touch my boys' delicate flesh.

MEDEA   I will not. Your words are all wasted.

JASON   O God, do you hear it, this persecution,
         These my sufferings from this hateful
         Woman, this monster, murderess of children?
         Still what I can do that I will do:
         I will lament and cry upon heaven,
         Calling the gods to bear me witness
         How you have killed my boys and prevent me from
         Touching their bodies or giving them burial.
         I wish I had never begot them to see them
         Afterward slaughtered by you.

CHORUS   Zeus in Olympus is the overseer
         Of many doings. Many things the gods
         Achieve beyond our judgment. What we thought
         Is not confirmed and what we thought not god
         Contrives. And so it happens in this story.

(Curtain.)

Bacchae

EURIPIDES

Characters

Dionysus

Chorus of Bacchae

Tiresias

Cadmus

Pentheus

Attendant

Messenger

Second Messenger

Agave

DIONYSUS   Unto this land of Thebes I come, Jove's son,
Dionysus; he whom Semele of yore,
'Mid the dread midwifery of lightning fire,
Bore, Cadmus' daughter. In a mortal form,
The God put off, by Dirce's stream I stand,
And cool Ismenos' waters; and survey
My mother's grave, the thunder-slain, the ruins
Still smouldering of that old ancestral palace,
The flame still living of the lightning fire,
Herè's immortal vengeance 'gainst my mother.

And well hath reverent Cadmus set his ban
On that heaven-stricken, unapproached place,
His daughter's tomb, which I have mantled o'er
With the pale verdure of the trailing vine.

And I have left the golden Lydian shores,
The Phrygian and the Persian sun-seared plains,
And Bactria's walls; the Medes' wild wintry land
Have passed, and Araby the Blest; and all
Of Asia, that along the salt-sea coast
Lifts up her high-towered cities, where the Greeks,
With the Barbarians mingled, dwell in peace.

And everywhere my sacred choirs, mine Orgies
Have founded, by mankind confessed a God.
Now first in an Hellenic town I stand.

Of all the Hellenic land here first in Thebes,
I have raised my revel shout, my fawn-skin donned,

Ta'en in my hand my thyrsus, ivy-erowned.

But here, where least beseemed, my mother's sisters
Vowed Dionysus was no son of Jove:
That Semele, by mortal paramour won,
Belied great Jove as author of her sin;
'Twas but old Cadmus' craft: hence Jove in wrath
Struck dead the bold usurper of his bed.

So from their homes I've goaded them in frenzy;
Their wits all crazed, they wander o'er the mountains
And I have forced them wear my wild attire.
There's not a woman of old Cadmus' race,
But I have maddened from her quiet house;
Unseemly mingled with the sons of Thebes,
On the roofless rocks, 'neath the pale pines, they sit.

Needs must this proud recusant city learn,
In our dread Mysteries initiate,
Her guilt, and humbly seek to make atonement
To me, for Semele, mine outraged mother —
To me, the God confessed, of Jove begot.

Old Cadmus now his might and kingly rule
To Pentheus hath given up, his sister's son,
My godhead's foe; who from the rich libation
Repels me, nor makes mention of my name
In holy prayer. Wherefore to him, to Thebes,
And all her sons, soon will I terribly show
That I am born a God: and so depart
(Here all things well disposed) to other lands,
Making dread revelation of myself.

But if this Theban city, in her ire,
With arms shall seek to drive from off the mountains
My Bacchanal rout, at my wild Mænads' head

I'll meet, and mingle in the awful war.
Hence have I ta'en the likeness of a man,
Myself transmuted into human form.
    But ye, who Tmolus, Lydia's strength, have left
My Thyasus of women, whom I have led
From lands barbarian, mine associates here,
And fellow-pilgrims; lift ye up your drums,
Familiar in your native Phrygian cities,
Made by your mother Rhea's craft and mine;
And beat them all round Pentheus' royal palace,
Beat, till the city of Cadmus throngs to see.
I to the Bacchanals in the dim glens
Of wild Cithæron go to lead the dance.

CHORUS From the Asian shore,
        And by the sacred steep of Tmolus hoar,
        Light I danced with wing-like feet,
        Toilless toil and labour sweet!
        Away! away! whoe'er he be;
        Leave our path, our temple free!
        Seal up each silent lip in holy awe.
        But I, obedient to thy law,
   O Dionysus! chant the choral hymn to thee

        Blest above all of human line,
        Who, deep in mystic rites divine,
        Leads his hallowed life with us,
        Initiate in our Thyasus;
        And, purified with holiest waters,
  Goes dancing o'er the hills with Bacchus' daughters.
        And thy dark orgies hallows he,
        O mighty mother, Cybele!

He his thyrsus shaking round,
All his locks with ivy crowned,
O Dionysus! boasts of thy dread train to be.

Bacchanals! away, away!
Lead your God in fleet array;
Bacchus lead, the ever young,
A God himself from Gods that sprung,
From the Phrygian mountains down
Through every wide-squared Grecian town.
Him the Theban queen of yore
'Mid Jove's fast-flashing lightnings bore:
In her awful travail wild
Sprung from her womb the untimely child,
While smitten with the thunderblast
The sad mother breathed her last.

Instant him Saturnian Jove
Received with all a mother's love;
In his secret thigh immured,
There with golden clasps secured,
Safe from Herè's jealous sight;
Then, as the Fates fulfilled, to light
He gave the hornéd god, and wound
The living snakes his brows around;
Whence still the wandéd Mænads bear
Their serpent prey wreathed in their floating hair.

Put on thy ivy crown,
O Thebes, thou sacred town!
O hallowed house of dark-haired Semele!

Bloom, blossom everywhere,
With flowers and fruitage fair,
And let your frenzied steps supported be
With thyrsi from the oak
Or the green ash-tree broke:
Your spotted fawn-skins line with locks
Torn from the snowy fleecéd flocks:
Shaking his wanton wand let each advance,
And all the land shall madden with the dance.

Bromius, that his revel rout
To the mountains leads about;
To the mountains leads along,
Where awaits the female throng;
From the distaff, from the loom,
Raging with the God they come.
O ye mountains, wild and high,
Where the old Kouretæ lie:
Glens of Crete, where Jove was nurst,
In your sunless caverns first
The crested Korybantes found
The leathern drums mysterious round,
That, mingling in harmonious strife
With the sweet-breathed Phrygian fife,
In Mother Rhea's hands they place,
Meet the Bacchic song to grace.
And the frantic Satyrs round
That ancient Goddess leap and bound:
And soon the Trieteric dances light
Began, immortal Bacchus' chief delight.

On the mountains wild 'tis sweet
When faint with rapid dance our feet;
Our limbs on earth all careless thrown
With the sacred fawn-skins strewn,
To quaff the goat's delicious blood,
A strange, a rich, a savage food.
Then off again the revel goes
O'er Phrygian, Lydian mountain brows;
Evoë! Evoë! leads the road,
Bacchus self the maddening God!
And flows with milk the plain, and flows with wine
Flows with the wild bees' nectar-dews divine;
And soars, like smoke, the Syrian incense pale —
The while the frantic Bacchanal
The beaconing pine-torch on her wand
Whirls around with rapid hand,
And drives the wandering dance about,
Beating time with joyous shout,
And casts upon the breezy air
All her rich luxuriant hair;
Ever the burthen of her song,
"Raging, maddening, haste along
Bacchus' daughters, ye the pride
Of golden Tmolus' fabled side;
While your heavy cymbals ring,
Still your 'Evoë! Evoë!' sing!"
Evoë! the Evian god rejoices
In Phrygian tones and Phrygian voices,
When the soft holy pipe is breathing sweet,
In notes harmonious to her feet,
Who to the mountain, to the mountain speeds;

> Like some young colt that by its mother feeds,
>   Gladsome with many a frisking bound,
> The Bacchanal goes forth and treads the echoing ground.

TIRESIAS Ho! some one in the gates, call from his place
          Cadmus, Agenor's son, who, Sidon's walls
          Leaving, built up this towered city of Thebes.
          Ho! some one say, "Tiresias awaits him."
          Well knows he why I am here; the covenant
          Which I, th' old man, have made with him still older,
          To lift the thyrsus wand, the fawn-skin wear,
          And crown our grey hairs with the ivy leaves.

CADMUS Best friend! with what delight within my palace
        I heard thy speech, the speech of a wise man!
        Lo! I am here, in the God's sacred garb;
        For needs must we, the son of mine own daughter,
        Dionysus, now 'mongst men a manifest God,
        Even to the utmost of our power extol.
        Where shall we lead the dance, plant the light foot,
        And shake the hoary locks? Tiresias, thou
        The aged lead the aged: wise art thou,
        Nor will I weary night and day the earth
        Beating with my lithe thyrsus. Oh, how sweetly
        Will we forget we are old!

TIRESIAS   Thou'rt as myself:
         I too grow young; I too essay the dance.

CADMUS Shall we, then, in our chariots seek the mountains?

TIRESIAS It were not the same homage to the God.

CADMUS The old man still shall be the old man's tutor.

TIRESIAS The God will guide us thither without toil.

CADMUS Of all the land, join we alone the dance?

TIRESIAS All else misjudge; we only are the wise.

CADMUS Too long we linger; hold thou fast mine hand.

TIRESIAS Lo! thus true yoke-fellows join hand with hand.

CADMUS I, mortal-born, may not despise the Gods.

TIRESIAS No wile, no paltering with the deities.
    The ancestral faith, coeval with our race,
    No subtle reasoning, if it soar aloft
    Even to the height of wisdom, can o'erthrow.
    Some one will say that I disgrace mine age,
    Rapt in the dance, and ivy-crowned my head.
    The Gods admit no difference: old or young,
    All it behoves to mingle in the rite.
    From all he will receive the common honour,
    Nor deign to count his countless votaries.

CADMUS Since thou, Tiresias, seest not day's sweet light,
    I, as thy Seer, must tell thee what is coming.
    Lo, Pentheus, hurrying homewards to his palace,
    Echion's son, to whom I have given the kingdom.
    He is strangely moved! What new thing will he say?

PENTHEUS I have been absent from this land, and hear
    Of strange and evil doings in the city.
    Our women all have left their homes, to join

These fabled mysteries. On the shadowy rocks
Frequent they sit, this God of yesterday,
Dionysus, whosoe'er he be, with revels
Dishonourable honouring. In the midst
Stand the crowned goblets; and each stealing forth,
This way and that, creeps to a lawless bed;
In pretext, holy sacrificing Mænads,
But serving Aphrodite more than Bacchus.
All whom I've apprehended, in their gyves
Our officers guard in the public prison.
Those that have 'scaped I'll hunt from off the moun-
      tains,
Ino, Agave who to Echion bare me,
Her too, Autonoe, Antæus' mother;
And fettering them all in iron bonds,
I'll put an end to their mad wickedness.
'Tis said a stranger hath appeared among us,
A wizard, sorcerer, from the land of Lydia,
Beauteous with golden locks and purple cheeks,
Eyes moist with Aphrodite's melting fire.
And day and night he is with the throng, to guile
Young maidens to the soft inebriate rites.
   But if I catch him 'neath this roof, I'll silence
The beating of his thyrsus, stay his locks'
Wild tossing, from his body severing his neck.
He, say they, is the new God, Dionysus,
That was sewn up within the thigh of Jove.
He, with his mother, guiltily that boasted
Herself Jove's bride, was blasted by the lightning.
Are not such deeds deserving the base halter?
Sin heaped on sin! whoe'er this stranger be.

But lo, new wonders! see I not Tiresias,
The prophet, in the dappled fawn-skin clad?
My mother's father too (a sight for laughter!)
Tossing his hair? My sire, I blush for thee
Beholding thine old age thus fatuous grown.
Wilt not shake off that ivy? free thine hand
From that unseemly wand, my mother's father!
This is thy work, Tiresias. This new God
Wilt thou instal 'mongst men, at higher price
To vend new auspices, and well paid offerings.
If thine old age were not thy safeguard, thou
Shouldst pine in chains among the Bacchanal women.
False teacher of new rites! For where 'mong women
The grape's sweet poison mingles with the feast,
Nought holy may we augur of such worship.

CHORUS   Oh impious! dost thou not revere the Gods,
Nor Cadmus, who the earth-born harvest sowed?
Echion's son! how dost thou shame thy lineage!

TIRESIAS   'Tis easy to be eloquent, for him
That's skilled in speech, and hath a stirring theme.
Thou hast the flowing tongue as of a wise man,
But there's no wisdom in thy fluent words;
For the bold demagogue, powerful in speech,
Is but a dangerous citizen lacking sense.
This the new deity thou laugh'st to scorn,
I may not say how mighty he will be
Throughout all Hellas. Youth! there are two things
Man's primal need, Demeter, the boon Goddess
(Or rather will ye call her Mother Earth?),
With solid food maintains the race of man.

He, on the other hand, the son of Semele,
Found out the grape's rich juice, and taught us mortals
That which beguiles the miserable of mankind
Of sorrow, when they quaff the vine's rich stream.
Sleep too, and drowsy oblivion of care
He gives, all-healing medicine of our woes.
He 'mong the gods is worshipped a great god,
Author confessed to man of such rich blessings
Him dost thou love to scorn, as in Jove's thigh
Sewn up. This truth profound will I unfold:
When Jove had snatched him from the lightning-fire
He to Olympus bore the new-born babe.
Stern Herè strove to thrust him out of heaven,
But Jove encountered her with wiles divine:
He clove off part of th' earth-encircling air,
There Dionysus placed the pleasing hostage,
Aloof from jealous Herè. So men said
Hereafter he was cradled in Jove's thigh
(From the assonance of words in our old tongue
For thigh and hostage the wild fable grew).
A prophet is our god, for Bacchanalism
And madness are alike prophetical.
And when the god comes down in all his power,
He makes the mad to rave of things to come.
Of Ares he hath attributes: he the host
In all its firm array and serried arms,
With panic fear scatters, ere lance cross lance:
From Dionysus springs this frenzy too.

   And him shall we behold on Delphi's crags
Leaping, with his pine torches lighting up
The rifts of the twin-headed rock; and shouting

And shaking all around his Bacchic wand
Great through all Hellas. Pentheus, be advised!
Vaunt not thy power o'er man, even if thou thinkest
That thou art wise (it is diseased, thy thought),
Think it not! In the land receive the god.
Pour wine, and join the dance, and crown thy brows.
Dionysus does not force our modest matrons
To the soft Cyprian rites; the chaste by nature
Are not so cheated of their chastity.
Think well of this, for in the Bacchic choir
The holy woman will not be less holy.
Thou'rt proud, when men to greet thee throng the gates,
And the glad city welcomes Pentheus' name;
He too, I ween, delights in being honoured.
   I, therefore, and old Cadmus whom thou mock'st,
Will crown our heads with ivy, dance along
An hoary pair — for dance perforce we must;
I war not with the gods. Follow my counsel;
Thou'rt at the height of madness, there's no medicine
Can minister to disease so deep as thine.

CHORUS   Old man! thou sham'st not Phœbus thine own god.
           Wise art thou worshipping that great god Bromius.

CADMUS   My son! Tiresias well hath counselled thee;
           Dwell safe with us within the pale of law.
           Now thou fliest high: thy sense is void of sense,
           Even if, as thou declar'st, he were no god,
           Call thou him god. It were a splendid falsehood
           If Semele be thought t' have borne a god;
           'Twere honour unto us and to our race.
           Hast thou not seen Actæon's wretched fate?

The dogs he bred, who fed from his own board,
Rent him in wrath to pieces; for he vaunted
Than Artemis to be a mightier hunter.
So do not thou: come, let me crown thine head
With ivy, and with us adore the god.

PENTHEUS   Hold off thine hand! Away! Go rave and dance,
And wipe not off thy folly upon me.
On him, thy folly's teacher, I will wreak
Instant relentless justice. Some one go,
The seats from which he spies the flight of birds —
False augur — with the iron forks o'erthrow,
Scattering in wild confusion all abroad,
And cast his chaplets to the winds and storms;
Thou'lt gall him thus, gall to the height of bitterness.
Ye to the city! seek that stranger out,
That womanly man, who with this new disease
Afflicts our matrons, and defiles their beds:
Seize him and bring him hither straight in chains,
That he may suffer stoning, that dread death.
Such be his woful orgies here in Thebes.

TIRESIAS   Oh, miserable! That know'st not what thou sayest,
Crazed wert thou, now thou'rt at the height of madness:
But go we, Cadmus, and pour forth our prayer,
Even for this savage and ungodly man,
And for our city, lest the god o'ertake us
With some strange vengeance.
                              Come with thy ivy staff,
Lean thou on me, and I will lean on thee:
'Twere sad for two old men to fall, yet go
We must, and serve great Bacchus, son of Jove.

What woe, O Cadmus, will this woe-named man
Bring to thine house! I speak not now as prophet,
But a plain simple fact: fools still speak folly.

CHORUS   Holy goddess! Goddess old!
         Holy! thou the crown of gold
         In the nether realm that wearest,
         Pentheus' awful speech thou hearest,
         Hearest his insulting tone
         'Gainst Semele's immortal son,
         Bromius, of gods the first and best.
         At every gay and flower-crowned feast,
         His the dance's jocund strife,
         And the laughter with the fife,
         Every care and grief to lull,
         When the sparkling wine-cup full
         Crowns the gods' banquets, or lets fall
   Sweet sleep on the eyes of men at mortal festival.
         Of tongue unbridled without awe,
         Of madness spurning holy law,
         Sorrow is the Jove-doomed close;
         But the life of calm repose
         And modest reverence holds her state
         Unbroken by disturbing fate;
         And knits whole houses in the tie
         Of sweet domestic harmony.
         Beyond the range of mortal eyes
         'Tis not wisdom to be wise.
         Life is brief, the present clasp,
         Nor after some bright future grasp.
         Such were the wisdom, as I ween,

Only of frantic and ill-counselled men.

Oh, would to Cyprus I might roam,
    Soft Aphrodite's isle,
Where the young loves have their perennial home,
    That soothe men's hearts with tender guile:
Or to that wondrous shore where ever
The hundred-mouthed barbaric river
Makes teem with wealth the showerless land!
O lead me! lead me, till I stand,
Bromius! — sweet Bromius! — where high swelling
Soars the Pierian muses' dwelling —
Olympus' summit hoar and high —
Thou revel-loving deity!
    For there are all the graces,
        And sweet desire is there,
        And to those hallowed places
    To lawful rites the Bacchanals repair.
    The deity, the son of Jove,
        The banquet is his joy,
    Peace, the wealth-giver, doth he love,
        That nurse of many a noble boy.
    Not the rich man's sole possessing;
    To the poor the painless blessing
    Gives he of the wine-cup bright.
    Him he hates, who day and night,
    Gentle night, and gladsome day,
    Cares not thus to while away.
    Be thou wisely unsevere!
    Shun the stern and the austere!
        Follow the multitude;

     Their usage still pursue!
       Their homely wisdom rude
  (Such is my sentence) is both right and true.

OFFICER Pentheus, we are here! In vain we went not forth:
    The prey which thou commandest we have taken.
    Gentle our quarry met us, nor turned back
    His foot in flight, but held out both his hands;
    Became not pale, changed not his ruddy colour.
    Smiling he bade us bind, and lead him off,
    Stood still, and made our work a work of ease.
    Reverent I said, "Stranger, I arrest thee not
    Of mine own will, but by the king's command."
    But all the Bacchanals, whom thou hast seized
    And bound in chains within the public prison,
    All now have disappeared, released they are leaping
    In their wild orgies, hymning the god Bacchus.
    Spontaneous fell the chains from off their feet;
    The bolts drew back untouched by mortal hand.
    In truth this man, with many wonders rife
    Comes to our Thebes. 'Tis thine t' ordain the rest.

PENTHEUS   Bind fast his hands! Thus in his manacles
    Sharp must he be indeed to 'scape us now.
    There's beauty, stranger — woman-witching beauty
    (Therefore thou art in Thebes) — in thy soft form;
    Thy fine bright hair, not coarse like the hard athlete's,
    Is mantling o'er thy cheek warm with desire;
    And carefully thou hast cherished thy white skin;
    Not in the sun's swart beams, but in cool shade,
    Wooing soft Aphrodite with thy loveliness.
    But tell me first, from whence hath sprung thy race?

DIONYSUS   There needs no boast; 'tis easy to tell this:
            All flowery Tmolus hast thou haply heard?

PENTHEUS   Yea; that which girds around the Sardian city.

DIONYSUS   Thence am I come, my country Lydia.

PENTHEUS   Whence unto Hellas bringest thou thine orgies?

DIONYSUS   Dionysus, son of Jove, hath hallowed them.

PENTHEUS   Is there a Jove then, that begets new gods?

DIONYSUS   No, it was here he wedded Semele.

PENTHEUS   Hallowed he them by night, or in the eye of day?

DIONYSUS   In open vision he revealed his orgies.

PENTHEUS   And what, then, is thine orgies' solemn form;

DIONYSUS   That is not uttered to the uninitiate.

PENTHEUS   What profit, then, is theirs who worship him?

DIONYSUS   Thou mayst not know, though precious were that
            knowledge.

PENTHEUS   A cunning tale, to make me long to hear thee.

DIONYSUS   The orgies of our god scorn impious worshippers.

PENTHEUS   Thou saw'st the manifest god! What was his form?

DIONYSUS   Whate'er he would: it was not mine to choose.

PENTHEUS   Cleverly blinked our question with no answer.

DIONYSUS   Who wiseliest speaks, to the fool speaks foolishness.

PENTHEUS   And hither com'st thou first with thy new god!

DIONYSUS   There's no Barbarian but adores these rites.

PENTHEUS   Being much less wise than we Hellenians.

DIONYSUS   In this more wise. Their customs differ much.

PENTHEUS   Performest thou these rites by night or day?

DIONYSUS   Most part by night — night hath more solemn awe.

PENTHEUS   A crafty rotten plot to catch our women.

DIONYSUS   Even in the day bad men can do bad deeds.

PENTHEUS   Thou of thy wiles shalt pay the penalty.

DIONYSUS   Thou of thine ignorance — impious towards the gods!

PENTHEUS   He's bold, this Bacchus — ready enough in words.

DIONYSUS   What penalty? what evil wilt thou do me?

PENTHEUS   First will I clip away those soft bright locks.

DIONYSUS   My locks are holy, dedicate to my god.

PENTHEUS   Next, give thou me that thyrsus in thine hand.

DIONYSUS   Take it thyself; 'tis Dionysus' wand.

PENTHEUS   I'll bind thy body in strong iron chains.

DIONYSUS   My god himself will loose them when he will.

PENTHEUS   When thou invok'st him 'mid thy Bacchanals.

DIONYSUS   Even now he is present; he beholds me now.

PENTHEUS   Where is he then? Mine eyes perceive him not.

DIONYSUS   Near me: the impious eyes may not discern him.

PENTHEUS   Seize on him, for he doth insult our Thebes.

DIONYSUS   I warn thee, bind me not; the insane, the sane.

PENTHEUS   I, stronger than thou art, say I will bind thee.

DIONYSUS   Thou know'st not where thou art, or what thou art.

PENTHEUS   Pentheus, Agave's son, my sire Echion.

DIONYSUS   Thou hast a name whose very sound is woe.

PENTHEUS   Away, go bind him in our royal stable,
       That he may sit in midnight gloom profound
  There lead thy dance! But those thou hast hither led,
  Thy guilt's accomplices, we'll sell for slaves;
  Or, silencing their noise and beating drums,
  As handmaids to the distaff set them down.

DIONYSUS   Away then! 'Tis not well I bear such wrong;
  The vengeance for this outrage he will wreak
  Whose being thou deniest, Dionysus:
  Outraging me, ye bind him in your chains.

CHORUS   Holy virgin-haunted water
       Ancient Achelous' daughter!

Dirce! in thy crystal wave
Thou the child of Jove didst lave.
Thou, when Zeus, his awful sire,
Snatched him from the immortal fire;
And locked him up within his thigh,
With a loud but gentle cry —
"Come, my Dithyrambus, come,
Enter thou the masculine womb!"
   Lo! to Thebes I thus proclaim,
"Twice born!" thus thy mystic name.
Blessed Dirce! dost thou well
From thy green marge to repel
Me, and all my jocund round,
With their ivy garlands crowned.
         Why dost fly me?
         Why deny me?
By all the joys of wine I swear,
Bromius still shall be my care.

Oh, what pride! pride unforgiven
Manifests, against high heaven
Th' earth-born, whom in mortal birth
'Gat Echion, son of earth;
Pentheus of the dragon brood,
Not of human flesh and blood;
But potent dire, like him whose pride,
The Titan, all the gods defied.
Me, great Bromius' handmaid true;
Me, with all my festive crew,
Thralled in chains he still would keep
In his palace dungeon deep.

Seest thou this, O son of Jove,
Dionysus, from above?
Thy wrapt prophets dost thou see
At strife with dark necessity?
    The golden wand
    In thy right hand.
Come, come thou down Olympus' side,
And quell the bloody tyrant in his pride.·

Art thou holding revel now
On Nysa's wild beast-haunted brow?
Is't thy Thyasus that clambers
O'er Corycia's mountain chambers?
Or on Olympus, thick with wood,
With his harp where Orpheus stood,
And led the forest trees along,
Led the wild beasts with his song.
    O Pieria, blessed land,
Evius hallows thee, advancing,
With his wild choir's mystic dancing,
    Over rapid Axius' strand
He shall pass; o'er Lydia's tide
Then his whirling Mænads guide.
Lydia, parent boon of health,
Giver to man of boundless wealth;
Washing many a sunny mead,
Where the prancing coursers feed.

DIONYSUS   What ho! what ho! ye Bacchanals
                Rouse and wake! your master calls.

CHORUS   Who is here? and what is he
        That calls upon our wandering train?

DIONYSUS   What ho! what ho! I call again!
        The son of Jove and Semele.

CHORUS   What ho! what ho! our lord and master:
        Come, with footsteps fast and faster,
        Join our revel! Bromius, speed,
        Till quakes the earth beneath our tread.
           Alas! alas!
      Soon shall Pentheus' palace wall
      Shake and crumble to its fall.

DIONYSUS   Bacchus treads the palace floor!
      Adore him!

CHORUS   Oh! we do adore!
         Behold! behold!
      The pillars with their weight above,
      Of ponderous marble, shake and move.
      Hark! the trembling roof within
      Bacchus shouts his mighty din.

DIONYSUS   The kindling lamp of the dark lightning bring!
      Fire, fire the palace of the guilty king.

CHORUS   Behold! behold! it flames! Do ye not see,
      Around the sacred tomb of Semele,
      The blaze, that left the lightning there,
      When Jove's red thunder fired the air?
        On the earth, supine and low,
        Your shuddering limbs, ye Mænads, throw!

The king, the Jove-born god, destroying all,
In widest ruin strews the palace wall.

DIONYSUS   O, ye Barbarian women, Thus prostrate in dismay;
Upon the earth ye've fallen! See ye not, as ye may,
How Bacchus Pentheus' palace In wrath hath shaken
down?
Rise up! rise up! take courage — Shake off that
trembling swoon.

CHORUS   O light that goodliest shinest Over our mystic rite,
In state forlorn we saw thee — Saw with what deep
affright!

DIONYSUS   How to despair ye yielded As I boldly entered in
To Pentheus, as if captured, Into the fatal gin.

CHORUS   How could I less? Who guards us If thou shouldst come
to woe?
But how wast thou delivered From thy ungodly foe?

DIONYSUS   'Myself, myself delivered, With ease and effort slight.

CHORUS   Thy hands, had he not bound them, In halters strong
and tight?

DIONYSUS   'Twas even then I mocked him: He thought me in his
chain;
He touched me not, nor reached me; His idle thoughts
were vain!
In the stable stood a heifer, Where he thought he had
me bound;
Round the beast's knees his cords And cloven hoofs he
wound.

Wrath-breathing, from his body The sweat fell like a
    flood:
He bit his lips in fury, While I beside who stood
Looked on in unmoved quiet.

                     As at that instant come,
Shook Bacchus the strong palace, And on his mother's
    tomb
Flames kindled. When he saw it, On fire the palace
    deeming,
Hither he rushed and thither, For "water, water,"
    screaming;
And every slave 'gan labour, But laboured all in vain.
The toil he soon abandoned. As though I had fled
    amain
He rushed into the palace: In his hand the dark sword
    gleamed.
Then, as it seemed, great Bromius — I say, but as it
    seemed —
In the hall a bright light kindled. On that he rushed, and
    there,
As slaying me in vengeance, Stood stabbing the thin
    air.
But then the avenging Bacchus Wrought new calam-
    ities;
From roof to base that palace In smouldering ruin
    lies.
Bitter ruing our imprisonment, With toil forspent he
    threw
On earth his useless weapon. Mortal, he had dared to
    do
'Gainst a god unholy battle. But I, in quiet state,

Unheeding Pentheus' anger, Came through the palace gate.

It seems even now his sandal Is sounding on its way:

Soon is he here before us, And what now will he say?

With ease will I confront him, Ire-breathing though he stand.

'Tis easy to a wise man To practise self-command.

PENTHEUS   I am outraged — mocked! The stranger hath escaped me

Whom I so late had bound in iron chains.

Off, off! He is here! — the man? How's this? How stands he

Before our palace, as just issuing forth?

DIONYSUS   Stay thou thy step! Subdue thy wrath to peace!

PENTHEUS   How, having burst thy chains, hast thou come forth?

DIONYSUS   Said I not — heardst thou not? "There's one will free me!"

PENTHEUS   What one? Thou speakest still words new and strange.

DIONYSUS   He who for man plants the rich-tendrilled vine.

PENTHEUS   Well layest thou this reproach on Dionysus.

Without there, close and bar the towers around!

DIONYSUS   What! and the gods! O'erleap they not all walls?

PENTHEUS   Wise in all wisdom save in that thou shouldst have!

DIONYSUS   In that I should have wisest still am I.

But listen first, and hear the words of him
Who comes to thee with tidings from the mountains
Here will we stay. Fear not, we will not fly!

MESSENGER   Pentheus, that rulest o'er this land of Thebes!
I come from high Cithæron, ever white
With the bright glittering snow's perennial rays.

PENTHEUS   Why com'st thou? On what pressing mission bound?

MESSENGER   I've seen the frenzied Bacchanals, who had fled
On their white feet, forth goaded from the land.
I come to tell to thee and to this city
The awful deeds they do, surpassing wonder.
But answer first if I shall freely say
All that's done there, or furl my prudent speech;
For thy quick temper I do fear, O king,
Thy sharp resentment and o'er-royal pride.

PENTHEUS   Speak freely. Thou shall part unharmed by me;
Wrath were not seemly 'gainst the unoffending.
But the more awful what thou sayst of these
Mad women, I the more on him who hath guiled
     them
To their wild life, will wreak my just revenge.

MESSENGER   Mine herds of heifers I was driving, slow
Winding their way along the mountain crags,
When the sun pours his full beams on the earth.
I saw three bands, three choirs of women: one
Autonoe led, thy mother led the second,
Agave — and the third Ino: and all
Quietly slept, their languid limbs stretched out:

Some resting on the ash-trees' stem their tresses;
Some with their heads upon the oak-leaves thrown
Careless, but not immodest; as thou sayest,
That drunken with the goblet and shrill fife
In the dusk woods they prowl for lawless love.
Thy mother, as she heard the hornéd steers
Deep lowing, stood up 'mid the Bacchanals
And shouted loud to wake them from their rest.
They from their lids shaking the freshening sleep,
Rose upright, wonderous in their decent guise,
The young, the old, the maiden yet unwed.
And first they loosed their locks over their shoulders,
Their fawn-skins fastened, wheresoe'er the clasps
Had lost their hold, and all the dappled furs
With serpents bound, that lolled out their lithe tongues.
Some in their arms held kid, or wild-wolf's cub,
Suckling it with her white milk; all the young mothers
Who had left their new-born babes, and stood with
   breasts
Full swelling: and they all put on their crowns
Of ivy, oak, or flowering eglantine.
One took a thyrsus wand, and struck the rock,
Leaped forth at once a dewy mist of water;
And one her rod plunged deep in the earth, and there
The god sent up a fountain of bright wine.
And all that longed for the white blameless draught
Light scraping with their finger-ends the soil
Had streams of exquisite milk; the ivy wands
Distilled from all their tops rich store of honey.
   Hadst thou been there, seeing these things, the god
Thou now revil'st thou hadst adored with prayer.

And we, herdsmen and shepherds, gathered around
And there was strife among us in our words
Of these strange things they did, these marvellous
        things.
One city-bred, a glib and practised speaker,
Addressed us thus: "Ye that inhabit here
The holy mountain slopes, shall we not chase
Agave, Pentheus' mother, from the Bacchanals,
And win the royal favour?" Well to us
He seemed to speak; so, crouched in the thick bushes,
We lay in ambush. They at the appointed hour
Shook their wild thyrsi in the Bacchic dance,
"Iacchus" with one voice, the son of Jove,
"Bromius" invoking. The hills danced with them;
And the wild beasts; was nothing stood unmoved.

And I leaped forth, as though to seize on her,
Leaving the sedge where I had hidden myself.
But she shrieked out, "Ho, my swift-footed dogs!
These men would hunt us down, but follow me —
Follow me, all your hands with thyrsi armed."
We fled amain, or by the Bacchanals
We had been torn in pieces. They, with hands
Unarmed with iron, rushed on the browsing steers.
One ye might see a young and vigorous heifer
Hold, lowing in her grasp, like prize of war.
And some were tearing asunder the young calves;
And ye might see the ribs or cloven hoofs
Hurled wildly up and down, and mangled skins
Were hanging from the ash boughs, dropping blood.
The wanton bulls, proud of their tossing horns
Of yore, fell stumbling, staggering to the ground,

Dragged down by the strong hands of thousand
    maidens.
And swifter were the entrails torn away
Than drop the lids over your royal eyeballs.
    Like birds that skim the earth, they glide along
O'er the wide plains, that by Asopus' streams
Shoot up for Thebes the rich and yellow corn;
And Hysiæ and Erythræ, that beneath
Cithæron's crag dwell lowly, like fierce foes
Invading, all with ravage waste and wide
Confounded; infants snatched from their sweet homes;
And what they threw across their shoulders, clung
Unfastened, nor fell down to the black ground.
No brass, nor ponderous iron: on their locks
Was fire that burned them not. Of those they spoiled
Some in their sudden fury rushed to arms.
Then was a mightier wonder seen, O king:
From them the pointed lances drew no blood
But they their thyrsi hurling, javelin-like,
Drave all before, and smote their shameful backs:
Women drave men, but not without the god.
    So did they straight return from whence they came,
Even to the fountains, which the god made flow;
Washed off the blood, and from their cheeks the drops
The serpents licked, and made them bright and clean.
This godhead then, whoe'er he be, my master!
Receive within our city. Great in all things,
In this I hear men say he is the greatest —
He hath given the sorrow-soothing vine to man
For where wine is not love will never be,
Nor any other joy of human life.

CHORUS I am afraid to speak the words of freedom
        Before the tyrant, yet it must be said:
        "Inferior to no god is Dionysus."

PENTHEUS 'Tis here then, like a wild fire, burning on,
        This Bacchic insolence, Hellas' deep disgrace.
        Off with delay! Go to the Electrian gates
        And summon all that bear the shield, and all
        The cavalry upon their prancing steeds,
        And those that couch the lance, and of the bow
        Twang the sharp string. Against these Bacchanals
        We will go war. It were indeed too much
        From women to endure what we endure.

DIONYSUS Thou wilt not be persuaded by my words
        Pentheus! Yet though of thee I have suffered wrong
        I warn thee, rise not up against the god.
        Rest thou in peace. Bromius will never brook
        Ye drive his Mænads from their mountain haunts.

PENTHEUS Wilt teach me? Better fly and save thyself,
        Ere yet I wreak stern justice upon thee.

DIONYSUS Rather do sacrifice, than in thy wrath
        Kick 'gainst the pricks — a mortal 'gainst a god.

PENTHEUS I'll sacrifice, and in Cithæron's glens,
        As they deserve, a hecatomb of women.

DIONYSUS Soon will ye fly. 'Twere shame that shields of brass
        Before the Bacchic thyrsi turn in rout.

PENTHEUS   I am bewildered by this dubious stranger;
            Doing or suffering, he holds not his peace.

DIONYSUS   My friend! Thou still mayest bring this to good end.

PENTHEUS   How so? By being the slave of mine own slaves?

DIONYSUS   These women — without force of arms, I'll bring
            them.

PENTHEUS   Alas! he is plotting now some wile against me!

DIONYSUS   But what if I could save thee by mine arts?

PENTHEUS   Ye are all in league, that ye may hold your orgies.

DIONYSUS   I am in a league 'tis true, but with the god!

PENTHEUS   Bring out mine armour! Thou, have done thy
            speech!

DIONYSUS   Ha! wouldst thou see them seated on the mountains?

PENTHEUS   Ay! for the sight give thousand weight of gold.

DIONYSUS   Why hast thou fallen upon this strange desire?

PENTHEUS   'Twere grief to see them in their drunkenness.

DIONYSUS   Yet gladly wouldst thou see, what see would grieve
            thee.

PENTHEUS   Mark well! in silence seated 'neath the ash-trees.

DIONYSUS   But if thou goest in secret they will scent thee.

PENTHEUS   Best openly, in this thou hast said well.

DIONYSUS   But if we lead thee, wilt thou dare the way?

PENTHEUS   Lead on, and swiftly! Let no time be lost!

DIONYSUS   But first enwrap thee in these linen robes.

PENTHEUS   What, will he of a man make me a woman!

DIONYSUS   Lest they should kill thee, seeing thee as a man.

PENTHEUS   Well dost thou speak; so spake the wise of old.

DIONYSUS   Dionysus hath instructed me in this.

PENTHEUS   How then can we best do what thou advisest?

DIONYSUS   I'll enter in the house, and there array thee.

PENTHEUS   What dress? A woman's? I am ashamed to wear it.

DIONYSUS   Art thou not eager to behold the Mænads?

PENTHEUS   And what dress sayst thou I must wrap around me?

DIONYSUS   I'll smooth thine hair down lightly on thy brow.

PENTHEUS   What is the second portion of my dress?

DIONYSUS   Robes to thy feet, a bonnet on thine head.

PENTHEUS   Wilt thou array me then in more than this?

DIONYSUS   A thyrsus in thy hand, a dappled fawn-skin.

PENTHEUS   I cannot clothe me in a woman's dress.

DIONYSUS   Thou wilt have bloodshed, warring on the Mænads.

PENTHEUS 'Tis right, I must go first survey the field.

DIONYSUS 'Twere wiser than to hunt evil with evil.

PENTHEUS How pass the city, unseen of the Thebans?

DIONYSUS We'll go by lone byways; I'll lead thee safe.

PENTHEUS Aught better than be mocked by these loose
      Bacchanals.
   When we come back, we'll counsel what were best.

DIONYSUS Even as you will: I am here at your command.

PENTHEUS 'So let us on; I must go forth in arms,
   Or follow the advice thou givest me.

DIONYSUS Women! this man is in our net; he goes
   To find his just doom 'mid the Bacchanals.
   Dionysus, to thy work! thou'rt not far off;
   Vengeance is ours. Bereave him first of sense:
   Yet be his frenzy slight. In his right mind
   He never had put on a woman's dress;
   But now, thus shaken in his mind, he'll wear it.
   A laughing-stock I'll make him to all Thebes,
   Led in a woman's dress through the wide city.
   For those fierce threats in which he was so great.
   But I must go, and Pentheus — in the garb
   Which wearing, even by his own mother's hand
   Slain, he goes down to Hades. Know he must
   Dionysus, son of Jove, among the gods
   Mightiest, yet mildest to the sons of men.

CHORUS O when, through the long night,
      With fleet foot glancing white,

Shall I go dancing in my revelry,
    My neck cast back, and bare
    Unto the dewy air,
Like sportive fawn in the green meadow's glee?
    Lo, in her fear she springs
    Over th' encircling rings,
Over the well-woven nets far off and fast;
    While swift along her track
    The huntsman cheers his pack,
With panting toil, and fiery storm-wind haste.
Where down the river-bank spreads the wide meadow
    Rejoices she in the untrod solitude.
Couches at length beneath the silent shadow
    Of the old hospitable wood.

    What is wisest? what is fairest,
    Of god's boons to man the rarest?
    With the conscious conquering hand
    Above the foeman's head to stand.
    What is fairest still is dearest.

    Slow come, but come at length,
    In their majestic strength
Faithful and true, the avenging deities:
    And chastening human folly,
    And the mad pride unholy,
Of those who to the gods bow not their knees.
    For hidden still and mute,
    As glides their printless foot,
The impious on their winding path they hound
    For it is ill to know,
    And it is ill to do,

Beyond the law's inexorable bound.
'Tis but light cost in his own power sublime
        To array the godhead, whosoe'er he be;
And law is old, even as the oldest time,
        Nature's own unrepealed decree.

What is wisest? what is fairest,
Of god's boons to man the rarest?
With the conscious conquering hand
Above the foeman's head to stand
What is fairest still is rarest.

Who hath 'scaped the turbulent sea,
And reached the haven, happy he!
Happy he whose toils are o'er,
In the race of wealth and power!
This one here, and that one there,
Passes by, and everywhere
Still expectant thousands over
Thousands hopes are seen to hover,
Some to mortals end in bliss;
        Some have already fled away:
Happiness alone is his
        That happy is to-day.

DIONYSUS   Thou art mad to see that which thou shouldst not see,
            And covetous of that thou shouldst not covet.
            Pentheus! I say, come forth! Appear before me,
            Clothed in the Bacchic Mænads' womanly dress;
            Spy on thy mother and her holy crew,
            Come like in form to one of Cadmus' daughters.

PENTHEUS　　Ha! now indeed two suns I seem to see,
　　　　　　A double Thebes, two seven-gated cities;
　　　　　　Thou, as a bull, seemest to go before me,
　　　　　　And horns have grown upon thine head. Art thou
　　　　　　A beast indeed? Thou seem'st a very bull.

DIONYSUS　　The god is with us; unpropitious once,
　　　　　　But now at truce: now seest thou what thou shouldst see?

PENTHEUS　　What see I? Is not that the step of Ino?
　　　　　　And is not Agave there, my mother?

DIONYSUS　　Methinks 'tis even they whom thou behold'st;
　　　　　　But lo! this tress hath strayed out of its place,
　　　　　　Not as I braided it, beneath thy bonnet.

PENTHEUS　　Tossing it this way now, now tossing that,
　　　　　　In Bacchic glee, I have shaken it from its place.

DIONYSUS　　But we, whose charge it is to watch o'er thee,
　　　　　　Will braid it up again. Lift up thy head.

PENTHEUS　　Braid as thou wilt, we yield ourselves to thee.

DIONYSUS　　Thy zone is loosened, and thy robe's long folds
　　　　　　Droop outward, nor conceal thine ankles now.

PENTHEUS　　Around my right foot so it seems, yet sure
　　　　　　Around the other it sits close and well.

DIONYSUS　　Wilt thou not hold me for thy best of friends,
　　　　　　Thus strangely seeing the coy Bacchanals?

PENTHEUS　　The thyrsus — in my right hand shall I hold it?
　　　　　　Or thus am I more like a Bacchanal?

DIONYSUS   In thy right hand, and with thy right foot raise it.
             I praise the change of mind now come o'er thee.

PENTHEUS   Could I not now bear up upon my shoulders
             Cithæron's crag, with all the Bacchanals?

DIONYSUS   Thou couldst if 'twere thy will. In thy right mind
             Erewhile thou wast not; now thou art as thou shouldst
                be.

PENTHEUS   Shall I take levers, pluck it up with my hands,
             Or thrust mine arm or shoulder 'neath its base?

DIONYSUS   Destroy thou not the dwellings of the nymphs,
             The seats where Pan sits piping in his joy.

PENTHEUS   Well hast thou said; by force we conquer not
             These women. I'll go hide in yonder ash.

DIONYSUS   Within a fatal ambush wilt thou hide thee,
             Stealing, a treacherous spy, upon the Mænads.

PENTHEUS   And now I seem to see them there like birds
             Couching on their soft beds amid the fern.

DIONYSUS   Art thou not therefore set as watchman o'er them?
             Thou'lt seize them — if they do not seize thee first.

PENTHEUS   Lead me triumphant through the land of Thebes!
             I, only I, have dared a deed like this.

DIONYSUS   Thou art the city's champion, thou alone.
             Therefore a strife thou wot'st not of awaits thee.

Follow me! thy preserver goes before thee;
Another takes thee hence.

PENTHEUS   Mean'st thou my mother?

DIONYSUS   Aloft shalt thou be borne.

PENTHEUS   O the soft carriage!

DIONYSUS   In thy mother's hands.

PENTHEUS   Wilt make me thus luxurious?

DIONYSUS   Strange luxury, indeed!

PENTHEUS   'Tis my desert.

DIONYSUS   Thou art awful! — awful! Doomed to awful end!
            Thy glory shall soar up to the high heavens!
                Stretch forth thine hand, Agave! — ye her kin,
            Daughters of Cadmus! To a terrible grave
            Lead I this youth! Myself shall win the prize —
            Bromius and I; the event will show the rest.

CHORUS   Ho! fleet dogs and furious, to the mountains, ho!
            Where their mystic revels Cadmus' daughters keep.
                Rouse them, goad them out,
            'Gainst him, in woman's mimic garb concealed,
            Gazer on the Mænads in their dark rites unrevealed.
            First his mother shall behold him on his watch below,
            From the tall tree's trunk or from the wild scaur steep;
                Fiercely will she shout —
            "Who the spy upon the Mænads on the rocks that roam

To the mountain, to the mountain, Bacchanals, has
    come?"
                    Who hath borne him?

        He is not of woman's blood —
           The lioness!
      Or the Lybian Gorgon's brood?
   Come, vengeance, come, display thee!
    With thy bright sword array thee!
      The bloody sentence wreak
      On the dissevered neck
Of him who god, law, justice hath not known,
    Echion's earth-born son.

He, with thought unrighteous and unholy pride,
'Gainst Bacchus and his mother, their orgies' mystic
    mirth
      Still holds his frantic strife,
And sets him up against the god, deeming it light
    To vanquish the invincible of might.
Hold thou fast the pious mind; so, only so, shall glide
In peace with gods above, in peace with men on earth,
    Thy smooth painless life.
I admire not, envy not, who would be otherwise:
Mine be still the glory, mine be still the prize,
      By night and day
    To live of the immortal gods in awe;
      Who fears them not
    Is but the outcast of all law.

    Come, vengeance, come display thee!
    With thy bright sword array thee!

The bloody sentence wreak
On the dissevered neck
Of him who god, law, justice has not known,
Echion's earth-born son.

Appear! appear!
Or as the stately steer!
Or many-headed dragon be!
Or the fire-breathing lion, terrible to see.
Come, Bacchus, come 'gainst the hunter of the
Bacchanals,
Even now, now as he falls
Upon the Mænads' fatal herd beneath,
With smiling brow,
Around him throw
The inexorable net of death.

MESSENGER   O house most prosperous once throughout all
Hellas!
House of the old Sidonian! — in this land
Who sowed the dragon's serpent's earth-born harvest —
How I deplore thee! I a slave, for still
Grieve for their master's sorrows faithful slaves.

CHORUS What's this? Aught new about the Bacchanals?

MESSENGER   Pentheus hath perished, old Echion's son.

CHORUS King Bromius, thou art indeed a mighty god!

MESSENGER   What sayst thou? How is this? Rejoicest thou,
O woman, in my master's awful fate?

CHORUS Light chants the stranger her barbarous strains;
        I cower not in fear for the menace of chains.

MESSENGER All Thebes thus void of courage deemest thou?

CHORUS O Dionysus! Dionysus! Thebes
        Hath o'er me now no power.

MESSENGER 'Tis pardonable, yet it is not well,
           Woman, in others' miseries to rejoice.

CHORUS Tell me, then, by what fate died the unjust —
        The man, the dark contriver of injustice?

MESSENGER Therapnæ having left the Theban city,
           And passed along Asopus' winding shore,
           We 'gan to climb Cithæron's upward steep —
           Pentheus and I (I waited on my lord),
           And he that led us on our quest, the stranger —
           And first we crept along a grassy glade,
           With silent footsteps, and with silent tongues
           Slow moving, as to see, not being seen.
           There was a rock-walled glen, watered by a streamlet,
           And shadowed o'er with pines; the Mænads there
           Sate, all their hands busy with pleasant toil;
           And some the leafy thyrsus, that its ivy
           Had dropped away, were garlanding anew;
           Like fillies some, unharnessed from the yoke;
           Chanted alternate all the Bacchic hymn.
           Ill-fated Pentheus, as he scarce could see
           That womanly troop, spake thus: "Where we stand,
               stranger,

We see not well the unseemly Mænad dance:
But, mounting on a bank, or a tall tree,
Clearly shall I behold their deeds of shame."
    A wonder then I saw that stranger do.
He seized an ash-tree's high heaven-reaching stem,
And dragged it down, dragged, dragged to the low earth;
And like a bow it bent. As a curved wheel
Becomes a circle in the turner's lathe,
The stranger thus that mountain tree bent down
To the earth, a deed of more than mortal strength.
Then seating Pentheus on those ash-tree boughs,
Upward he let it rise, steadily, gently
Through his hands, careful lest it shake him off;
And slowly rose it upright to its height,
Bearing my master seated on its ridge.
There was he seen, rather than saw the Mænads,
More visible he could not be, seated aloft.
The stranger from our view had vanished quite.
Then from the heavens a voice, as it should seem
Dionysus, shouted loud, "Behold! I bring,
O maidens, him that you and me, our rites,
Our orgies laughed to scorn; now take your vengeance."
And as he spake, a light of holy fire
Stood up, and blazed from earth straight up to heaven.
Silent the air, silent the verdant grove
Held its still leaves; no sound of living thing.
They, as their ears just caught the half-heard voice,
Stood up erect, and rolled their wondering eyes.
Again he shouted. But when Cadmus' daughters
Heard manifest the god's awakening voice,

Forth rushed they, fleeter than the wingéd dove,
Their nimble feet quick coursing up and down.
Agave first, his mother, then her kin,
The Mænads, down the torrents' bed, in the grove,
From crag to crag they leaped, mad with the god.
And first with heavy stones they hurled at him,
Climbing a rock in front; the branches some
Of the ash-tree darted; some like javelins
Sent their sharp thyrsi through the sounding air,
Pentheus their mark: but yet they struck him not;
His height still baffled all their eager wrath.
There sat the wretch, helpless in his despair.
The oaken boughs, by lightning as struck off,
Roots torn from the earth, but with no iron wedge,
They hurled, but their wild labours all were vain.
Agave spake, "Come all, and stand around,
And grasp the tree, ye Mænads; soon we will seize
The beast that rides thereon. He will ne'er betray
The mysteries of our god." A thousand hands
Were on the ash, and tore it from the earth:
And he that sat aloft, down, headlong, down
Fell to the ground, with thousand piteous shrieks,
Pentheus, for well he knew his end was near.
His mother first began the sacrifice,
And fell on him. His bonnet from his hair
He threw, that she might know and so not slay him,
The sad Agave. And he said, her cheek
Fondling, "I am thy child, thine own, my mother!
Pentheus, whom in Echion's house you bare.
Have mercy on me, mother! For his sins,

Whatever be his sins, kill not thy son."
She, foaming at the mouth, her rolling eyeballs
Whirling around, in her unreasoning reason,
By Bacchus all possessed, knew, heeded not.
She caught him in her arms, seized his right hand,
And, with her feet set on his shrinking side,
Tore out the shoulder — not with her own strength:
The god made easy that too cruel deed.
And Ino laboured on the other side,
Rending the flesh: Autonoe, all the rest,
Pressed fiercely on, and there was one wild din —
He groaning deep, while he had breath to groan,
They shouting triumph; and one bore an arm,
One a still-sandalled foot; and both his sides
Lay open, rent. Each in her bloody hand
Tossed wildly to and fro lost Pentheus' limbs.
The trunk lay far aloof, 'neath the rough rocks
Part, part amid the forest's thick-strewn leaves
Not easy to be found. The wretched head,
Which the mad mother, seizing in her hands
Had on a thyrsus fixed, she bore aloft
All o'er Cithæron, as a mountain lion's,
Leading her sisters in their Mænad dance.
And she comes vaunting her ill-fated chase
Unto these walls, invoking Bacchus still,
Her fellow-hunter, partner in her prey,
Her triumph — triumph soon to end in tears!
I fled the sight of that dark tragedy,
Hastening, ere yet Agave reached the palace.
Oh! to be reverent, to adore the gods,

This is the noblest, wisest course of man,
Taking dread warning from this dire event.

CHORUS
Dance and sing
In Bacchic ring,
Shout, shout the fate, the fate of gloom,
Of Pentheus, from the dragon born;
He the woman's garb hath worn,
Following the bull, the harbinger, that led him to his doom.
O ye Theban Bacchanals!
Attune ye now the hymn victorious,
The hymn all glorious,
To the tear, and to the groan!
Oh game of glory!
To bathe the hands besprent and gory,
In the blood of her own son.
But I behold Agave, Pentheus' mother,
Nearing the palace with distorted eyes.
Hail we the ovation of the Evian god.

AGAVE
O ye Asian Bacchanals!

CHORUS
Who is she on us who calls?

AGAVE
From the mountains, lo! we bear
To the palace gate
Our new-slain quarry fair.

CHORUS
I see, I see! and on thy joy I wait.

AGAVE
Without a net, without a snare,
The lion's cub, I took him there

CHORUS
In the wilderness, or where?

AGAVE   Cithæron —

CHORUS   Of Cithæron what?

AGAVE   Gave him to slaughter.

CHORUS   O blest Agave!

AGAVE   In thy song extol me,

CHORUS   Who struck him first?

AGAVE   Mine, mine, the glorious lot.

CHORUS   Who else?

AGAVE   Of Cadmus —

CHORUS   What of Cadmus' daughter?

AGAVE   With me, with me, did all the race
             Hound the prey.

CHORUS   O fortunate chase!

AGAVE   The banquet share with me!

CHORUS   Alas! what shall our banquet be?

AGAVE   How delicate the kid and young!
             The thin locks have but newly sprung
             Over his forehead fair.

CHORUS 'Tis beauteous as the tame beasts' cherished hair.

AGAVE Bacchus, hunter known to fame!
             Did he not our Mænads bring

On the track of this proud game?
  A mighty hunter is our king!
 Praise me! praise me!

CHORUS   Praise I not thee?

AGAVE Soon with the Thebans all, the hymn of praise
 Pentheus my son will to his mother raise:
  For she the lion prey hath won,
  A noble deed and nobly done.

CHORUS   Dost thou rejoice?

AGAVE   Ay, with exulting voice
  My great, great deed I elevate,
   Glorious as great.

CHORUS Sad woman, to the citizens of Thebes
 Now show the conquered prey thou bearest hither.

AGAVE Ye that within the high-towered Theban city
 Dwell, come and gaze ye all upon our prey,
 The mighty beast by Cadmus' daughter ta'en;
 Nor with Thessalian sharp-pointed javelins,
 Nor nets, but with the white and delicate palms
 Of our own hands. Go ye, and make your boast,
 Trusting to the spear-maker's useless craft:
 We with these hands have ta'en our prey, and rent
 The mangled limbs of this grim beast asunder.
  Where is mine aged sire? Let him draw near!
 And where is my son Pentheus? Let him mount
 On the broad stairs that rise before our house;
 And on the triglyph nail this lion's head,
 That I have brought him from our splendid chase.

CADMUS Follow me, follow, bearing your sad burthen,
        My servants — Pentheus' body — to our house;
        The body that with long and weary search
        I found at length in lone Cithæron's glens;
        Thus torn, not lying in one place, but wide
        Scattered amid the dark and tangled thicket.
        Already, as I entered in the city
        With old Tiresias, from the Bacchanals,
        I heard the fearful doings of my daughter.
        And back returning to the mountain, bear
        My son, thus by the furious Mænads slain.
        Her who Actæon bore to Aristæus,
        Autonoë, I saw, and Ino with her
        Still in the thicket goaded with wild madness.
        And some one said that on her dancing feet
        Agave had come hither — true he spoke;
        I see her now — O most unblessed sight!

AGAVE Father, 'tis thy peculiar peerless boast
        Of womanhood the noblest t' have begot —
        Me — me the noblest of that noble kin.
        For I the shuttle and the distaff left
        For mightier deeds — wild beasts with mine own hands
        To capture. Lo! I bear within mine arms
        These glorious trophies, to be hung on high
        Upon thy house: receive them, O my father!
        Call thy friends to the banquet feast! Blest thou!
        Most blest, through us who have wrought such splendid
            deeds.

CADMUS Measureless grief! Eye may not gaze on it,
        The slaughter wrought by those most wretched hands.

Oh! what a sacrifice before the gods!
All Thebes, and us, thou callest to the feast.
Justly — too justly, hath King Bromius
Destroyed us, fatal kindred to our house.

AGAVE   Oh! how morose is man in his old age,
And sullen in his mien. Oh! were my son
More like his mother, mighty in his hunting,
When he goes forth among the youth of Thebes
Wild beasts to chase! But he is great alone,
In warring on the gods. We two, my sire,
Must counsel him against his evil wisdom.
Where is he? Who will call him here before us
That he may see me in my happiness?

CADMUS   Woe! woe! When ye have sense of what ye have done,
With what deep sorrow, sorrow ye! To th' end,
Oh! could ye be, only as now ye are,
Nor happy were ye deemed, nor miserable.

AGAVE   What is not well? For sorrow what the cause?

CADMUS   First lift thine eyes up to the air around.

AGAVE   Behold! Why thus commandest me to gaze?

CADMUS   Is all the same? Appears there not a change?

AGAVE   'Tis brighter, more translucent than before.

CADMUS   Is there the same elation in thy soul?

AGAVE I know not what thou mean'st; but I become
Conscious — my changing mind is settling down.

CADMUS Canst thou attend, and plainly answer me?

AGAVE I have forgotten, father, all I said.

CADMUS Unto whose bed wert thou in wedlock given?

AGAVE Echion's, him they call the Dragon-born.

CADMUS Who was the son to thy husband thou didst bear?

AGAVE Pentheus, in commerce 'twixt his sire and me.

CADMUS And whose the head thou holdest in thy hands?

AGAVE A lion's; thus my fellow-hunters said.

CADMUS Look at it straight: to look on't is no toil.

AGAVE What see I? Ha! what's this within my hands?

CADMUS Look on't again, again: thou wilt know too well.

AGAVE I see the direst woe that eye may see.

CADMUS The semblance of a lion bears it now?

AGAVE No: wretch, wretch that I am; 'tis Pentheus' head!

CADMUS Even ere yet recognised thou might'st have mourned
him.

AGAVE Who murdered him? How came he in my hands?

CADMUS Sad truth! Untimely dost thou ever come!

AGAVE   Speak; for my heart leaps with a boding throb.

CADMUS   'Twas thou didst slay him, thou and thine own sisters.

AGAVE   Where died he? In his palace? In what place?

CADMUS   There where the dogs Actæon tore in pieces.

AGAVE   Why to Cithæron went the ill-fated man?

CADMUS   To mock the god, to mock the orgies there.

AGAVE   But how and wherefore had we thither gone?

CADMUS   In madness! — the whole city maddened with thee.

AGAVE   Dionysus hath destroyed us! Late I learn it.

CADMUS   Mocked with dread mockery; no god ye held him.

AGAVE   Father! Where's the dear body of my son?

CADMUS   I bear it here, not found without much toil,

AGAVE   Are all the limbs together, sound and whole?
         And Pentheus, shared he in my desperate fury?

CADMUS   Like thee he was, he worshipped not the god.
         All, therefore, are enwrapt in one dread doom.
         You, he, in whom hath perished all our house,
         And I who, childless of male offspring, see
         This single fruit — O miserable! — of thy womb
         Thus shamefully, thus lamentably dead —
         Thy son, to whom our house looked up, the stay
         Of all our palace he, my daughter's son,

The awe of the whole city. None would dare
Insult the old man when thy fearful face
He saw, well knowing he would pay the penalty.
Unhonoured now, I am driven from out mine home;
Cadmus the great, who all the race of Thebes
Sowed in the earth, and reaped that harvest fair.
O best beloved of men, thou art now no more,
Yet still art dearest of my children thou!
No more, this grey beard fondling with thine hand,
Wilt call me thine own grandsire, thou sweet child,
And fold me round and say, "Who doth not honour
    thee?
Old man, who troubles or afflicts thine heart?
Tell me, that I may 'venge thy wrong, my father!"
Now wretchedst of men am I. Thou pitiable —
More pitiable thy mother — sad thy kin.
O if there be who scorneth the great gods,
Gaze on this death, and know that there are gods.

CHORUS Cadmus, I grieve for thee. Thy daughter's son
        Hath his just doom — just, but most piteous.

AGAVE Father, thou seest how all is changed with me:
       I am no more the Mænad dancing blithe,
       I am but the feeble, fond, and desolate mother.
       I know, I see — ah, knowledge best unknown!
       Sight best unseen! — I see, I know my son,
       Mine only son! — alas! no more my son.
       O beauteous limbs, that in my womb I bare!
       O head, that on my lap wast wont to sleep!
       O lips, that from my bosom's swelling fount
       Drained the delicious and soft-oozing milk!

O hands, whose first use was to fondle me!
O feet, that were so light to run to me!
O gracious form, that men wondering beheld!
O haughty brow, before which Thebes bowed down!
O majesty! O strength! by mine own hands —
By mine own murderous, sacrilegious hands —
Torn, rent asunder, scattered, cast abroad!
O thou hard god! was there no other way
To visit us? Oh! if the son must die,
Must it be by the hand of his own mother?
If the impious mother must atone her sin,
Must it be but by murdering her own son?

DIONYSUS   Now hear ye all, Thebes' founders, what is woven
By the dread shuttle of the unerring Fates.
Thou, Cadmus, father of this earth-born race,
A dragon shalt become; thy wife shalt take
A brutish form, and sink into a serpent,
Harmonia, Ares' daughter, whom thou wedd'st,
Though mortal, as Jove's oracle declares.
Thou in a car by heifers drawn shalt ride,
And with thy wife, at the Barbarians' head:
And many cities with their countless host
Shall they destroy, but when they dare destroy
The shrine of Loxias, back shall they return
In shameful flight; but Ares guards Harmonia
And thee, and bears you to the Isles of the Blest.
     This say I, of no mortal father born,
Dionysus, son of Jove. Had ye but known
To have been pious when ye might, Jove's son
Had been your friend; ye had been happy still.

AGAVE   Dionysus, we implore thee! We have sinned!

DIONYSUS   Too late ye say so; when ye should, ye would not.

AGAVE   That know we now; but thou'rt extreme in vengeance.

DIONYSUS   Was I not outraged, being a god, by you?

AGAVE   The gods should not be like to men in wrath.

DIONYSUS   This Jove, my father, long hath granted me.

AGAVE   Alas, old man! Our exile is decreed.

DIONYSUS   Why then delay ye the inevitable?

CADMUS   O child, to what a depth of woe we have fallen!
Most wretched thou, and all thy kin beloved!
I too to the Barbarians must depart,
An aged denizen. For there's a prophecy,
'Gainst Hellas a Barbaric mingled host
Harmonia leads, my wife, daughter of Ares.
A dragon I, with dragon nature fierce,
Shall lead the stranger spearmen 'gainst the altars
And tombs of Hellas, nor shall cease my woes —
Sad wretch! — not even when I have ferried o'er
Dark Acheron, shall I repose in peace.

AGAVE   Father! to exile go I without thee?

CADMUS   Why dost thou clasp me in thine arms, sad child,
A drone among the bees, a swan worn out?

AGAVE   Where shall I go, an exile from my country?

CADMUS   I know not, child; thy sire is a feeble aid.

AGAVE   Farewell, mine home! Farewell, my native Thebes!
              My bridal chamber! Banished, I go forth.

CADMUS To the house of Aristæus go, my child.

AGAVE   I wait for thee, my father!

CADMUS   I for thee!
              And for thy sisters.

AGAVE   Fearfully, fearfully, this deep disgrace,
              Hath Dionysus brought upon our race.

DIONYSUS   Fearful on me the wrong that ye had done;
              Unhonoured was my name in Thebes alone.

AGAVE   Father, farewell!

CADMUS   Farewell, my wretched daughter!

AGAVE   So lead me forth — my sisters now to meet,
              Sad fallen exiles.
                        Let me, let me go
              Where cursed Cithæron ne'er may see me more,
              Nor I the cursed Cithæron see again.
              Where there's no memory of the thyrsus dance.
              The Bacchic orgies be the care of others.

PLAYS

THE ORESTEIA TRILOGY: Agamemnon, the Libation-Bearers and the Furies, Aeschylus. (0-486-29242-8)

EVERYMAN, Anonymous. (0-486-28726-2)

THE BIRDS, Aristophanes. (0-486-40886-8)

LYSISTRATA, Aristophanes. (0-486-28225-2)

THE CHERRY ORCHARD, Anton Chekhov. (0-486-26682-6)

THE SEA GULL, Anton Chekhov. (0-486-40656-3)

MEDEA, Euripides. (0-486-27548-5)

FAUST, PART ONE, Johann Wolfgang von Goethe. (0-486-28046-2)

THE INSPECTOR GENERAL, Nikolai Gogol. (0-486-28500-6)

SHE STOOPS TO CONQUER, Oliver Goldsmith. (0-486-26867-5)

GHOSTS, Henrik Ibsen. (0-486-29852-3)

A DOLL'S HOUSE, Henrik Ibsen. (0-486-27062-9)

HEDDA GABLER, Henrik Ibsen. (0-486-26469-6)

DR. FAUSTUS, Christopher Marlowe. (0-486-28208-2)

TARTUFFE, Molière. (0-486-41117-6)

BEYOND THE HORIZON, Eugene O'Neill. (0-486-29085-9)

THE EMPEROR JONES, Eugene O'Neill. (0-486-29268-1)

CYRANO DE BERGERAC, Edmond Rostand. (0-486-41119-2)

MEASURE FOR MEASURE: Unabridged, William Shakespeare. (0-486-40889-2)

FOUR GREAT TRAGEDIES: Hamlet, Macbeth, Othello, and Romeo and Juliet, William Shakespeare. (0-486-44083-4)

THE COMEDY OF ERRORS, William Shakespeare. (0-486-42461-8)

HENRY V, William Shakespeare. (0-486-42887-7)

MUCH ADO ABOUT NOTHING, William Shakespeare. (0-486-28272-4)

FIVE GREAT COMEDIES: Much Ado About Nothing, Twelfth Night, A Midsummer Night's Dream, As You Like It and The Merry Wives of Windsor, William Shakespeare. (0-486-44086-9)

OTHELLO, William Shakespeare. (0-486-29097-2)

AS YOU LIKE IT, William Shakespeare. (0-486-40432-3)

ROMEO AND JULIET, William Shakespeare. (0-486-27557-4)

A MIDSUMMER NIGHT'S DREAM, William Shakespeare. (0-486-27067-X)

THE MERCHANT OF VENICE, William Shakespeare. (0-486-28492-1)

HAMLET, William Shakespeare. (0-486-27278-8)

RICHARD III, William Shakespeare. (0-486-28747-5)